BLESSED McGILL

Novels by Edwin Shrake

Blood Reckoning
But Not For Love
Blessed McGill
Peter Arbiter
Limo (with Dan Jenkins)
Strange Peaches
Night Never Falls
The Borderland
Billy Boy
Custer's Brother's Horse

TEXAS LITERARY CLASSICS

BLESSED MCGILL

BY EDWIN SHRAKE

JOHN M. HARDY PUBLISHING

ALPINE & HOUSTON

2007

First Printing: September 2007

ISBN 0-9798391-0-6

First published: 1968
Doubleday & Company

Printed and Bound in the United States of America

Cover Photo - Bill Wittliff

Cover Design - Leisha Israel

John M. Hardy Publishing
Houston, Texas

www.johnmhardy.com

BLESSED MCGILL

1

Spring is good in this land. From my house on the rim of the plateau I smell cedars still wet from the rain, and I hear the river running over rocks in the valley. The river runs down from the high mountains, where it snowed thirty feet during the winter, and so there is much snow-water to bring down the canyon and through the valley and on out to where the river meets the Rio Grande gorge. From along the river I hear the bells of sheep in the meadows around the village of Valdez with its adobe buildings and pole fences, and I can smell piñon smoke coming up from the chimneys of Spaniard sheepherders whose people have lived in Valdez since Coronado passed through here three hundred years ago. I hear water in the irrigation ditches that must be cleaned now that the ice is melting. Soon I should begin to plant, were this an ordinary time.

The yellow light of my whale-oil lamp flutters and pops on these pages as my pen moves. My lion's tooth dangles on my chest beside the silver images of Our Lady of Guadalupe and St. Jude. Outside I hear my noble mule Excelsior rubbing his flanks against the wall of my house to rid his hide of some pestiferous itch. Excelsior! What a fine beast he is for a mule! Before much longer, maybe in the next few minutes, for I have no way of seeing into the mind of my enemy any more than he can see into mine, I must mount Excelsior and ride down into the valley for the meeting with Octavio, also called Gotch Eye, once called Jacob Charles Gerhardt. It is odd in the midst of so much life all around me, new with the spring, to know that I must go meet Octavio, for he will surely murder me.

Yet I must go. The truth is I am less afraid of Octavio and his renegades than of Excelsior slipping on the mud and rocks of the trail down the valley wall. It is a preposterous situation, but I at least have a reason to die whereas noble Excelsior does not. According to the view of my Franciscan friend Father Higgins, I have been a wicked man and my sins are piling up on my head or would be if I reckoned on sin. Since I was a boy I have hit, shot, stomped, got drunk with, spraddled or even loved most everybody who appeared in my path and many that I had to chase. I have seen that there is unity in all things, and as a result I do not so much mind dying.

I have observed more death than most, have caused a devil's pleasure of it. Death is not a too awful confrontation. A fellow hollers or does not and then he is gone and all that is left is a punky bag of flesh. No, I don't mind dying as much as I hate to give up the light. Discounting times when I was wounded or unconscious, I have been as long as ten years without sleeping more than five hours at a stretch, which is a handy habit for a scalp hunter, scout, buffalo shooter, gambler, brawler, gold seeker, and family man like myself. You might wonder why if I do not mind dying I feel the urge to write down my recollections. The fact is I do not know why. Father Higgins would say it is my need to confess and ease my immortal soul, but one who has spent as much time in the high mountains and among savages of all kinds as I have can judge what is immortal and what is not, and there is nothing to do about it.

A man can only guess at his intentions. Regardless of why I write it, this is my chronicle. I tell it not in order but as it arrives in my head, hopping over the more boring parts since I am in a hurry for cause you can understand. There is a lantern hanging on a *viga* outside my door to guide Octavio's messenger, and there is no predicting when he may turn up. Octavio will probably send Eagle Dancer, a stinking coon if there ever was one. It is likely Eagle Dancer will be drunk on tiswin or out of his mind on peyote buttons mixed with grape brandy, and I will hear him falling and crashing and howling through the junipers long before he reaches my house. If Eagle Dancer is not drunk I will not hear him except for the stirring of Excelsior but in sensing him will look up from my lamp and papers and see his ugly face at the door. It is a temptation to blow a hole in him for the sport of it. But that would not please Father Higgins nor alter my course, and this is how it must be.

My name is McGill. How I came to be here is my story. I am a man of some fair education, for which thanks be to my mother. From her I received also my keenness for reading and my love and distrust of words. Words can conceal the mean or commonplace as the chaparral conceals a wild pig. I have observed a number of gentlemen and thieves of my acquaintance covering themselves with words to disguise their low desires. But I do admire and respect those who use words as they are meant to be used, which is to speak the truth or to make poetry. I have found all sorts of things will pass as truth. There is the truth that Father Higgins speaks, for I now know it to be a kind of truth. There is the truth that Badthing speaks, which is more like poetry. What the final truth is I do not comprehend, nor am I certain there is such a quality separate from the whole, nor am I convinced that it matters. My father told me that birth is real, death is real, and all between is a game. It is hard to quarrel with that.

2

I will come to those things in other places. Of the moment I must continue as I began if I am to finish before Octavio has need of me. My name McGill came from my father John Patrick McGill, who was an Irishman and a fighter. His education of books was scanty, being only what my mother taught him, but his knowledge of life was broad and included a sea journey when he came from Ireland and landed in the Port of New York. I have been to New York on a trip to buy rifles from the Sharps factory in Connecticut and found the place a sewer. Man was not meant to live in such wretched conditions as prevail where thousands are crowded together fouling the atmosphere. Some leaders of our country are concerned about spreading our population too thin by the westward movement of families, but it is not good to mash people together. A horse Indian requires from ten to twenty square miles of land to support himself in good temper as well as health. White men need less and white women go crazy with that much space to occupy. If this country ever gets overcrowded it will be because women can't stand to be alone.

So my father made his way to the West with many adventures such as shootings, etc. After roaming in the mountains of Tennessee, he went to St. Louis for the commerce, as he had heard tales of wondrous trading in furs and hides. He was a bullwhacker on the high-wheeled freight wagons of the Santa Fe Trail fifty years ago. Having no head for business, he did not prosper but he did earn his own saddle, rifled musket, provisions, and three horses, and set forth for Texas in the days when she was becoming a Republic independent of the State of Coahuila, Mexico.

In the old mission town of San Antonio de Bexar he met my mother. She was a beautiful young woman I am sure, as she was beautiful when I knew her. Her name is Josefina María de Avila Guzman McGill. She is a *gachupín*, Spanish born, daughter of a Spaniard merchant who I am told did not like my father and resented his attentions. Fortunately for me, the Spaniard merchant was dispatched by a party of Penetakas while traveling in the vicinity of the Comal River. Possibly he had irritated them in some way, such as by cheating. Had they been Apaches the reason would be clear, as Apaches consider the sight of a Mexican or Spaniard provocation for murder, but my father insisted they were the Honey Eaters, who also in those days needed little excuse for rascality. I had the idea the señor could have been killed by Texans, for the battle at the Alamo, to which my mother was witness from outside the walls, had not been long over, and the territory was full of quarrelsome people as well as outlaws. The death of the Spaniard merchant left my mother without family, her own mother having died of fainting fits. Once my father agreed to recommence being a Catholic, as he had been in childhood, she consented to marry him and the banns were announced at the Mission de San Juan by an uncle from Matamoros.

It was my mother who gave me my Christian name of Peter Hermano McGill. She called me Peter after the Anglo name for San Pedro and Hermano after the Mexican word for brother. I acquired a Comanche name that means Refuses-to-Die later, though I was still quite young, as the result of several scrapes and episodes, some of which I will relate. My mother has never heard me called by such a name and would have done penance of ten thousand Hail Marys had she ever, for it would be to her blasphemy of the worst sort. I myself did not like the name, considering it bad luck for some period until I did perceive that I seemed to be charmed in that I stood while others fell, and soon enough I became accustomed to it and would answer to it if addressed in a friendly tone. But I always listened for the hint of mockery in the use of the name, and it went hard on those who so abused it. So you will see, as I do now, that there has been a pattern to my life and that the design has brought me here.

My father, of course, was part of the pattern. Although he told me tales of his experiences on the Santa Fe Trail and in Texas, he related nothing of Ireland other than that he was born there.

"Ireland is where I come from and that is all you need to know about the place," he would tell me. "Whatever of Ireland that is in you will show itself soon enough."

If I questioned him about his own father he would grow silent. Once he replied that he had no family worth mentioning and that he had worked his passage to America as a cabin boy. I do know that he hated the English, but that is not unusual. He came into Texas in 1835 and took part in the first siege of Bexar, about a year before the battle at the Alamo and the building of Fort Coleman, which were accomplished in the spring and summer of 1836. Being a good shot and of robust nature, and owning his own horses and weapons, he served for nearly two years with Captain Tomlinson's Rangers, patrolling the Colorado River for a wage of $1.25 per day paid mostly in Republic of Texas redback currency. He engaged in numerous fracases during those times. In 1838 he hunted buffalo with Lamar around Brushy Creek and other environs. In 1839 he fought Juan Flores and his outlaws at the North San Gabriel River. He emerged from that affair as a hero by riding across a ford in the river and coming down through some cottonwoods to the outlaws' flank. With his new Paterson five-shot pistol in hand, he jumped his horse over a brush barricade and surprised the outlaws. Discharging his pistol at close quarters, he killed one outlaw outright and then leaped from his horse and did off with another by sticking his knife in the Mexican's brisket. Immediately he came upon the Mexicans he began yelling and screaming in the fiercest manner—an unnerving trick that I learned from him, for a great show of violence and ferocity not only excites the blood but often accomplishes more than actual physical activity—and, fearing there were other Rangers behind him, the poor fellows were in panic, allowing the Rangers to rush them from the front and chase them through the woods like wild cattle.

The next year my father fought the Kiowas at Little River with Captain John Bird in an engagement in which a half-dozen Rangers, including Bird, were killed. Returning to Austin, my father discovered the Comanches had rid him of a certain problem by puncturing the merchant with arrows and removing his hair along with two wagon-loads of coffee, sugar, salt, flour, mirrors, butcher knives, hoes, homespun cotton, beads, corn whiskey, and other trade goods, some of which had been intended for presentation to the Comanches in return for buffalo robes which the Indians wound up able to barter elsewhere. Hastening to San Antonio, my father approached my mother, who was pledged to him. But in line with the rules of her faith, they had to wait a decent interval for mourning the late Spaniard merchant while the crawly things of the earth reclaimed his body. During that period of waiting, my father, thinking to make his fortune, joined the Texas expedition to Santa Fe de San Francisco in 1841.

Peculiar how his thoughts turned so often toward Santa Fe and how mine have directed me to this area where I have built my house north of Taos. He thought of Santa Fe in terms of commerce. Or he spoke of it in those terms. But I suspect that rather than the commerce it was the mystery of the land that beckoned, as the mountains drew me. There is a feeling of ancientness in the mountains and the pine forests and the deserts, in the rivers and the canyons. There is a feeling that life began here. Some of the tribes that we call Pueblos believe that the Ancient Ones came up from a hole in the earth. Father Higgins is trying very hard to talk them out of that idea. He says that during the years when the Franciscans were not active in the mountains the Indians backslid greatly in the matter of religion, for which he blames the Campbellites and the Presbyterians. I do not believe the Pueblo tribes or any other Indians truly changed their ideas of religion even when the Franciscans were strongest but merely assumed those parts of the Catholic trappings that appealed to them, particularly admiring the beautiful silver statues of Our Lady and the paintings, robes, candles, and singing. To me it is as sensible to believe the Ancient Ones came up from a hole in the earth as to believe that first there was one man and one woman in Paradise, especially if the Ancient Ones came up at the direction of spirits that live in this area. When I am in a high mountain meadow and the snow peaks above me rise into the clouds and I am camped by a stream amongst yellow and blue wild-flowers, then I am sure that whatever God there is must dwell in this place, for how could He be so foolish as to not?

The Texan expedition to Santa Fe in 1841 was not for Christianizing. The Texans have always felt that the New Mexico Territory to the source of the Rio Grande del Norte is theirs. After beating the Mexicans at San Jacinto and estab-lishing the Republic, though fretted with border troubles and Mexican threats, the Texans began to covet the moun-tain country. Lamar issued a proclamation inviting the citizens of New Mexico to join the Texans in a new nation. Some have explained the 1841 expedition in terms that would make it sound glorious and patriotic, but my father was frank about his reasons for going. He did not know exactly how he planned to do it, but he intended to make his fortune at Santa Fe de San Francisco and perhaps occupy some land there and send for his future wife.

The Texans gathered a force of more than three hundred men under General Hugh McLeod. Lamar himself spent the night in their camp and spoke to my father of their buffalo hunting adventures together. The Texans had pack mules, wagons, beef cattle, merchants, a doctor, and a cannon. There was band music, with drums and trumpets, and the Lone Star flag was carried as they rode out to begin a journey of some one thousand miles. Before they had ridden very many days they received word that the Mexicans in Santa Fe were sorely frightened and were causing trouble to the Anglo colonists there. My father recalled that a cheer went up from the men, reaffirmed in their cause by the ambition to rescue the Anglos and meanwhile to give the Mexicans another whipping. That exuberance departed before they arrived in the vicinity of Santa Fe. The Mexican militia that rode out to meet the Texans was genuinely afraid, my father said. Many of the Mexicans were armed only with bows and arrows and old muskets more dangerous to the shooter than to the target. They were prepared to flee at the opening cannon blast. At least one of their officers, in fact, having urged them to give battle, had already ridden off hastily in the opposite direction under view by Texan scouts.

The Texan position was located in the Pecos River Valley and the pitiful Mexican militia prepared itself with trembling and concern. Then the Mexicans beheld a sight that amazed them. In place of an invincible army, the Mexicans saw a poor, shabby, starving ragbag of men. Crossing the desert had been a severe hardship. Most of the animals were gone. A Kiowa attack in northwest Texas had resulted in the deaths of several men and the loss of many horses and cattle. The men were sick and thirsty and had no fight in them. They shamefully surrendered. My father said it was the lack of discipline and leadership that did them in, as many in the expedition were nothing more than rowdies to begin with. I have made that journey myself numerous times and found it not overly difficult.

The Mexicans reacted to their triumph as could have been expected. They subjected their captives to scorn and ridicule, though not taking them into Santa Fe, and then marched them down to the prison in Chihuahua with orders that the sick, weak, or malingering should be shot and their ears sent to the Governor at Santa Fe. I have heard stories of five pairs of ears tacked to the wall in that gentleman's office. We were told years later that of those who arrived in Chihuahua, every fourth man was shot. The Mexicans made the selections for execution by having the prisoners draw beans. The black beans meant death. It is a Mexican game that they delight in, but I suppose it is no worse than many other forms of justice practiced hereabouts for centuries. I have seen men murdered with less of a chance than one in four.

My father, however, was enterprising. With two others, he escaped the Mexicans while on the march, accepting a rifle ball in his right leg as the price for freedom. The Mexicans did not disturb themselves seriously about the escape. After a brief chase my father and his companions were consigned to the will of the desert, which was then—in that stretch called Jornada del Muerte—undergoing a blizzard. My father's leg was broken and the wound got infected and pained him so that he was delirious. He awoke one morning with sufficiently clear head to realize that his companions had abandoned him. He did not blame them, as it was the sensible thing to do, but he did not admire them for it either. He struggled to sustain his life by eating a chuckwalla and chewing cactus pulp and Spanish dagger flowers and drinking snow. Another day or two passed—in his deliriums he could not track the time—and when he awoke again, almost frozen, his vision was of the legs of ponies. He looked up to see a dozen Apaches gazing down on him as buzzards circled above. They were Mimbreños or Copper Mine Apaches with black greasy hair and bright headbands. This was not long after a massacre of Mimbreño warriors by scalp hunters who were paid one hundred dollars for a head of male Apache hair by the governments of Chihuahua and Sonora and were said to be financially induced also by the owners of the copper mines at Santa Rita del Cobre. In that massacre the great Mimbreño chief Juan José had been killed by a howitzer loaded with nails and concealed under bags of flour. The Mimbreños responded by slaughtering the miners and their families and making a stronghold of the mountains around the Santa Rita mines, the Indians not caring a whit for the copper itself except as ornament. In addition to having heard about this, my father also noted two fresh scalps hanging from the lances of two warriors and so believed that it was his moment to die.

Instead of killing him, the Mimbreños took him to their camp. Perhaps it was his delirious raving that saved him and perhaps it was only an Indian whim. Although one tribe is as different from another as the Dutchmen from the Spaniards, as a rule Indians are not sentimental toward white strangers. But they can be hospitable and friendly when not faced with danger. Certainly my father was no danger to them. Because of his condition and his being a white man, the shaman would not touch him, but in the Mimbreño camp was a Mexican woman captive, a wife of Mangas Colorado, who had some knowledge of orthodox medicine. She persuaded the council to allow her to set my father's broken and poisoned leg, which they found humorous. The splinting of the bone and the cleaning of the wound were nearly the death of him. He told me later that had it not so entertained the coons, he might have chosen to die. Then the shaman took over with his poultices of mud and herbs and hot prickly pears and his magic charms, and my father began to heal. He stayed six months in the camp of Mangas Colorado. In their direct fashion, the Indians called my father Bad Walk and ceased to be interested in him as he hobbled about the camp on the hickory crutch he had carved for himself. The Mimbreños were at peace with the Republic of Texas and had no doubt enjoyed the prospect of the Texans journeying up to Santa Fe to whip the Mexicans although were less satisfied with the result, as a Mexican victory seldom pleased an Apache from any angle.

Mangas Colorado became somewhat friendly with my father. The chief was a great flat-faced fellow whose name, in a faulty rendering of Spanish, meant Red Sleeves. He got that name for his practice of dipping his arms in the blood of

Mexicans he had killed, although he may not have done that grisly performance more than once if the truth were known. Eventually Mangas Colorado did admit that the two scalps my father had seen on the lances belonged to his former companions, but my father did not report that when he returned to Austin. He allowed the relatives of the two men to believe they were slain by Mexican guards. There was scant honor to be had in any case, but it was better for the families of the dead not to know their men had died from Apache arrows while abandoning a comrade. Mangas Colorado explained to my father in Spanish that his warriors had mistaken the Texans for Mexicans, which was quite possible owing to seasoning by the weather. My father was wise enough not to press the issue, as he was relieved that his own life was still in his possession. When my father could move about well enough on his crutch, the Mimbreños delivered him to a party of buffalo hunters who in turn delivered him to a patrol of Rangers, and so he arrived back in Austin after a series of adventures fed up with commerce for a while.

3

It is now a little more than two hours since I began to write my chronicle. I have paused for a supper of beans, jerked beef, and coffee. I have built a fire of piñon wood in my mud-brick fireplace. I do not hear Excelsior outside, but I feel that he is there. I talk to that mule as Indians talk to their ponies. I find him a loyal companion who is never boring.

Looking around my house, I see articles that have a history for me. There is an old powder horn of my father's, a gilt clock that my wife bought in Santa Fe after the merchant assured her that it was imported from Copenhagen, a short-handled hatchet with a wrist thong, some books in Spanish with leather covers that my mother admired, a doll carved from wood and dressed in calico, an albino buffalo robe that might bring two hundred dollars in St. Louis, my baby's Navajo blanket woven in patterns of blue and green and yellow, many other items. It is sweet and sometimes comic to remember how each item came to be here. But there is no use lingering on them, as I have little time to rely on.

I was writing of my father before I paused. When he

returned to Austin after the 1841 expedition, he took a job working for a wagoner. He did not resume his romance with my mother, although she was pledged, for he figured that he was now lacking in parts, as his leg had not mended properly and had left him a gimp. Word was coming back of those who had died in Chihuahua and also of the fate of the Mier Expedition into Mexico. He regretted, he told me, having returned at all but wished he had gone to California and allowed my mother to believe he had perished in the desert. When she heard of his presence in Austin, my mother came in her carriage to see him and persuaded him that she wished to be held to her vow. The idea that she could love him caused him astonishment. He protested, but she was firm. She is a small woman, five feet in height, but she has the strength of the Conquistadores. Against her, my father's arguments were worse than useless. They were married in Bexar and came back to Austin to live. With her dowry, my father established his own wagon-making business and began to earn a decent living. In the first years of their marriage he carried a derringer pistol in his belt at all times and was quick to produce it if he thought he was being joked as a cripple. He was so touchy about it that he blew holes in two cowherders in four years, though both survived. He also maimed a fellow with his crutch in Dutch John's Saloon on Congress Avenue.

In 1844 he bought the farm of a man who had been killed by Indians on West Pecan Street. My father paid twelve dollars an acre for the land and the cabin on the east bank of the Colorado. It was a good investment. To the west he could look across at the cedar hills. There were many wildflowers. Cottonwood, sycamore, and cypress trees grew along the creeks and streams. In abundance were oak, chinaberry, elm, hackberry, and willow trees, sage and cedar, so that he had no want for fuel or fencing. The city is built on hills and in the valley of the Colorado and to the west are higher hills. My mother and father enjoyed sitting of an evening and looking out at the blue hills and the smoke rising from the cabins. He had thought originally of settling in Montopolis but was happy with his choice, especially since the land south of the river bend was flooded more often than is entertaining.

There were bad times in Austin during that period. There were lights over where the government should be located, as many citizens of the Republic preferred to have it in Houston. Raiders tried to steal the archives and move them down to the bayous. Grass grew in the streets of Austin, my father told me. The Republic joined the United States despite the protests of some Yankee politicians who said the ten million dollars paid to settle part of Texas's debts was too high a price for dust, cockleburs, cactus, and wild Indians. My father did well with his wagon business. In 1850 I appeared, though I was not baptized until 1852 in the St. Patrick's Church.

One of my earlier memories is of crossing the river on Swisher's Ferry. I recall my mother wearing a bonnet and a long skirt and sleeves on the ferry. Thereafter, following a discussion with my father, she returned to her more Spaniard style of dress. I recall also my first visit to Franck's Bath House north of Swisher's Ferry. I could not have been more than five or six years of age and my mother took me into the tubs with her, as there were at that time no bathing rooms for men. When I was about eight years old the Army Camel Corps brought in its strange beasts and camped south of the river, causing a stompede of a cow herd that was crossing the Colorado. When I was ten they put gas lamps and a piano into the saloon at Buaas' Hall. I was not allowed inside, of course, but I did look in after my father and thought it an elegant place. In the town we had horse races, barbecues, circuses, minstrel shows, and actors, ample in the way of amusements, particularly for a boy capable of finding his own. That same year the War Between the States was coming and there were many parades and speeches.

I remember the Unionists having a parade with a band drawn in a chariot and putting up a U.S. flag at Hancock's Store. The Secessionists came and sang and there were brawls. The Secessionists flew a Texas flag atop a one-

hundred-foot pole near the old capitol building and wore
Lone Star flags in their hats. By then I was a student at the
German Free School and took to learning rapidly in the
fields of literature and philosophy and was good at history,
mental arithmetic, spelling, grammar, and punctuation. We
used to ride over and play around the brickyard at Shoal
Creek, and there were apothecary shops and jewelry shops
to look in the windows of. We could fish and hunt without
much pestering from Indians, of which there were Caddo,
Tonkawas, Wacos, Wichitas, Comanches, Kiowas, some
Lipans and others occasionally in the vicinity. But as youths
we began to feel the bitterness. When the news came to us
in the spring of 1861 about the fight at Fort Sumter, my
father was distraught, saying we all faced hard and bloody
days. The next year Texas voted itself into the Confederacy.
Old Man Sam Houston did not answer roll call and so
refused to pledge himself and was replaced as Governor.
There was quite a commotion about that, as I recall.

A law was passed making all men between eighteen and
fifty eligible for military service. My father, having but one
capable leg, was not acceptable, not that he would have
gone anyhow. He was opposed to slavery but believed, as
some do today, that there should be more than one nation
between the Atlantic and the Pacific, Mexico and British
America. I remember my father complaining about the
taxes, which were not so bad when paid with Confederate
money but difficult when paid in kind, and about the
drought. The black tongue killed many animals. The Travis
Rifles were organized, and the Quitman Rifles and Tom
Green Rifles and the Austin City Light Infantry. The Tom
Green Rifles sent back one of their battle flags with sixty
bullet holes in it. My father denounced it as tomfoolery.

There was a reward of thirty dollars a head for the
Mountain Rangers, as some of the Union sympathizers in the
hills called themselves. There were murders and hangings
around town. We ground corn and rye for coffee and used
corn to make molasses. At Waller Creek they were making
cannons out of brass carted from Mexico. There was a big

powder mill in the Cypress Creek valley. My father was in more than one fight in this period, as was I. Fighting was one thing I had a talent for and took pleasure in. There was never a time, once I could walk, when I was not ready to engage in a scrap of any sort for the slimmest of reasons. My mother objected, certainly, but concentrated for the main on keeping my head in my books whenever she could. She like-wise saw to it that I attended Mass with her at St. Patrick's. There was many a Mass that I observed through swollen eyes and many a response that came from cracked lips.

Maybe none of this is very interesting and I should not have gone on about it, but this was my background. Of my childhood I will relate no more except for two or three inci-dents. One took place in the summer of 1863 as I was going on thirteen years of age. It had quite a telling effect on my life, as you will see.

My father gave me a treat that morning. As it was June, and most lovely, with a sort of soft yellow light laying over the town, and the smell of honeysuckle and sound of bees making me too sleepy to do much work in the big shed behind our house on West Pecan Street, and as there was no school at the moment, my father asked me to go with him to deliver a new spring wagon we had built for a Dutchman farmer out in the hills. I had been fiddling around all morning. I was supposed to be working on the bed of a freight wagon we were building for a leather goods merchant, but it was one of those mornings when a hammer seemed very heavy, and I would sit for long moments between driving each nail and would stare out the big open door of the shed. Beyond the shed, across the dirt road, was a field of bluebonnets and an oak tree with a rope swing hanging from one limb. Who knows what I may have been thinking about? Most likely, nothing. Most likely I was simple-mindedly warming from the sun and lazing like a hound. Then I saw my father had come in the door and had been watching me, and I went to hammering like hail stones on the roof. He came over to me scowling. He got around on a cane when we were at home. In the matter of standing, he was all right and could even hop about some. But when it came to walking very far, it took determination on his part. Sweat would appear on his face and he would stick out his chin and his mustache would rise up and thrust out like horns. In damp weather his leg hurt him fiercely. Or when he had walked much his leg hurt, although at those times he was liable to become kind and patient and good-humored, not wanting to allow the pain to get the best of him.

"Climb down out of there, Peter," he said to me.

I descended from the wagon with quaking heart, for I was sure he had seen me loafing. When he felt good he was apt to wallop me for sins that would otherwise have passed.

"I ain't disturbing you too much, I presume? If you'd rather stay back here and hammer nails I could take Luther with me instead," he said.

Luther Freeman was an old Negro who worked for us. My father bought Luther and then set him free, whereupon he took the name Freeman as so many did. Luther was a mean old coon and arrogant toward me and I didn't miss many chances to devil him. Luther was standing by the forge listening with his head bent to one side and sweat shining on his black face. Although I say he was old, he was probably not more than forty then. Luther had big arms and a fondness for the sweet yellow wine from El Paso, and I was about half scared of him catching me some time when he was drunk and my father wasn't around. I supposed I would have to kill him if he did. My father had just bought me one of the new Dance Brothers & Park .44-caliber percussion revolvers that they had begun making over at Columbia. It was a fine weapon with a rifled barrel, a brass trigger guard, and a blade front sight. I was pretty accurate with it up to about twenty yards, but ammunition was hard to come by and I didn't have much chance to practice.

Anyhow, I guessed what was on my father's mind and ran to hitch the mules to the new Gerhardt wagon. What we would do was drive out in the new wagon and ride back on the mules, thus saving on the ferry fees. Swisher was charging a dollar for unloaded wagons but only fifty cents for a mounted man. Without taking along an extra wagon to drive back in, we could get across for a dollar and a half, including the twenty-five cents for each passenger, and back for a dollar, so we would save a dollar and a half, a sum not to ignore. My father had paid twenty dollars for my new pistol and besides had recently bought himself a Henry rifle that he had been wanting. It was a lever-action magazine rifle that used a .44-caliber rim-fire cartridge, and it was his joy. The Henry was a delicate piece of machinery and had to be pampered, but it would shoot sixteen times without reloading. He had bought it off a veteran of the Quitman Rifles who had taken it off one of Sherman's troopers someplace. It had a brass frame with the words New Haven Arms Co., New Haven, Connecticut, on it, plus Henry's Patent October 16, 1860, and my father had decorated the offside of the stock with brass tacks that spelled out *JPM*. He was talking about the rifle as we drove along the road toward the ferry with white caliche dust coming up behind us and hanging in the air before settling, as there was not enough breeze to scatter it.

"If I'd had me this Henry rifle when I was in the Rangers, there would be a fearful number less of brown boogers." he told me. That was how he talked. I recall that he was wearing his big hat with the brim that turned up in front, and the hat had a string that went around his neck to save him from chasing it in event of a sudden wind or jounce. "Some of them boogers was dreadful clever, you see. They used to dash up a few bravo boys to draw fire from our old single-shots—some of us even had muzzle-loading muskets—and oncet we had fired they would proceed to tumble all the rest down on top of us like mad devils, sending a lot of arrers whistling in while still out of range of our hand guns to make us duck our heads and when we looked up, why, boy, we was looking straight into the eyeballs of a swarm of crazy bucks who had ever intention of jerking the hair off our heads. It would take nearly a minute to reload one of them muzzle-loaders, and in that time a horse Indin could ride two or three hundred yards and shoot fifteen arrers. Now, there is cowardly brown boogers same as cowardly Englishmen, but not in no great amounts. Any brown Indin that lives on the desert or the plains or anywhere in all of Texas and the Hill Country, or up in the high mountains, has got more heart than a thicket full of bobcats. Even their sissy-men [by which my father meant those Indians called *berdaches* who prefer their own kind to women] is braver and tougher than the thugs that does such a bluster over at Dutch John's or such places, and don't you ever forget it if you intend to get a lot older."

So passed the morning in pleasant conversation. We crossed on the ferry, with some joshing about the raising of the prices, and went out on the road through the hills. The limestone cliffs that reared up from the water were white in the sun and past them were many a swale and valley, with slanting green meadows that had sheep in them. The hills went on, row after row covered in cedar with good timber in the valleys and good clear water flowing over limestone in the streams. We would come to a ridge and be able to see more ridges stretching far on out toward the Llano Estacado. The Llano Estacado is a huge broad plain on a plateau covered with high grass and in winter more buffalo used to roam there than a man could count. My father said he had once sat on a piece of high ground and watched buffalo pass in a herd ten miles wide from dawn to dark. You could hear their thunder and smell their stink for miles, and their dust blotted out the sun. That was near Yellowhouse Canyon at the foot of the plains. In those days few white men had ever seen the Llano Estacado, as the Comanches and their friends the Kiowas fought to protect their buffalo park. Even today, in this advanced and modern time, I doubt if there are more than two or three thousand white people in the whole area between Fort Worth and El Paso. But I believe my father's buffalo story. I saw much the same thing only four years after he told me.

At noon we rested a bit and watered our mules at Bee Creek and ate the lunch my mother had prepared. "Boy, you got the finest mother and I got the finest wife that ever breathed the air," my father said, chewing on a fried chicken leg. "If ever you hear a man call her a Meskin, you break his head right on the spot without another word being spoke. She is a Spaniard. Being a Spaniard is something to be proud of. It's nowhere near like being a Meskin mongrel such as the trash and vermin we got to chase out of Texas now and then. A Meskin is half snake, half coon, and all scum. He is nowhere near as good as a one hundred-percent nigger and usually even smells worse, although his skin may not be as unseemly looking. A Spaniard is entirely different from a Meskin. You can tell a Spaniard the second you see one. He stands up. Any race that turns out a woman like your mother knows enough to be proud of itself."

I myself have got along very well with most Mexicans and in fact have favored a number of them highly. But the wars and border troubles were not far from my father's memory, and it is natural to hate people who contest you for what you want. The idea of being friendly with Mexicans, as many on both sides were doing in the War Between the States, struck my father not only as foolishness but as a moral outrage. Union sympathizers were continually trying to slip down across the Rio Grande and ship out of Vera Cruz to join up with the Union Army. Some Union-loving families went to Mexico and stayed there, just as some Confederacy-loving families did after the War. Meanwhile the Mexicans were sending us brass for our cannons and were conducting a lively trade with us and were accepting citizens of either persuasion who escaped from New Orleans or Galveston.

"Tomfoolery and humbug," said my father. "The Meskins are playing both sides and that is a sin. In any quarrel, boy, you can't go two ways at oncet. You either stay out or you choose one side and stick with it."

"What are you doing now in this war but playing both sides?" I asked as we lay beside the river.

"Boy," my father said to me, "it is too nice a day to spoil it by beating you for your ignorance and lack of respect. So I think I will not, though I might yet if you open your mouth oncet more. I am for the Union in the matter of principle.

But I love Texas and have shared dangers with my Confederate friends here and have come to depend on them. A man should never go back on a friend no matter what the principle, for it is never worth it. Do you have any further comment?"

"No sir," I said.

"That is a lucky thing for both of us," said my father.

I hitched up the mules again and we resumed our drive to Gerhardt's farm. I had seen Gerhardt once before, when he came into my father's shop to order the wagon. My father had been dubious about Gerhardt's ability to pay, as the farmers in the hills were having lean times and high taxes. But Gerhardt was a tidy, thrifty fellow, like most Dutchmen, and soon he returned with the entire sum—part in gold, part in wool, and the rest in various produce that was worth more to us than money. Gerhardt was a short, round-headed man with pink skin and blond side whiskers. My father learned Gerhardt had come to Texas some fifteen years earlier along with a number of other Dutchmen who settled in the hills between San Antonio de Bexar and Fredericksburg. The Dutchmen managed to live in fair safety as the result of one of their leaders, a Baron von Meusebach, who was called El Sol Colorado by the Indians because of his red beard, making peace with several bands of Comanches at a meeting on the San Saba River. There were Dutchmen scattered here and there over millions of acres between the Colorado and Llano rivers, but they were good workers and did not try to bully or pester the Indians, nor did they slaughter the buffalo. Generally the Indians were content to accept gifts of coffee and sugar and cloth and occasional livestock and leave the Dutchmen to their labors.

This Gerhardt, my father told me as we drove along, had an unusual wife. She was a Lipan woman who had been captured by the Mexicans in a raid on an Apache *rancheria* near the old town of Zodiac, which is near to Fredericksburg, which is about a hundred miles west of Austin. In the fight her husband, a Lipan war chief called Bear That Walks, was killed. The Mexicans were scalp hunters, an unwholesome profession, as I can attest, but the woman being comely for a Lipan, was spared for other uses until the Mexicans wearied of her or could sell her as a slave. Gerhardt, whose own wife had died on the trip from their German state to Galveston, came across the Mexicans and observed their vile treatment of the woman and also overheard their plans for her. He persuaded the Mexicans to sell her to him for twice the price of her scalp, which in those days would have brought about twenty-five dollars.

The woman worked very hard for Gerhardt, as was her habit. He was not disappointed to learn she had been pregnant when captured. Two hard-working Indians were better than one, according to the Dutchman's reasoning. The woman bore a son. Together, Gerhardt and the woman built his farm. You might suppose the woman would have run off to join her own people. But hard as she worked for Gerhardt, it was nothing to how hard she had worked for Bear That Walks. With Gerhardt she was never hungry, never had to walk long distances with heavy loads, was seldom beaten and had a warm, dry place to sleep. Evidently she became fond of the little Dutchman, who called her Hilda, after his dead wife, and who eventually married her—which act required courage—and had the son baptized Jacob Charles Gerhardt. The boy's mother, the Lipan Hilda, named him Bear That Sings, for he was husky, like his father, and demonstrated a sweet singing voice as a child. It was not until later that he acquired his other names, Octavio being his favorite.

The Gerhardt farm was in a small valley below a humpbacked ridge. Through the valley ran a stream that had recently gone down after spring flooding, leaving bits of driftwood and other debris clinging to the cedars and littering the grazing land of Gerhardt's sheep. Behind the house, as we approached, was a peach orchard. The house was built of stone and we could see the sun striking the tin roof while we were still far off. The corral and outbuildings were of wood, though neatly put together. It was an industrious-looking place and very comfortable. The first we knew something was wrong was when we found a spotted cur laying dead near the barn. The cur's throat had been cut so that the poor beast's head was turned around backward.

"Indins," my father said, taking up his Henry rifle from the seat.

With a feeling of excitement and some apprehension, I produced my Dance Brothers & Park revolver and we drove in the wagon around to the front of the house where we beheld the source of the disturbance.

Half a dozen ruffians were getting ready to hang Mr. Gerhardt. They had heard us coming. Before we could react, a couple more of them stepped out from the side of the house with handguns aimed at us and ordered us to throw down our weapons. We had no choice but to oblige. I was so surprised that I sat and gaped. My father began cursing in his eloquent fashion and the ruffians laughed.

"In God's name, save me, Mr. McGill!" cried the Dutchman. His hands were tied behind his back and the noose was around his neck. The maguey rope had been tossed over a limb of a pecan tree. Gerhardt was very pale and wet looking. His wife was trussed up with peales and was lying in the dirt with a hunk of her deerskin skirt torn off and stuffed into her mouth as a gag. Her eyes were big as gold pieces. The boy was standing beside the porch while one of the ruffians held a shotgun at his back. The boy was a healthy specimen about my age, dark and muscular with his black hair loose in Dutchman style.

"What is it you're aiming to do?" my father said.

"Why, we are aiming to hang this feller, as you should be able to see," said one of the ruffians who seemed to be the leader. He was tall and skinny and had a bandanna handkerchief over his face, as did the others, and was wearing a pair of good black Mexican boots with silver buckles on the sides.

"Save me!" the Dutchman cried.

"What harm has he did you?" inquired my father.

"What harm he has did to us is no concern of yours," the

skinny ruffian said. "If you choose to make it so, we might have to hang you, too. We got no need to explain the reasons for hanging a Yankee-loving Dutch booger and Jew."

"I'm not a Jew. I'm a Lutheran," said Gerhardt.

"You look like a Jew to me. And it is well known that I hate Jews," the leader said.

The others nodded and said they felt likewise.

I did not know for sure what a Jew was or why it should be bad to be one, but I could tell it did not look good for the Dutchman. His wife had begun to moan and thresh about. One of the ruffians prodded her with his toe and made a remark I will not repeat, and the others laughed. The boy, Jacob, had not moved even his eyes except to glance at us when we appeared but was gazing steadfastly at the tall, skinny man in the Mexican boots.

"As loyal citizens of the Confederate States of America, we are going to confiscate your cattle, sheep, and other possessions, you Jew booger, and we sentence you to death for being a Yankee spy," said the leader.

"They are the Haengebund," the little Dutchman said to my father.

That was what the Dutchmen farmers called them. Under guise of being Confederate patriots, groups of ruffians roamed the hills creating trouble for the Dutchmen, most of whom were Union sympathizers and had no use for slavery, never having been raised on the notion. My father had told me about the Haengebund, but I had not paid it much attention as it had been no menace to me personally. Looking at the trembling little Dutchman with the rope around his neck, however, I made up my mind that the Haengebund were patriots we could do without.

"You are no better than thieves and murderers," said my father.

The leader cocked his pistol and pointed it at my father's head. "What did you say?" the leader said.

"I said you are a goat-breathed skunk," replied my father, "and also a yellow snake with a peanut for a heart."

The leader thought that over for a moment.

"You got the warter and I got the duck's back. I will attend to you some other time, gimp," the leader said.

"I swear you will get your chance, for I will recognize your ugly face no matter how many bandannas you cover it up with," said my father.

"Shoot him," a ruffian said.

"Hang the Jew," said another.

"Yes, hang the Christ killer," said another.

"Even if this man is a Jew, which he ain't, he don't deserve hanging. And besides Christ was killed two thousand years ago," my father said.

"Well, I ain't my own self got around to doing anything about it till now," said the leader. "Haul him up, boys."

"Oh Lord God in heaven deliver me," the Dutchman said. "Oh sweet Jesus Christ save me for I have done nothing to these men that they should want to kill me." His face looked pitiable, solemn, and frightened, with his eyes rolled up toward the skies as though he really hoped God might elect to come down and save him but could not see his way to believing it entirely.

"God!" said the boy Jacob in a loud voice. "You save this man, God!"

The ruffians laughed again, though somewhat nervously.

"Listen to me, God! You save this man!" said Jacob.

"God don't listen to a filthy Indin," one of the ruffians said. "Nor does He save a Yankee Jew," said another.

"Not especially a Yankee Jew that don't speak good English and consorts with Indins," said another.

"Haul him up!" the leader said.

Gerhardt began singing "Lead, Kindly Light." The boy Jacob joined in. He did in fact have a strong clear singing voice, and I have never heard a hymn sound more sincere or prayerful than what that boy sang that day. Two men grabbed the rope and started hauling on it. The rope squeaked and scraped on the limb and the men cursed and pulled, digging their heels into the ground, as Gerhardt rose up on his toes and kept singing until the maguey cut into his neck and even then his voice came out in little squeals like a rat's.

Gerhardt was not a heavy man, not more than a hundred and fifty pounds at most. But that is a considerable weight to haul up on a rope that is merely tossed over a tree limb. Another of the ruffians ran to help the first two. Jacob kept on singing. Gerhardt's neck was stretching and his eyes bugging out. Then several things happened at once.

My father jumped off the wagon seat, landed on his bad leg, fell to the ground, and the leader kicked him in the head, knocking him up against the hub of a wheel and rendering him dizzy. I jumped, too, and was thrown down and sat on by the biggest of the ruffians. And the tree limb broke with a crack, dumping Gerhardt in a heap and sending the three ruffians who had been hauling on the rope tumbling over backward.

"Thank you, God," said Jacob.

"Shut up, you dirty Indin," said the leader. "God didn't bust that limb and if you think this Jew booger is saved you are dumber than most coons."

By then the other ruffians had got up and were dusting off their pants and cursing. The leader went to his horse and got a rawhide peal about four feet long. It was the sort of cord that cowherders use for tying the legs of a calf. Proceeding to where Gerhardt lay, the leader cut the rope from the Dutchman's neck and yanked him to his feet, whereupon Gerhardt fell promptly back down again. This action was repeated three or four times before Gerhardt found the strength to stand. Naturally, he was a bit short on wind.

"I am saved," the Dutchman croaked when he regained his voice.

"No chanct of that, Jew," said the leader, looping the peal around the Dutchman's neck and grasping each end of it in his hands like a garrote.

"Rotten pig-hearted such-and-such," my father said, approximately, sitting up and touching the back of his head where it was bursted open and bloody.

The leader, who was in quite a rage by now, started pulling on the peal in such a manner as to throttle the Dutchman.

"God! You save this man!" said Jacob, who began singing again.

The leader's bandanna dropped down and his face twisted up with effort and sweat poured off his long nose as he pulled on the peal. The Dutchman's eyes bugged out again. He kicked and squirmed. The leader pulled and sawed on the peal until it cut his hands and they began to bleed. Disgusted, he dropped the peal and looked at his hands. "Look what you have did to me!" the leader said. Gerhardt fell down. There was blood on his neck and on his cotton shirt, but he was still alive.

"Thank you, God," said Jacob.

The leader wrapped his bandanna around his right hand, which was cut the worst.

"I'll be danged if I ever knowed it was so hard to kill a Jew," said the leader.

"Let's leave him be," said another ruffian.

"Yeah, we punished him for sure," another said.

"We've showed him what happens to Yankee spies."

"Boys, I come here to kill a Yankee-loving Jew booger and I ain't leaving till I have killed one," said the leader.

Gerhardt, lying on the ground, sounded like he was gargling. But he was trying to talk. What he was saying was that he was not a Jew and moreover that he did not care for Jews himself and that he was certainly not a Yankee and that there was a terrible mistake being made and if they would only leave him alone they could have all his cattle and sheep. A few of the ruffians listened as if they were impressed by what he was saying, but the rest were in a state of agitation and began arguing among themselves about whether to ride off in a hurry, shoot us all and then ride off, or go ahead and hang the Dutchman before riding off. The big fellow who was sitting on me was the only one who seemed undisturbed. "This is some chicken scratch," he kept saying. "This here is some chicken scratch indeed, my boy." I thought less of Gerhardt for his carrying-on, but I suppose it was reasonable of him to protest even if it was useless. After all he had been hanged and choked and that can tangle a man's thinking. It was a little surprising he hadn't tried that dodge earlier. But in a minute or two Gerhardt quit saying how he didn't like Jews and took to praying again. It was sort of gargle gargle gargle gargle but you could get the drift of it—God save me, I didn't kill Christ, I'm no Yankee-lover, I'm a simple farmer, I'm a decent Christian, I tithe for a regular ten percent, I say my prayers every day, I never saw these men before, and so forth. Quite a number of words gargled out of those poor bloody swollen lips.

"They's a bigger tree yander," said one of the ruffians, pointing toward a large oak tree beside the stream.

"Stand up, Jew," the leader said to Gerhardt. That command wasn't worth the breath it took to utter it. Even if he could have stood up, which was unlikely, the Dutchman wasn't about to march down to that other tree so they could hang him again. "Stand up or I will put a bullet in you." That command likewise did not make much impression. "These here Jews is sure stubborn and unfriendly," said the leader, kicking Gerhardt in the ribs.

"All of you must go now," said Jacob.

"Haw, listen at that crazy Indin," the leader said.

"God, I am telling You to make them go now," said Jacob. "Indin thinks he can boss God," one ruffian said.

"That's a crime against religion," said another.

"I am telling You!" Jacob said and resumed his sweet singing.

The Lipan woman, Hilda, was no longer struggling but lay quiet watching the scene as I have since seen Indians do when they know death is certain and fighting is aimless. I saw my father tense himself as though about to spring up, but a handgun poked against his ear made him sit back again.

"Boy," said the fellow on top of me, "I am willing to let you up so's you can watch this here fine chicken scratching from a better vantage if you will promise not to make me no woes."

"Don't promise him nothing," my father said.

"Let's get on with this," said a ruffian. "I got chores to do at home."

"I need to be getting back, too," another said, looking at his pocket watch and glancing at the sun.

"Stand up, Jew," said the leader.

When Gerhardt did not move, but kept on gargling, the leader bent over and tried to lift him. But the leader's hands were too tender and he was somewhat tired by now.

"All right you hard-necked old cow fleck of a Jew, I'll show you a trick or two about killing," the leader said.

He went over and got the maguey rope he had cut off the Dutchman's neck. Fashioning a slipknot, he lifted up the Dutchman's head by the hair and replaced the rope around his neck. He tied the other end of the rope to the horn of his saddle. Jacob was singing very loud.

"Git!" the leader yelled and slapped his horse on the flank.

The horse slowly backed off until the rope was tight and then stopped. Clearly that was a horse trained for cow work, where the practice is to keep the rope taut on a downed beast while the cowherder rushes to it and binds its feet. The rope had tightened up so that Gerhardt's face turned a blotchy blue, but if Gerhardt didn't move any more the horse wouldn't either. That put the leader out of his head with fury. He grabbed a Mexican quirt from his saddle and raised it to strike the horse.

Jacob's song changed to a scream. He leaped at the leader of the ruffians. The fellow with the shotgun fired at him, missed and hit one of his own companions in the leg, shattering the kneecap and blowing out bits of bone, flesh and denim trouser. The man howled, sat down and looked at the meat of his knee. Jacob was to the leader in two bounds. The leader swung his quirt and slashed it across the boy's left eye. Jacob fell yelping and crying and trying to get up again. The quirt had cut through his eyebrow and eyelid and on down his left cheek for two or three inches. I saw his eyeball come out in a gush of soppy matter. The eyeball was sliced almost in half and lay on his cheek like an onion. Everybody was yelling all at once save for Hilda, who had not moved.

Of course the commotion and racket scared the horse who bolted.

And there went Gerhardt, the little Dutchman, bouncing and banging and skidding across the grass at the end of the rope as the horse galloped toward the creek.

That deed used up the remainder of the ruffians' nerve. Loading their wounded man into the new wagon, they then fetched the leader's horse and cut Gerhardt loose. In their hurry, they did not take the sheep or cattle nor any other plunder and did not even pause long enough to steal our guns which still lay where we had thrown them. They rattled off with our mules pulling the new wagon and with horsemen all around. My father shot three times at them with his Henry before it jammed from the dirt, and they fired three or four shots back as they rode into the woods. I heard a bullet pop as it went past my head.

Hilda put Jacob's ruined eyeball back in its socket and tied a bandage around his face. I hitched a team to the Dutchman's old wagon and my father and I lifted the body into the bed. Gerhardt's head was the size of a pumpkin. His broken neck was twice as long as it was supposed to be.

Coming around to the back of the wagon, Hilda looked at the bottoms of the Dutchman's shoes.

"I command you to leave us now," she said, talking to his spirit. "I command you not to bother us while we live, for we loved you and did the best we could."

"We will get a doctor for the boy and you will stay with us until we are sure the danger is over," my father said.

Hilda nodded. Like all Lipans, she was afraid of ghosts and eager to be gone, for the Lipans believe the dead want their relatives to join them. When there is a death, the Lipans move away quickly and never mention the dead person's name again. Hilda was barely Christianized enough to allow the corpse to ride in the wagon with us, and we could tell she was uneasy about it. After a bit she began to sway from side to side and croon.

We drove back the way we had come, past the orchard and around the ridge. It was still a lovely day, with the light the color of ripe peaches. In the fields were large patches of red and yellow wildflowers called Indian blankets, and we passed a hillside of bluebonnets. We could see gray sheep moving in a meadow with no cur sheepdog to keep them from straying. The cows raised their heads to watch us go by. A mockingbird dived from the branches of a cottonwood, nearly hit my father's hat, then flashed back up to the branches and twittered at us for coming too close to his nest. Jacob spoke once on the way back to Austin.

"That God up there is useless," is all he said.

That same week the Rangers found the wagon by Hamilton's Pool, with the mules tied nearby. Mule stealing was a serious offense. In the back of the wagon was much dried blood, too much, I would say, for the man who bled it to have lived afterward.

4

I have been outside for a look around or, more truthfully, for a listen. I could hear nothing except the rumbling stomach of Excelsior and the water running in the river and in the irrigation ditches. The Spaniards dug the first of those ditches to irrigate the land along the rim of the plateau. To do so, water had to be brought up from the valley in the mother ditch. How the Spaniards arranged it I have never understood, not having a knack for engineering, but the water comes nearly a thousand feet up the side of the cliff at about a forty-five-degree angle. Upon reaching the rim, the water is dispersed into the network of ditches and is controlled by sluice gates. Shutting off a man's sluice gate to divert more water for yourself is a guarantee of a fracas. The result is that the farms along the rim grow much beans, squash, corn, pumpkins, and other victuals. As the rim is five miles long, this is a rich area. But to stand down in the valley and look at that mother ditch climbing the wall, you would think it impossible.

It is a clear night now that the rain has gone. The stars are close and the air is so clean that it is a delight to breathe it. I saw one small fire in the mountains across the valley. Whoever lit it to warm his camp does not know Octavio is near. I stood at the edge of the rim and looked across the valley to the dark shapes of the mountains and took in their feeling of strength. The lights of Valdez are out, although I can still smell the piñon smoke, as that smell is never entirely absent from this place. To the west is the great gorge of the Rio Grande and beyond is the desert. I did hear the yapping of coyotes, but in this high clear air it is difficult to tell how far off they are, for voices carry great distances at night.

Writing has cramped my fingers. To restore them I rubbed and patted Excelsior and chatted with him about the difficulty of putting down so many words and trying to force them to make sense. Excelsior was sympathetic but not overwhelmed. That is his usual stance. He blew his white breath and twitched his ears and caused his hide to jump as I scratched him. I fear my endeavors in this house at this table in this lantern light are lost on him. He views this as conceit and would rather I were up to more honorable work.

Also I find I am hungry again. I will settle for a cup of coffee, as I brought a tin of Father Higgins' best from the mission though I brought few other provisions. The beans, bacon, and flour are almost gone, but there is plenty of salt and brown Mexican sugar and there is enough beef hanging in the smokehouse to last me longer than I will likely need it. Thinking of food, I feel a craving for buffalo tongue roasted over a low hot fire of buffalo or antelope chips. I recall that in the prime hunting days, before the herds were so diminished, more than once I had buffalo tongues in front of me in piles higher than my head. Often I used to cut open a fresh-killed buffalo and eat its liver sprinkled with bile, after the practice taught me by the Tanima Comanches. They were a brave group and good hunters, but their table manners would never have suited my wife. She was not fond of Comanches.

I remember a dinner I had in an Antelope Comanche camp one evening about ten years ago, which was about ten years after the hanging of the Dutchman and a while before

Octavio decided to kill me. I had come upon the Antelopes very suddenly, to the shock and displeasure of both me and them. It was in the spring and I was alone, riding generally west from Hermosillo in Sonora. I had been in the Sierra Madre Occidental on the west coast of Mexico hunting for gold and otherwise disporting myself. In returning to Texas I made a wide detour to the south of the Chisos Mountains, where some very nasty-tempered Kiowa Apaches had a *rancheria* at the time, and came up across the Rio Grande at Eagle Pass and so proceeded north through the brush until I climbed onto the plateau of Texas and went into the Hill Country. I was traveling at a leisurely pace with no place to go, a condition that I enjoyed. It was in my mind to hire a couple of skinners and wagons and go on a buffalo hunt, although this was far from the best time for it. Late spring is the calving season. The bulls were ill-humored at this period, circling the herd and attacking wolves that came too close. Also the great beasts were shedding. Their hair was falling off in large patches, making them a haven for flies, mosquitoes, and ticks. Late spring was a time to take meat, not hides, but it had already got so that the professional hunters would shoot any sort of scraggly hide and leave the meat for the wolves, vultures, coyotes, carrion crows, and worms.

Idling along, it also went through my mind to turn off to San Antonio for a spot of gambling or veer out toward the Mimbres Mountains in New Mexico Territory and poke about for another lost mine I had heard of. I had two good horses— a fine Kentucky mare I was riding and a shaggy little Indian pony—and a strong pack mule, nearly a thousand dollars in gold from the Sierra Madre Occidental and three hundred dollars' worth of gold onzas I had been paid by the Governor of Chihuahua. I crossed the Nueces River west of San Antonio where I would have to turn at once if I so decided. I walked up a sandy bank, leading my horses and mule through difficult footing, and went out of the shadows of the willows and saw them looking at me.

They had pitched camp in a meadow along the river above the bank and behind the willows. There were some twenty tepees of the usual sort, with sixteen to eighteen poles stacked together to join at the top and fan out at the bottom to form a framework that was covered by buffalo hides. Immediately the dogs, who had allowed the spring weather to dull their wits as much as I, began to bark and run at me in a series of short dashes. Many Indians train their dogs not to bark, but most, being dogs after all, persist. I stood rooted. My Sharps buffalo gun was packed onto my mule and my father's old Henry rifle was in a deerskin scabbard on my saddle. All I wore on my person in the way of armament were my Colts revolver in a holster on my right leg, a derringer in my belt, a Bowie knife in a scabbard on my left leg and a dagger in my right boot. I was fair dressed for an evening in the dance halls, but before I could have reached my Henry one of the bucks I saw pick up his short *bois d'arc* bow could have shot two dogwood arrows clean through my person.

So I dropped the reins and held out my empty hands, moving my right hand, palm up, toward the fellow with the bow and then making with that same hand a general sweep to include the camp. I wanted no misunderstanding. Looking around with only my eyes, I saw two more bucks had appeared with a couple dozen women and children and all were watching me. One particular dog, a cur that had some mastiff in him, was uncomfortably near. I could see his yellow teeth and his slavering tongue as he whined and snarled and drew nearer, emboldened by the fact that I had not moved. There appeared to be confusion in the camp. More women and children came into view but no more bucks. In front of several of the tepees were deerskins pegged out for scraping. In the middle of the camp fires smoldered beneath eight or ten pots and kettles set on piles of blackened stones or hanging from rigs made of barrel hoops. Drying meat hung on tree limbs out of reach of the dogs. The odor of the Indians came out to greet me even if they did not—it was a scent of wet dog, grease, blood, dung, animal fat, spoiled meat, sweet and sour breath; an odor so pungent that I could smell it although I myself had been riding for five days without pausing for a bath and was extremely ripe. I was about as gamy as I care to get. To that social offense I attribute my not having smelled the Indians earlier, as I had approached from downwind. I do not know how to attribute my not having sensed them, for my sense of danger by then, when I was twenty-three or thereabouts, was so keen that I have awakened from a slumber when an enemy was yet a half-mile off. Berating myself for my lazy brain, I stood motionlessly with my arms out, palms up, and waited and watched the cur edging toward me.

One of the braves lifted his right hand—his left holding the bow—and touched his index finger to his forehead above the left eye and drew the finger across his brows; then pointed toward me and back toward the camp with a shrugging gesture. White man, he was saying in a not unfriendly manner, what do you want with us?

I again made the motion for peace. I motioned that I recognized them as Comanches—which sign is to wriggle the index linger backward to indicate the stealth of a snake—but asked which band they were. In this area I would have expected them to be the Penetakas, also called the Honey Eaters or the Wasps, but would not have been surprised to find they were Tanimas or Tanawas, except I had heard all three of those bands had gone up to the reservation. It was on a buffalo hunt with the Tanimas, when I was seventeen, that I first undertook to eat raw hot fresh liver, from which indulgence the Tanimas got their name of Liver Eaters, although the practice was not uncommon among most buffalo Indians. But I had since fallen out with their band over some quarrel or other and I sincerely hoped these were not they. Nor was I on such good terms with the Penetakas, but that is another tale.

There was muttering in the group around the tepees. The cur was almost close enough for me to kick him. The other dogs were yapping around me and mine in a circle. The brave, touching himself, made the sign for Human Beings, which is what the Comanches and many other tribes call themselves, our name for them coming from Komantcia, which is a Spaniard corruption of the Ute word for enemy. The brave made the sign with his right hand for the swiftness of running, and again I was surprised. They were the Quahadi or Antelope band. I had thought them to be much farther west at that time. This was a sub-band of Antelopes who had split off from the others of their tribal affiliation for some purpose—either political disagreement or to set up a temporary base for war or raiding. A war or raiding party would account for the absence of most of the braves. In a camp of that size there should have been at least fifteen or twenty braves. There never were very many Antelopes and a party of twenty braves was a large party. If they were out for war, there was no better moment to make my run than the present. However, I detected past the tepees a considerable remuda of horses and perhaps a hundred head of cattle whose presence, along with the lack of paint on the four braves I saw, could mean they were merely on a stealing expedition and would allow me to pass.

I motioned that I wished to proceed. The brown coons spoke among themselves, the women giving shout to various opinions and the braves unable to decide. But it seemed to me that the argument was not going in my favor.

I kicked the dog. I was wearing my favorite boots—of Ute make, with rawhide soles and with buckskin uppers that were soft enough for comfort but tough enough to fend off thorns or mute the strike of a rattler—but I wished I had been wearing the heavier, clumsy boots of the cowherder, for I did wish injury to that cur. The dog did a grand somersault, yowling and kicking, back into the pack. Meanwhile I stepped quickly around to the side of my Kentucky mare, putting her between me and the Antelope braves and putting myself beside the oiled butt of my Henry, seeing very clearly the old *JPM* in brass tacks.

"*No vaya tan aprisa, mi amigo,*" a voice said behind me. "*El viento ha cambiado.*"

There was a second then when I might have died.

When I heard the voice my knowledge told me it was an Indian speaking Spanish and my instincts told me that I would not have the leisure to reach for the Henry but should draw my Colts and shoot while turning, maintaining a slight chance to mount the mare, cut the mule and pony free and ride toward the willows to my left. It would mean turning myself broadside to the camp, but I would be down on the left side of the mare's neck. It would also mean exposing my back to whoever was behind me, but I had to take the risk that perhaps he was a lone buck returning from the river. And of course it was probable that when I turned I would kill the buck or vice-versa and the problem would solve itself in that respect.

But in the wink that it required me to make these computations, other impressions commenced: What the voice said ("Don't be in such a hurry, my friend. The wind has changed.") was not necessarily menacing; there was the sound of hoofs plodding in the sandy bank and of leather creaking; I got the smell and sense of many people.

When I turned it was with my hands held up and out, as previously, in the gesture of peace.

Behind me, as I had feared, were the rest of the braves. A look at their paint and costume confirmed that they had been out for war and that they had been successful. If it had not been a profitable trip, the members of the party would have come in singly with their faces painted black and the tails and manes lopped off their horses. But these were in wahoo regalia. All that was lacking was the rejoicing and wild galloping about, and that would have been because they had tracked me into camp and so had arrived by stealth.

What a fantastic sight they were! Their faces and lances were painted red, green, and yellow. They carried buffalo-hide shields painted with bright mystic symbols and designs and ringed with eagle and turkey feathers—the eagle being a symbol of power and the turkey of cunning—and with horse tails and bits of fur and plumes. Each man wore around his neck or elsewhere on his person an amulet containing his magic which was his secret and his power, be it merely a little bag of bird claws or a snake skin or a colored stone or whatever, and usually several mixed items. The horses were painted red and ocher and other colors and some had ribbons in their tails and manes.

A few of the men wore headdresses of buffalo horns fashioned from the skull of the beast with the hair left on, and some wore deer antlers. One wore a badger fur with the head of the animal leering atop the Indian's own head. Another wore a U. S. Cavalry hat adorned with eagle feathers, and still another wore a woman's cotton sunbonnet from which dangled feathers and strings of beads. Their long hair fell in braids to the sides of their faces; the braids were bound up in fur, bird claws, cloth, or gewgaws; a scalp lock hung down in another thin braid. Most had on moccasins, breechclout, and leggings, for they had been through shinnery country, but their torsos were naked and were painted in designs of green, blue, yellow, black, red, and white. At a glance I saw at least three scalps, one of them blond, on willow hoops.

I was trying to make out the fellow who had addressed me. He was the leader, sitting on a pad saddle atop his pony. The pony had a war bridle of braided rawhide with the free end of it tucked into the rider's belt so that he could retrieve the pony if thrown. A loop was braided into the pony's mane so that the rider could suspend himself along the animal's neck as I had been prepared to do with my mare, whose neck had a leather strap around it for that function.

The fellow looked at me solemnly. I suppose it was solemnly, for he was so painted up it was difficult to tell his expression. A slash of black went across his eyes from ear to ear, causing a fearful flutter when he blinked. A similar slash went across his mouth, and the two were connected by lightning bolts of red. Two strings of bear claws hung on his chest. His torso, which was well-muscled but starting to sag at the breast in aging, was covered with daubs of paint, some for magic and some for decoration. He had a copper bracelet at his left bicep and gold earrings in his ears. His shield and lance were in such a profusion of feathers and battle honors that they seemed to be constantly moving, which was one reason for those ornaments. He had a short hunting bow in his left hand and in his right an arrow that was already strung to the sinew, the dark iron tip ready to fly. Around him the other braves came up in a semicircle, glancing from him to me in some puzzlement.

"Why do you not greet me?" the fellow asked in Spanish, or rather in border Tex-Mex that many Indians can speak.

"Meaning no offense," I said in Spanish, "but I can't place you. Though you call me friend, and I prefer to be your friend, in honesty I cannot bring forth your name," etc., etc. I went on about it in a convivial tone for some time, as Comanches are ornate speakers and love an orator and also as I was in quite a mess.

They heard me out. They were pretty interested in at what length I could say something as simple as "Who, me?" Eventually, when I had finished, the fellow turned his buffalo-skull headdress from one rank of braves to the other and addressed them in the Comanche tongue, which is like the northern Shoshone, though of course with variations of dialects in the different bands. In Comanche and with signs I can handle a basic discourse, though am at a loss for genuine oratory.

"My lion-hearted, fire-breathing comrades," the chief began, near as I could understand, "today we have earned for ourselves great glory, not to mention many fine horses and Longhorn cattle and other booty which is ours by right of having taken it…" I saw the braves start to fidget. They had probably ridden a long way, splitting up after the ambush of some farmer and his family, and rejoining at another place and then driving those horses and cattle back to this camp. They came in without having had a man killed, although I saw one who had what appeared to be a bullet wound in his shoulder and had patched it with mud and grass after allowing blood to mingle grandly into his paint. For them the party was a huge success, and what they had wanted to do was to ride into camp and start the festivities. They wanted to dance, shout, brag, smoke, drink if possible, eat and frolic with the women. Speechmaking was for later. But the leader's magic had evidently been potent, and if the spirit urged him to speak the braves would listen. The Comanches

were respectful to speakers. If this one was outside the
bounds of proper behavior, they would at least sit through
his harangue, for, other than it being the courteous thing to
do, who knew but what the spirits that possessed him might
turn dangerous?

"...and this person here, while not a Human Being, yet is
well known to us and it is my request that he be allowed safe
passage through our territory," the fellow said, meaning me.
That was presumptuous of him, as this was not his territory
any more than it was mine, but the words heartened me.
"Now let us celebrate our victory," he said and the whooping
and shouting began. To me in Tex-Mex he said: "You will
smoke with me and share my beer."

"Beer?" I said.

"It is all that I have kept of our plunder," the chief said.
"The rest I have divided among the braves who followed me,
for to do less would be to show doubt in my magic and my
ability to do it again. But you know the custom." He sounded
regretful for a moment, though the movement of his lips and
the blinking of his eyes made him look like the spook-face a
child imagines is peering in the window at night. "Yet I do
have that beer," he said, cheering up. "I have a great barrel of
it. I think it comes from the new beermaking place beside
the river near Austin, for I believe I recognize the markings,
and I wish to share it with you."

So saying, the chief dismounted, dug the rein out of his
belt, handed over his horse—a U. S. Cavalry mount, by the
way, reshod with rawhide—to a boy, bade the boy take my
horse, mule and pony also, and began walking toward the
tepee. That Cavalry mount must have belonged to an officer,
for it was a fine dun gelding, though I guessed it was not
quite fine enough to be the chief's war horse. On a raid the
Comanches liked to take two horses each, one for transporta-
tion and one for riding in action. They knew the value of a
fresh mount and preferred to save their really good horses for
the actual raid or for the buffalo chase or for a big race. A
Comanche on a really good, fresh horse was one of the
wildest, bravest boogers anybody ever saw. A Comanche on a

bad or tired horse tried to keep out of the way and would run from a fight without a twinge of conscience. They were not lacking in brains when it came to making war.

I followed through the screaming mob. I noted there were no small children or old people. They must have been left back with the main band, as a war-raiding party, even one that would pause to set up camps like this one, must of necessity travel fast and requires able bodies. There were more warriors than I had counted on, too. But it is frequently true that a war-raiding party will have more than one man per lodge. In times of peril the Comanches do not mind sharing their women.

The women had taken the three scalps on the willow hoops and were hooting and yelping and dancing about in disgusting fashion. The dogs were barking, including the cur I had kicked. The warriors had gone to sit in front of their tepees and light their pipes and relax in glory. The medicine man went into the medicine lodge to do some hocus-pocus. We walked past one fellow, unpainted, who sat before his tepee in a nasty sulk; I recognized him as the man with the bow I had first seen in the meadow. I figured him to be a *pukootsie*, or backward fellow, who had got his ire up and had decided to be as nasty and difficult toward himself and all forms of activity as possible. He did not look at us but sat and stared at a small mound of colored glass that was piled between his bare feet.

"Hopping Crow chose not to go with us," the chief said. The Comanches practiced a sort of cooperative anarchy in which a man did not have to do anything he did not want to do. Once the raid was under way, the war chief or raid leader was the boss, which was only common sense. But at any moment up until then, anybody could turn around and go home if he saw fit. The chief was the chief because people decided to follow him, not because there were laws that ordered them to. "Hopping Crow is grieving," the chief said, walking through the mob. "A ghost visited him the night we were preparing to leave on our raid. We were parading around the camp, singing our songs, smoking our pipes, getting ready to leave before daylight. Poor Hopping Crow went into the trees to eliminate. As he squatted, the ghost came. The ghost was a short man. He had been scalped and his fingers and genitals had been cut off. He was very unhappy. At first Hopping Crow thought the ghost was one of his own victims who was doomed to wander the spirit world forever in that miserable condition because of Hopping Crow's mutilations. Being a brave man, though sensibly not wishing to offend a ghost, Hopping Crow denied any knowledge of having killed the person and asked him to be off."

The chief put down his shield and lifted his tepee flap, which faced downwind, and the odor nearly bowled me over. Inside it was dim and hot, with fire burning under a cooking pot in the center of the lodge and smoke rising through the smoke hole. Several buffalo robes were scattered about. Motioning for me to sit, the chief then himself sat and wearily removed his buffalo-skull headdress. Hanging from a medicine stick that leaned against the wall was a full war bonnet of eagle feathers.

"That was presented to me by friends," the chief said, noticing my eyes on the bonnet. "But my vision told me not to wear it on this raid. Ah, my vision. It was a considerable vision. One of the very finest. But I was speaking of Hopping Crow."

The chief took up his pipe and lit it with a brand from the cooking fire. He presented the pipe to the four directions as he puffed. The smoke smelled sweet and earthy, of mud and roots. I accepted the pipe and smoked it, making the four gestures in the proper ceremony. The taste was hot but not unappealing, though the Comanches could and did smoke anything that would burn and one had to be cautious. I saw the red painted part in the chief's hair as he bowed his head and mumbled an incantation to himself. The painted part was coming to signify membership in the peyote cult, which was spreading among many tribes. Then he looked up and for the first time I thought maybe I did recognize him.

"The ghost," he said, "told Hopping Crow that his magic would not avail him if he went on the raid with us. The ghost said he had seen Hopping Crow plainly in a vision and that he had marked a magic ring around Hopping Crows heart. Into that ring would go a bullet. Hopping Crow tried to argue, but there is no disputing the word of a ghost, as any fellow of the slightest wit will agree. So Hopping Crow stayed here. He needed the horses and other fine things we got, but he would not go against the ghost. It was a wise decision. One of the persons at the farm we raided was short. He shot the bullet into Knows Nothing's shoulder, after which of course we cut off that person's fingers and genitals. Had Hopping Crow been with us, the short man's bullet would have killed him."

The chief smoked for a few minutes in silence.

"So you see," he said at last, "it is not absolutely required to obey a ghost. One can elect to die instead."

From outside we heard a fearful ruckus. The women were yelling in a different manner from their victory chanting. Someone screamed and began to protest in English. The chief sighed, rose from his cross-legged position without using his hands, and went through the flap with me following.

The Antelope women had a white girl down on the ground near the cooking fires and were beating her with sticks. They had ripped off her dress and several warriors were sporting pieces of it. Her petticoat was rapidly disappearing as hands clutched at her between blows. She had very long black hair and was quite well formed as I could quickly tell although she was doing her hest to conceal her body from the gaze of the warriors.

"Cease this!" the chief said, or words to that effect, and after another blow or two the women stopped beating the girl. She lay on the ground crying and covering her breasts. Her face was smeared with dirt through which the tears made little rivulets. Bruises and welts were beginning to appear.

"This ignorant unspeakable cast her shadow across the cooking fire," said one of the women.

"A grave offense," the chief said. "Remove the food from that pot and bury it at a safe distance. However, the girl is young and stupid. She must not be killed. At least, not yet. She is valuable."

When the girl perceived that the beating had stopped, she opened her eyes. Seeing me, she leaped up and ran to me, crying, holding up her petticoat with one hand and covering her breasts with the other.

"Oh, I knew they would send someone to save me," she said.

She was about sixteen years of age and had a most satisfactory face as well as figure. She was perhaps an inch taller than my mother, so that the top of her head came nearly to my shoulder. That she expected me to rescue her was not only clear but reasonable. To do it was another matter. The braves and the women were crowded around in the mood for some lively game, such as skinning both of us. But as she pressed her sobbing face against my chest I felt a stirring that I have seldom felt, and my resolve to mind my own business faded away.

"Calm yourself," I said.

She looked up at me with large, wet gray-green eyes.

"They did send you, didn't they?" she said.

"Didn't who?" I said.

"You're not from the Army or the Rangers?" she said.

"No ma'am."

"But you're a white man, looks like," she said. "You take me away from here." Then she began to vilify me. "What are you doing here with these murdering savages? What kind of a criminal and bully are you? Get me out of here at once! You must be one of those filthy squaw men or despicable traders. Get me out of here. Oh, I should have known you were not to be trusted!"

She talked on in that nature for a moment, being hysterical with pain and fright. My position with the Antelopes was not so secure that I could proceed with any dramatic rescue, though she did not discern that.

"Maybe we should beat her some more," said the chief after listening to her.

"That would only spoil her looks," I said.

"Then spoil them!" shouted a fat woman waving a buffalo-horn spoon.

"No, my friend is right," the chief said. "She is a handsome girl even if she is too pale for a man of taste. I believe I will take her for myself." To me in Tex-Mex he said: "I brought but one woman, as one of my wives is in her period of bleeding and thus is repulsive, another wife is with child, and a third I left in the bed of my brother for luck. I will use this girl here as my own, for I should have something due me more than a barrel of beer. After all, I was the one who dragged her out of the house."

The chief announced his intentions in Comanche. There were grumblings from a couple of young bucks and from several of the women.

"Look at her," said the fat woman. "She is hideous and much too old ever to become a Human Being."

"Well," an older brave said, "the white men have odd tastes. Just as this one here"—he pointed to me with the shin-bone of a deer—"is not pleasing to look at, she is not either. But in the white villages they don't know a pretty thing when they see one."

"This one is much too white and much too tall to be hand-some in anyone's way of thinking," said a little, fat, bow-legged warrior whose hair was plastered with buffalo grease. Again, meaning me.

"This talk makes my head hurt," the chief said.

Eventually they resumed their dancing and shouting, as the chief did not seem about to change his mind. The fat woman carried off the cooking pot to be emptied. The girl was looking back and forth from the chief to me.

"Go to this man's tent and stay there," I told her.

"You are a hooligan and a scum," she said and ran weeping to the chief's tepee.

As the day progressed into evening, with much dancing

and yelling, I learned of the girl's plight. The Antelopes had left their horses in a grove of elms and had crept up on foot to her father's sod farmhouse near Bee Caves, which is a few miles west of Austin, early in the morning of the previous day. The father, mother, and brother were outside doing chores—chopping weeds in the vegetable garden, milking the cows, slopping the hogs, all such things as farmers do—when the Antelopes appeared. The chief rushed up and touched the father twice with a short-handled battle-ax to count coup. That is considered a very brave thing to do. But meanwhile the father fetched his rifle from the doorway and shot a hole in Knows Nothing. The chief then killed the father with an ax and took his scalp while the mother and brother were meeting a similar fate. They found the girl in the kitchen, as these events had required only two or three minutes and she had not known how to behave. Admiring her appearance, the leader made her a captive. When I asked if they were not concerned about the Army punishing them, the chief laughed.

"Not the Army," he said. "They walk and can't shoot much. Maybe we would not like to fight the Rangers, who ride good horses and shoot six times or more with one gun. But we don't worry about the Army. Now we eat."

The girl was summoned from the tepee and made to serve us. She had repaired her petticoat and had wrapped a deerskin around her shoulders, but her attitude toward me had not improved. She kept turning toward me glances of loathing. The leader spoke frankly about his intentions toward her—mentioning her physical features in particulars, speculating about her experience, discussing what he planned to do and how he would go about it and how it would affect him. The other braves made suggestions. Fortunately the girl could not understand a word of it, but the laughter of the braves and the women gave her a good hint. There was nothing for me to do but keep silent and wait. The poor girl, so recently deprived of her family and now on the verge of losing another possession she no doubt thought of as precious, was kept hustling about in the delivery of victuals and was sped at her tasks by being poked with sticks. As if that was not bad enough, the sight of the Antelopes' dinner made her sick.

The main course was a boiled horse's head. The Comanches preferred not to eat horses unless necessary, as horses were vital to their lives, but the chief savored horse meat above all else and this was his special dish. A hole had been chopped in the skull so the brains could be spooned out. The unfortunate white girl, seeing fingers and spoons dipping into the gray mess while the horse looked at her from empty sockets, began to retch, which earned her another beating. She endured this beating well, being more accustomed to it and having by now absorbed so many shocks in one day that she was becoming numb. She still kept looking at me, though, as if I was supposed to whisk her to safety; the fact that I made no motion to do so proved to her that I was a renegade and worse than the Antelopes.

Also on our menu was curdled milk taken from the slit udders of some of the girl's late father's cows, as well as horse tripe that had been brushed through the grass for cleaning before being dumped into a pot. The Comanches would not eat fish or fowl if they could help it and would not ever use the same pot for both boiling and broiling, but that was about the limit of their fastidiousness. We had rabbit, onions, radishes, dried plums and peaches, corn meal, ash cakes, a bottle of brandy that went around for one swig each. I was presented a large chunk of raw horse liver, sliced with a knife on a flat rock, by the chief, whose friendly grunts and eagerness as he watched me eat it were meant to show he knew of my association with the Tanimas. For I had now figured his identity, though none others in this band did I recall having seen before.

We drank much of the hot, flat beer. One brave who had been chewing peyote buttons as a tonic for his appetite went crazy, leaped about humorously, tried to pick up a handful of fire, and had to be knocked senseless. There were many speeches. Each man who had been with the party stood up and recounted his role in it. They repeated in florid style having seen the chief count coup on the girl's father. Another coon named Stands-in-the-Willows had counted coup on the brother. The way they told it, this party sounded like one of the grandest battles of history rather than what it was—an incident of two dozen or so Antelopes murdering a man, woman and boy, capturing a girl and stealing livestock. But as I have said, two dozen Antelope warriors assembled in one place is about as large a number as most folks ever saw, disregarding a few important battles or some of the big winter camps, and so this party would indeed enter their lore.

At length, the chief arose to speak. People were sitting around the fires as at a picnic or barbecue along the river at home, looking up at the fellow's splendid brass and copper ornaments glinting in the firelight. With his torso bare and a gourd of beer sloshing in one hand, he described the fight all over again as if nobody had ever heard of it before. From the cries and gasps of the crowd, that appeared to be the truth. The talk went on until I, thinking of the girl in a most nagging and curious way, and being also full of beer and liver, began to drowse. What woke me was hearing my Comanche name and realizing the chief was telling them about me.

"Many winters ago"—he began, though it had been only six years before, when I was seventeen—"this person, who is a mighty hunter of all animals including Mexicans, and wears the mighty lion's tooth on his chest with the White Painted Lady and a Bearded One, was hunting buffalo with the Liver Eaters. . ."

It is not my intention to give the Antelope chief less than his due in my chronicle or to be reluctant to describe his speech, but as he was so windy and as I will have more to say of this man later if there is time, I will relate briefly and from my own viewpoint the story he told the Antelopes at the victory dinner, for this does have a bearing on my current situation.

I was hunting buffalo with the Tanimas. We were up along the Pecos River in the month of December. There were many low buttes and mesas rising at random out of miles of sage, mesquite, and gray winter bunch grass. On the cold clear days you had the feeling you could see to the edge of the earth; out in the far distance the ground met the sky in a blending of gray that made the horizon indistinguishable. You could smell the sage and dust, but the air had the dampish tinge of a coming blue norther. We had a good hunt. When I decided to return to San Antonio de Bexar, where I had been living with my mother, I took only a few of the best hides and a haunch and a couple of hams and a few tongues and packed them onto my mules. After a farewell to the Tanimas, I set out riding southeast, thinking to travel by the most direct route.

The first night I made camp in a dry stream bed at the base of a bluff out of the wind, for the norther was blowing up and smelled of snow. My two horses and two mules were loose-hobbled. I built a low but warm fire of antelope chips and then put some mesquite brush on it for a good blaze. That was a foolish thing. But I was feeling good. I had my saddle for a pillow and some good blankets and a thick hairy buffalo robe and some hot coffee with plenty of sugar and some cigars and a New Testament to ponder over and wanted some light. I was frying bacon when I noticed my animals beginning to fret.

I looked up from the fire and at the edge of the light were six Comanches. They identified themselves as Penetakas, said they were a hunting party and asked me for coffee and sugar. The Penetakas were generally friendly toward white men by then and most were on the reservation. From the appearance of these six, I guessed they were thieves and scoundrels who hung around the agencies. I supplied them with coffee. They wanted more. I noticed two of them lingering beside my mules and ordered them to step into the light, which they did. I refused to give more coffee, showing that I had little left, but did give them tobacco and corn husks to roll it in. All six came around the fire and sat and smoked. They were evil-looking fellows, dark and dirty. At least two were drunk. One short, bandy-legged brave with a Chinaman-face began to get abusive. I ignored him as much as possible and talked of all my friends among the various bands, exaggerating some and wishing I had friends among the Penetakas.

The Chinaman-face informed me they intended to take my robes, meat, mules, and one of my horses. I disputed that and said some ungodly killing would be the result. I asked their names. They were quiet. It was ominous, I thought. Touching my lion's tooth and Our Lady and St. Jude, I began scooching toward my saddle roll where my pistol was. Then I felt a hard bump and was confused for a second as to what had happened before I realized—mostly from the colors I saw and from a strange, disembodied sensation—that I had been hit on the skull with a club by someone who must have leaned down from the bluff behind me.

I knew, hurt as I was, that to delay would be fatal. Three of the coons still sat drinking my coffee and smoking my tobacco, but the others were up and coming toward me with clubs and knives. I leaped at the saddle roll and felt another bump, a blow, and looking down saw the feathers of an arrow protruding from my deerskin coat. I yanked out the arrow, leaving the tip buried in me, and glanced at the blood on the shaft. "Lord," I thought, "I am killed." As yet there was no pain but only the strange, lightheaded feeling, and I was aware my hair was wet.

Not slowing, I lunged for the pistol. But Chinaman-face beat me to it. He cocked the hammer and fired a shot that hit the wall of earth behind me, splattering dirt and pebbles. I rushed past him and ran toward my horse, whereupon I felt yet another blow and knew I had been hit by another arrow. I got my hands on my horse's neck but my hands were slippery and I fell off. Rolling over, I crashed into the legs of Chinaman-face and knocked him down, and by some emergence of strength that comes when peril is the greatest, I climbed up the bank of the bluff, a height of some six feet, nimbly as a cougar.

At the top I met the fellow who had clubbed me. He proceeded to club me again and I fell. The others, at least three of them, were after me at once. I could not move then. A fold of my forehead was hanging across one eye but I could see several dark figures against a sky sparkling cold with stars. They gathered around and beat me with their clubs—knobby sticks about two feet long, studded with nails or flints or glass. One brave stabbed me a couple of times. I made not a sound. Through it all my mind was insanely clear, observing the colors, resenting the blows that made my body jerk, marveling that I was now a dead man. Many Indians believe the spirit leaves the body through the mouth as breath, which is one reason they object so violently to hanging or strangulation, as that entraps the spirit in a corpse. But for me, as I died, the spirit or whatever—what I suppose Father Higgins would call the soul—left me all of a piece, from everywhere but especially from the eyes. I saw it go out from my eyes in two long thin vapory strings that kept rising like smoke from a campfire, and I knew that once it was all out it could never be brought back and that I should concentrate my will on drawing it back in me.

I felt a ringing, clanging sensation—a sort of whoom whoom *WHOOM*, growing louder, then receding, then growing louder than before—and saw everything in a coppery glow, artificial-looking, each bush of sage or mesquite, each dark figure, looking cutout or made-up and placed there like a piece of scenery in a stage play. My body was full of a gassy feeling, as though I needed greatly to belch, and my heart was floating in the gas, and I knew that the moment I belched I would cease to exist, as that would blow out the rest of the vapor, though I knew also that the relief would be great and it was an overwhelming temptation to do so. It was incredible how much vapor there was, still rising. I was thinking of nothing except that. Not of my mother, not any curiosity as to what came next, but merely observing the sensations, perhaps wondering a bit whether to struggle against them or to let go and vanish, watching the vapor. The copper faded and all was black, with the whoom whoom *WHOOM* whoom still going on and the clanging louder. I felt that the next *WHOOM* would not recede but would be the final one.

Then I was in the air floating. I lay in the air for a long while, delicious-feeling, touching nothing but seeing the earth rising slowly to me. I landed in a pile of rocks. One large rock was against my cheek and I saw a dark blotch of blood forming on it in the moonlight. The whooming and clanging were gone, but I was still lightheaded and giddy, feeling that my limbs had no weight and that I was having a grand experience. Like a drunk with single-minded dedication to find a place to sleep, I began to crawl.

Next I knew the Penetakas were screaming and running away.

Next I knew after that, I was enclosed in a hard bundle of some sort and there was not an inch of my body that did not pain me.

As the story was eventually put together by both the Antelopes who found me and the Penetakas who ran, the robbers had thrown me off the bluff after convincing themselves they had beaten, shot, and stabbed me to death. They had not scalped me because my head was in such a ruined condition and also because of my reddish hair, which Chinaman-face considered unlucky. They had not mutilated me because they were in a hurry and the Comanches are not so insistent upon mutilation as the Kiowas and intended to retrieve the arrows so as to conceal the source of the crime. I had crawled away, back to the top of the bluff. As the Penetakas below in the firelight argued over dividing my possessions, I appeared erect on the edge of the bluff, my arms outstretched, my face a ghastly sight, the second arrow sticking out of my coat, the moon outlining me and the fire shining up on my wounds that were made more grisly by the shadows.

The Penetakas swore I said: "I refuse to die." In Comanche, this would have been *Ka-Teu-Wie*.

I doubt I could have said anything, but then I would also doubt having been able to crawl to the top of the bluff and to stand. The coons below were convinced they were dealing with a ghost. Either that or with a man of supernatural medicine. In neither case did they wish to remain in the vicinity. They fled into the night, leaving all my possessions. The next morning the Antelopes found me and took me to the lodge of Bull Chaser, who had great powers of curing, and there in a few weeks I healed. From then on I was known to the Comanches as Ka-Teu-Wie, or No-Die or Refuses-to-Die, and the many misfortunes that later befell the Penetakas were claimed by quite a number to have been caused by abusing me. When I did return to Austin and San Antonio, the tale had preceded me on the lips of a French trader.

Some time after that I had the pleasure of skinning Chinaman-face, who was alive when I began but of course did not survive the project.

5

This chief, Charlie Otter, who was speaking, had been in that Antelope camp. The story he told was elaborated with superhuman activities—for example, he said the two arrows had pierced my heart and a very potent spirit had sealed the wounds—but an Indian is not inclined to disbelieve a good story. When Charlie Otter finished I had to stand up and go through the tale once more. I had their whole attention. The white girl was outraged that I was entertaining the heathens, but every so often one of them would whack her with a stick for being slow, so she did not have the idleness to use in hating me.

At the conclusion of my version of the tale, in which the truth was spared once again, we drank more beer, ate more entrails and horse's brains, and the dancing took up anew. Charlie Otter began eying the white girl in a way that left no doubt what he had in mind. To delay him, I encouraged him to talk and continued pouring beer into his gourd. He made frequent trips to urinate and his walking was wobbly and his speech was getting addled. A Comanche on foot, just walking around, is as awkward and lost as a Comanche on horseback is graceful and sure, and a drunk Comanche on foot is a sight for the circus. But the chief knew what he wanted. As the other braves began to slip into the shadows with their ladies, Charlie Otter began listening to me with nothing more than politeness.

"Charlie Otter, my old friend, warrior of unparalleled valor," etc., etc., I said in a long build-up, "sell me that ugly, weak, useless white girl. I will give you my pony, twenty cartridges, a half-pound of coffee, fifty dollars in gold specie that will buy many valuable items from the Comancheros, three cigars, a mirror, and a new pair of tweezers."

His plucked brows raised at that and the glaze nearly went out of his eyes. He took a long swallow of beer.

"No," he said.

"But white women are notoriously bad workers, must be beaten often which is tiresome, eat too much, are usually sick, cannot walk far, have irksome tongues, are constantly dying in childbirth, are ignorant of the ways of the Human Beings and other important matters, complain much, are selfish and faithless," I said.

"I don't care," said Charlie Otter. "I want to—."

"This girl is too sniveling for pleasure, has an unwholesome palor, smells revolting so as to make a warrior sneeze, and is almost a midget. Her hands have no strength, she thinks without logic, she is stupid and inclined to be hysterical. I will increase my offer by another fifty dollars in gold."

"Fine," said Charlie Otter. He slapped me on the shoulder. "A good price for such a worthless creature. We shake hands."

We shook hands. He belched.

"Done," I said. "I will tell her."

"Tomorrow," he said. "You tell her tomorrow. Tonight I want to—."

"She will not be worth as much," I said. She was looking at us and trying to guess what we were saying.

"I could get that much in Santa Fe."

"It is far to Santa Fe."

"So I will keep her," he said.

"You are clever at bargaining."

"What is mine is mine," said Charlie Otter.

Well, I thought, hello trouble, welcome home. The chief made a display of getting up, with many grunts and sighs and a clacking of his bear tooth necklace. I looked at the girl and my heart moved another dab. She stood a few feet from us, eyes downcast, expression piteous, covered in filthy skins, torn petticoat, and bruises. She had a slender neck and a well-made rosy body, with nice, plump bosom, hips, thighs and ankles. It has been my opinion for most of my life, excluding periods bordering on lunacy, that there are few things lower or more treacherous than cowherders, goats or white women, with hardly any exceptions, and that belief enabled me to speak with some passion in bargaining with Charlie Otter. But, looking at this girl, I was aware that not only was she of my kind, and thus deserving of my loyalty to an extent, but also that she was exceedingly helpless, very attractive to me, and not beyond the possibility of improving enough to become the woman I could be pleased with.

And here was Charlie Otter giving every sign of coming to know her sooner than I. There is no supposing what I might have done that night. I felt the dagger snug against my right leg and the Bowie knife at my left hip; my other arms were with my livestock. Wild ideas were going through my head—of quietly murdering Charlie Otter, no feat in itself, of scattering the Antelopes' horse herd, of escaping the camp in the night with the girl. That the plan could be brought off I had little doubt, as I never lacked in confidence unless a partner's abilities were also involved. I preferred not to have to do that, since Charlie Otter was a friend. However, a man does as he must.

But then there was a clamor from the south edge of the camp, near where I had come across the river, and Badthing appeared.

The few Antelopes who were still around the fire, and the even fewer who were sober enough to do more than groan and gag, took up a sudden excited silence at the

BLESSED MCGILL

apparition that marched into the firelight clanging a sheep's bell. Badthing was a mysterious figure, muchly feared, who roamed from Galveston to the Arkansas River, from the Sierra Madre to the California missions, going through the country of the Apache, Pueblo, and Plains tribes with impunity. It was said he was a god or a devil, the two being difficult to tell apart in many schemes of being, not born of man but of the earth, though some said his mother was a very clever coyote. The Indians, frankly, did not know what to make of him, nor did anyone else.

I have heard his age estimated by white men who have encountered him at from thirty to ninety years. The Indians seldom bothered with that sort of guesswork. To them you were either a baby, a child, young, prime, or old, depending on your own facility. I happened to know Badthing was a Karankawa, descendant of an ancient and mostly died-out tribe that once lived along the Gulf Coast. He was a small man and wondrously dressed in tall black silk hat, red tunic buttoned on backward, long dirty breechclout of gold-leaf cloth, Ute boots like mine except with intricate beadwork and tiny silver chimes, a pearl necklace, and a brass ring in his nose. The ring, it was said, was placed there when Badthing was sold into slavery as a child by the Comancheros in Santa Fe.

"What luck is mine," said Charlie Otter in a sour tone.

"Maybe he brings good fortune," I said.

"Maybe a pig is a horse," said Charlie Otter.

Anxious as he was to retire, for the shakedown dance would begin early in the morning, there was an etiquette to follow. Charlie Otter finished getting unsteadily to his feet and stood with his arms folded, watching Badthing come nearer.

In one hand Badthing carried a cedar bow taller than he. Over his right shoulder in a quiver were a dozen cane arrows, each three feet or so in length. With that bow he could fire those arrows two hundred yards and at a lesser range could shoot an arrow through the body of a deer with

59

EDWIN SHRAKE

such force that the arrow would travel another forty yards and stick into a tree. As Badthing stood there clanging his sheep's bell, the Antelopes were transfixed, some with drunkenness and some with awe. They detested sorcercers who used their powers wickedly, but they were not sure of anything about Badthing except that when possible he was to be avoided and when in his company he was to be treated well. Some believed he was a Little Person, an elf with great magic, capable of turning himself into a bird or a brook or a cottonwood tree, anything that found his fancy.

Behind Badthing was his wife, No Nose, leading a pony and two mules. Her nose, so I had heard, had been cut off as punishment for adultery, a not uncommon justice on the plains, but the mutilation had rendered her so unattractive that her Kiowa husband had been unable to sell or trade her and so had simply kicked her out of camp and she had taken up with Badthing. Though a woman of some intelligence, she was very disagreeable looking. Her hair was hacked off short and her clothes were full of lice which she killed by chewing the seams, the lice and nits popping as she bit on them.

"I wish permission to set up my ba-ak near your fire, Charlie Otter, and maybe to have a little snack of your tasty horse head for myself and my woman," said Badthing. "I will play my whistle and my tambourine for your dancers. My intentions are, as always, peaceful. I am on my way toward the setting sun to locate a great buffalo herd that was revealed to me by an extremely old buffalo I spoke to recently. If you wish, I will deliver your people to the location of that herd, also."

"Hmmm," Charlie Otter said. Seeing me, Badthing spoke again:

"My salute to you. I discover you in the camp of the Antelope people, which is no surprise. It is wise to rest in the camp of the most unrelenting enemies and fiercest killers of the Apaches, for I have been told by an eagle and once again by a turkey and once more by a wise mustang that except for Octavio, or Gotch Eye, of the Lipan outlaws, many Apaches have sworn to murder you by torture, my friend."

60

"This is the truth?" said Charlie Otter, blinking at me.

I nodded and Charlie Otter said, "Then we will kill them with you."

"I have matters that need attending in the white towns," I said. "We will kill them later."

"As you wish," said Charlie Otter.

"Now I have a riddle," Badthing said. "It is a riddle for all who wish to think on it. Observe the sky. Observe the stars."

"What for?" asked Charlie Otter.

"Observe and listen. But first let me ask another riddle. Why is it that when a bluecoat shoots his rifle at you the puff of smoke appears before you hear the sound of the shot?" The Antelopes who were able were listening curiously, although Charlie Otter was rocking back and forth in his attempt to stand and was getting impatient. Seeing this, Badthing went on: "The reason is because seeing is faster than hearing."

"Everybody knows that," said Charlie Otter. "Why else would we signal with smoke or mirrors?"

"But if seeing is faster than hearing, then something must be faster than seeing," Badthing said. "And that is knowledge. But wait. Do you think you see the puff of smoke the moment the rifle is fired, or does it take a moment for the vision of the smoke to reach your eyes? I will tell you that it takes a moment to reach your eyes, just as the sound of the shot takes two moments to reach your ears. Now observe the stars. Suppose we see a new star that appears in the heavens for the first time. We call it a new star and we learn to trail by it. But there is no star there. What we see is a light that we call a star."

"What is the difference?" said Charlie Otter.

"That is my riddle," Badthing said. "Suppose a great and powerful spirit—maybe the White Painted Lady—struck a spark far, far up in the heavens. That spark burned for an instant and then went out forever. That spark was struck long, long ago, long before there were Human Beings on this earth, long before the huge birds left their tracks in the stone, long before the rivers or the trees or the mountains. The spark was struck so far away that it has taken all this time for the light to travel to our eyes as the puff of smoke travels to our eyes from a rifle. But tonight that spark has become visible in the heavens and so now we call it a star. But is it a star or is it not? The spark went out long ago but we just now see it, so is what we see the star or is it only a picture of a star, as a picture of a buffalo drawn on a deerskin is only a picture of a buffalo and not the buffalo itself? The spark has vanished at its source, but does that make the light we see less real? Can we call that light a star although it no longer exists?"

"I will have to think about that," Charlie Otter said. "I will tell you the answer in the morning."

"The answer is our relationship to the spirits," said Badthing.

"Well, of course," Charlie Otter said.

"One more thing," said Badthing. "When a spark glows, such as when a flint is struck with steel, there is heat. Suppose that heat has been traveling with the spark, though not as fast, as the sound does not travel as fast as the sight of smoke. Tonight we see the light. Tomorrow night the heat arrives and the heat is of such magnitude that it sets fire to the earth and burns us all up. Suppose that."

"I had rather not. Set up your ba-ak," Charlie Otter said.

"Thank you," said Badthing. He motioned to No Nose. She began setting up his lodge by shoving the sharpened ends of willow poles into the ground in a circle and bending them together at the top to make a framework that would be covered with hides. She could set it up in a few minutes.

"One more riddle," Badthing said.

"No, no, that's enough," said Charlie Otter. He made a speech of welcome to Badthing, mainly so he would not have to hear any more riddles. The speech was shorter than usual, for the audience began further to dwindle and Charlie Otter had to search for words in his drunkenness. When he finished, Charlie Otter looked around as if wondering what it was he had been about to do before he was interrupted.

His eyes discovered the white girl and he recalled. Beckoning to her, he walked toward his tepee. The wife he had brought along—the fat woman who had carried off the spoiled pot and had wanted to beat the white girl—arose to follow but he waved her away.

Badthing sat down and began to play his reed flute and shake his tortoise-shell tambourine, pretending not to watch us. The girl looked from me to Charlie Otter.

"Come along," I said, taking her by the arm.

She started sobbing.

"Don't make me do this," she said. "Let me die. Please give me your knife and I will kill myself."

"It's not as bad as all that," I said.

Her heart broke at those words and she gave up hope of being saved from Charlie Otter. Sobbing piteously, as though some vent had opened to let out her sorrow, she stumbled along with me half dragging her. Charlie Otter fell down three times on the way to his tepee. Each time he rolled over, sat up, put his palms on the ground, squatted like a frog with his scalp lock dangling before his eyes, then heaved himself up, tottered about for a step or two, and resumed his course. He nearly knocked over his tepee by walking upright into it. But he found the flap, fell again, and crawled inside. By the time I pulled the girl in, he had divested himself of his breechclout and was kneeling beside a robe. Being drunk and tired, he had allowed his old belly to droop, but even so it was plain to see that he had the desire to do what he had brought the girl there for.

"Hurry up," he said.

The girl covered her eyes. Charlie Otter clutched at her petticoat. I could not help but admire her appearance, even in such circumstances. Reaching out with a brown hand that had crusted blood on it, he took the girl by the thigh and pulled her down on the robe. He tore off the deerskin that had concealed the upper part of her body and he yanked her hands away from her eyes. She looked at me and covered her eyes again. Once more he removed her hands and I thought he was about to tie her arms with rawhide, but this time she did not cover her eyes and I seemed to detect in her some curiosity as she lay back on the robe and looked full at Charlie Otter. He had forgotten about me as surely as if I had never been born. The girl was resigned now and showed pluck, though tears still streamed her cheeks. Charlie Otter knelt above her, weaving.

"Don't hurt me," she said in the voice of a child.

I pulled out my seven-pound Bowie knife, intending to hit Charlie Otter on the temple. But as I raised my hand he gave a long sigh and fell over unconscious from drink.

Trying to be discreet, I rolled Charlie Otter off the girl and directed her to get dressed. She was astonished but complied. "Don't open your mouth until we're out of this camp," I said. I went to the flap and called in Charlie Otter's fat wife.

"Your man has had much beer and is weary from raiding and fighting," I told the Indian woman. "He has sold me the white girl and he wishes to sleep now. I will leave the agreed-upon goods with you but must be off immediately to Fredericksburg."

The Indian woman nodded. She smiled and her cheeks puffed up to cover her little black eyes. She helped the white girl wrap herself in skins, for she had not enjoyed the prospect of Charlie Otter taking a pretty young wife. The Indian woman spread a robe over Charlie Otter and went to saddle my horse.

When we came out of the tepee, the fire was deserted except for a few braves who had followed the example of their chief and for Badthing, who looked up from his flute and grinned as pleasantly as he could considering the birds and flowers painted on his face.

"I will tell Charlie Otter you will meet him in the time before the snow to hunt buffalo with him, for I have seen in a vision that you will be there and so will I," said Badthing in Spanish. "We will meet near the Double Mountain. Do not worry, my friend. I will remain in this camp. Charlie Otter will not chase you, nor will he long blame you for this, for the spirits have caused it and so it is to be desired. You and the girl will know each other well. I have seen it."

I thanked him. Not wishing to take needless chances, I hurried to prepare our departure. Leaving the pony and the other items for Charlie Otter, I mounted the girl behind me on my mare and we rode off toward Austin. It was some miles through the darkness before she spoke.

"Why did you do it?" she said.

"Lady," I said, "I did not want you to think me a common garden variety of lout."

6

It is coming daylight. I have been out to give oats to Excelsior and to stand on the rim and watch the dawn. The valley is deep in shadow and to the west the desert sleeps, but there is light like a halo in the clouds around the mountain peaks. Roosters are crowing down in the valley and along the rim. There is the smell of a fine day when trees will blossom.

I have made it through another night.

Somehow I expected to. I didn't think Octavio would send for me so soon. He appreciates the agony of apprehension. He is a strange creature. I sit now at my oak table, unsleepy but filled instead with energy and excitement, drinking coffee and thinking of Octavio. There is enough about him to occupy a man's mind. He has been the frustration of a dozen colonels on this side of the border and of more Mexican generals than one would care to consider. It was in Mexico, raiding the haciendas of Chihuahua, Coahuila, and Sonora, that he got his name Octavio. I have never understood that name. One version I heard was that Octavio came from the musical term, for the boy Bear That

Sings became a man of powerful voice. Another story was that a Mexican governor saw this savage Lipan renegade wearing a garland of oak leaves and compared him to the Roman commander Octavian, though if it was for style or appearance I could not say, for I have to my regret learned little of Roman history. However it would have been easy for the peons to corrupt the name into Octavio and for the Lipan to admire the sound of it. I did not ask him, even when we were friends. It is impolite to inquire about a name.

I recall now the day my father and I took Octavio, then called Jacob, and his mother back to Austin in the spring wagon after the death of the Dutchman farmer. We arrived after dark and when we ushered the silent boy and the shy Lipan woman into our kitchen, my mother had just finished baking a pan of sour dough biscuits and making cream gravy from flour, fresh milk, and pork chop grease. From the stove she took a platter of pork chops and put it on the kitchen table. She set out a bowl of field peas and a mound of boiled potatoes, a jar of butter, a pitcher of cold milk, and a pot of coffee strong enough to make your toes ache. My father drank a bit of the coffee and then went to take the Dutchman's body to the Rangers' office, not that reporting the murder was liable to do much good. In those times murder was common in the hills and the Comanches and Kiowas were being pesky. The Rangers had plenty to do without worrying about the death of one Dutchman who could have been a Union spy anyhow.

Jacob had been raised as a Christian more or less, and his mother had lived with one long enough that they did not entirely observe the Lipan mourning customs. The widow did not weep or shave her head or sprinkle herself with pollen or tear her clothes. Instead they both fell to eating the food my mother had prepared. I gathered they were very relieved when my father drove off with the body.

Hungry though I was, I could not eat much, only putting away five or six pork chops and maybe eight biscuits covered with gravy, plus a few helpings of peas and potatoes. I watched our visitors curiously, not at that time having ever lived among the Lipans. Both the woman and boy were very clean. The Dutchman had introduced them to soap. The woman Hilda wore her hair long in a single braid down her back. Jacob's hair was cut in the white manner, being long but not of shoulder length. Whereas my hair was roanish of color and tended toward the curly, his was straight and shiny black. Blood had dried black on the bandage and on his cheek. His uncovered right eye was like one of those black shiny desert stones they call Apache tears. His neck was thick and muscular and his face was full with strong chin and beakish nose. His expression as he chewed on the pork chops was pensive. Luther, the ex-slave and mean coon, appeared in the doorway. Neither Indian looked at him, but he did not take his eyes off them while my mother fixed him a dinner plate.

"Who is they, Mistress McGill?" he asked at last.

"Guests," my mother said, handing him his plate. "Go off now."

Then she came around the table and stood beside Jacob, who was wiping up gravy with his last biscuit. Tiny and beautiful, with hair black as theirs but bound up in a knot on top of her head, she spoke to them in classic, elegant Spanish with her musical voice.

"The boy is injured. May I examine his eye?"

Hilda nodded. Jacob reached up and pulled off the bandage. I am not the squeamish sort, but I will admit that I almost gagged. Besides the deep, meaty cut, the socket was filled with what looked like squashed grape. My mother did not flinch.

"We must take him to the doctor," she said.

"For what?" said Hilda, shrugging. "The eye is dead. Could the white doctor give him a new eye that will see? I think not."

"But we must at least clean the wound to prevent infection."

"I do not know that word. The wound heals itself. We

close the wound and it draws together and in time is healed. But the eye will not see."

"Maybe Our Jesus Christ will fix it," said Jacob, smiling a bit.

"Hey there," I said. I was never what could be described as a good, devout Catholic, as my mother is, but in my youth, as I have said, I was a churchgoer and was aware that blasphemy brought vengeance from the heavens.

"Do you not think Our Jesus Christ can fix it?" Jacob said, turning his good eye toward me.

"He could if He elected to." said I.

"And Our Sure Enough Father in the sky? Could He fix it if He elected?" Jacob said.

"Sure."

"And White Painted Lady, Mother of Our Jesus Christ? Does She look down from the clouds at us?"

"I suppose so," I said. I caught my mother's look and said, "Sure She does."

"All right then," said Jacob, "I leave it to Them to fix my eye so that I can see the whereabouts of those who murdered one who was once among us."

"God's ways are mysterious," my mother said.

"They are indeed," said Jacob.

"Killer-of-Enemies will punish them," Hilda said.

"I will punish them," said Jacob.

"Killer-of-Enemies has given you the knowledge and strength to do so," Hilda said.

That was the first I ever heard of Killer-of-Enemies, a Lipan god or spirit that created all animals and taught the Lipans to hunt, steal, and kill.

"For that I am grateful," said Jacob. "Our Jesus Christ says in the words from the Spirit Book that I should not punish them. Our Jesus Christ says I should leave them to the underworld where fire will torture them and snakes and lizards will crawl over their bellies. I prefer to torture them myself. I have depended on Our Sure Enough Father to protect me from my enemies, and I have found it does not work so well."

"Don't you believe in God and Jesus?" I asked, leary of thunderbolts.

"What do you mean?" said Jacob.

"I mean don't you believe that God and Jesus are real?"

"Why of course I do," Jacob said.

So ended my first theological discussion with Octavio. My mother gave my bedroom to Hilda, who was more tired than she had let on and went right to sleep after placing a clean bandage over her son's eye. For me and Jacob, it was blankets and straw beds in the stable, where Luther slept. Luther sat in the doorway of the stable with his dinner plate on his knee and watched us make our beds ready. I went back into the kitchen to help my mother wash the dishes. Our kitchen in that house on West Pecan Street always smelled of flour and coffee and frying meat. It was a good smell and was so much a part of my growing up that I can smell it now by looking at the coffee grounds in the bottom of my cup.

"It was crude of you to argue with that poor boy," my mother said. "He is hurt and overwrought and didn't know what he was saying."

"He seemed pretty positive."

"It is even cruder of you to argue with me," she said. "But you have reason to be overwrought, too."

It hadn't occurred to me that I might be overwrought, but it was not a bad arrangement for my mother to think so, as she claimed I might drop the dishes if I handled them. So I sat at the table and contented myself with a bowl of hot peach cobbler covered with cream and melted butter. Being overwrought had its advantages, as a number of women have since demonstrated to me. I told my mother the story of what had happened to the Dutchman. It did not upset her, though she did make fitting sympathetic comments. She was a tough little lady, accustomed to the ways of the country despite her handsome and aristocratic bearing. After a while my father came in and ate his dinner which she had kept warm on the stove.

"I don't know what we're going to do with these folks,"

he said. "But they won't go back to that farm, you can bet. I figure we'll keep them around here until something turns up."

I asked him what the Rangers had said about Mr. Gerhardt.

"They didn't cry and take on about him," said my father. "Being as we didn't know none of these fellows that done him in, the Rangers say they must of come from north of the Red River or some such place. So I left off the Dutchman at the undertaker's, and I suppose we'll bury him tomorrow."

"It appears to me that somebody ought to care at least a little," I said.

"We care, boy, and that's better mourning than most folks get," said my father.

I remember how he leaned across the table with a dab of gravy on his mustache and looked hard at me, as if he wanted to tell me something but didn't know how to go about it. His face was sunburned but his forehead was white and I could see the wrinkles in his neck and the squint-marks at his eyes and the hairs in his nose. His cane was hooked over the back of the chair.

"What you keep in mind," he said, "is that most folks are mostly scum, no matter how pleasant they may act. Also most of them ain't too bright and if you ain't wary you will outsmart yourself. That's all I got to say about that."

I went out to the stable and crawled onto my straw bed. Jacob was still awake, his one eye looking up at the roof where he could see a crack of moonlight. His eye must have been hurting very much, but he had not let out a whimper.

"Does the nigger speak this language?" he asked me in Tex-Mex.

I glanced over toward the corner by the door where Luther lay wrapped in a blanket.

"I don't believe so," I said.

"Good. Then I will always talk to you in this language."

"You don't like Luther?"

"Like? If you mean is he my friend, then I do not. I have

smelled him and he is a coward and a bad man. But you are my friend."

"Okay by me," I said.

"But you must admit," he said, "that the way you think about Our Sure Enough Father is very dangerous."

Throughout all that summer, Jacob and I were seldom more than ten feet apart. We were such close pals that we traded our secrets and sat up nights whispering in our straw beds in the stable. We had the measles and the mumps together. We built a hideout in a high fork of an oak tree over by the river and watched for Comanches or Kiowas. I would sit up there on a plank platform that we had concealed with leaves and vines and Jacob would crouch beside me. I had my Dance Brothers & Park revolver and he had an old shotgun. One day we did see some Indians coming down the river, but they were just a few helpless old Tonks. We dug what we called a cave, though it was only a hole in the ground that we roofed with boards and covered with dirt. There was a password to get in. We hunted wild turkeys without much luck and caused the death of a hundred cottontails and a few jackrabbits. We captured a mother possum and kept her in a pen while she raised her babies. When she disappeared we found that she had become dinner for Luther. So we put a scorpion in his boot and how he did howl. We went to the horse races and sneaked out to hide in the shadows and watch the barbecues and other frolics. Jacob's eye cut had healed, leaving a bad scar, and his eyeball was like a white pebble. Usually he wore a black handkerchief tied across that eye. Some of the boys tried to hoorah him a little bit at first, but they soon learned better. He took to fighting as naturally as a wild cat. He was about the best horseman I ever saw. There is a saying that a white man will ride a horse until it's worn out and then a Mexican will get on that horse and ride two more days and then an Indian will get on the same horse and ride wherever he wants to go. Even mounted bareback on an old mule, Jacob cut a superb figure.

Jacob made us each a four-foot bow out of mulberry and

taught me to shoot it until I was about as good as he was. It was a wonder how he had picked that up from his mother. He made each of us a medicine bag out of buckskin, and what went into his was one secret he wouldn't tell me. He dressed like a white boy, but there was never any mistaking what he was. He used to talk about the Lipans, telling me the old stories about how they came from an underworld and were great hunters before their enemies banded together and drove them south and east out of the mountains and onto the plains. He had a particular hate for Comanches. He said he had a vision of himself leading the Lipans against the Comanches. We talked a lot about war and killing, as all boys do. He went to Mass with us some, though Hilda never did, and he loved Bible stories, but during the prayers I would look around and catch him smiling and studying the people in church with his good eye. We avoided any more arguments about religion.

Hilda was a help to my mother. The Lipan woman tended our garden and took care of the chickens and cooked and cleaned house and occasionally went into town with my mother in the carriage, but the loafers made remarks that stopped that and resulted in my father challenging the entire assembly at Dutch John's one night. My father and I drove out to the Dutchman's farm now and then to tidy up the place. Jacob and his mother would not go near it. We sold their livestock and gave them the money, but they didn't have much idea what to do with it. We tried to sell the farm, but the war news was bad and nobody was buying. My father became increasingly depressed and agitated at the war news. People were returning to Austin with arms and legs shot off and with holes in their persons. An escaped Yankee prisoner was caught wearing a woman's dress and bonnet and was hanged at the corner of Congress and Pecan. Sam Houston died that summer over in Huntsville. We heard the news about Gettysburg and Vicksburg. There wasn't much food and we were asked to share what we had with families of Confederate soldiers. As the news got worse and the Yankees came to Galveston, Luther became meaner and sassier to me, Jacob, and Hilda. He didn't like it at all when he was pressed into service as a volunteer to help build Magruder's Fort south of town on a bluff near the Post Road. He got himself some corn whiskey someplace and came home drunk three nights in a row and Jacob and I would listen to him muttering and grumbling as he lay on his blanket in the stable. One evening he sat sharpening his knife on a sandstone and talking about what a big man he was going to be when Mr. Lincoln got there. Hilda avoided him as though he had the cholera. Jacob never spoke to him. I think Luther was a little scared of Jacob and never spoke to him directly, though we would hear him talking out loud to himself about Indians being no good.

In the dog days of late summer, when it was hot and the leaves hung without moving, I came home from the German Free School one afternoon, Jacob having refused to go, and found nobody in the house or the wagon shed. My father had gone off on an errand in town with my mother. Leading my mule on a rawhide halter, I went into the stable. There was Luther, huge and mean drunk with his shirt open and sweat on his black chest holding a knife on Jacob and Hilda.

"You come round here too Master McGill," Luther said, waving the knife. His eyes were wide and yellow-white and there was a jug of corn whiskey on a hay bale. "This here red Indin slut won't have nothing to do with me. She call me a black nigger. I'm going to fun her some."

"Put up that knife, Luther." I said.

"Oh but I'll whale you, too," he said.

"My father will whip your impudent back," I said.

"No sir, he won't do that," Luther said laughing. "Mr. Lincoln is on his way. If your daddy touch me, Mr. Lincoln shoot him so full of rifle balls that it take eight men to carry him to the grave."

"You're drunk," I said.

"Yes, sir, I sure am that," said Luther.

"My father has been kind to you," I said. He set you free and he doesn't beat you."

"Well, thank a-plenty," said Luther. "Yes sir, I do thank you, Master McGill. What right your daddy got to set me free anyhow? Huh? What right he got to beat me anyhow? Mr. Lincoln say he don't have no right at all. Mr. Lincoln will fix his wagon, I tell you that. Soon as Mr. Lincoln get here, I be the boss of this house. You and your daddy and your mama got to serve me like a boss. I be Master Luther. How you like that, eh?"

"You're drunk. Go sleep it off," I said.

"Yaa-hoo!" yelled Luther. "Drunk! Drunk, he say! Am I drunk! Yaa-hoo!"

He did a scuffing dance around the hay bale, took another swig of corn whiskey, wiped his mouth with his hand and looked at Hilda grinning.

"Now some Indin skut," he said. "Now some, for a fact."

"Leave her alone," I said.

"This is my fight," said Jacob. It was the first time he had spoken English in Luther's presence.

"It be that, boy, for a fact," Luther said.

Hunching over, holding the knife in his right hand, Luther began to shuffle back and forth in a half-circle around me, Hilda and Jacob. I could see he was too drunk to reason with and I was wishing I had my pistol, which is a great reason-maker. Just then, Jacob moved. Fast as a snake, he ducked under the knife and ran out the door. I was shocked. Luther gaped at the sight of Jacob running from him. Then Luther started laughing.

"That some vicious Indin," Luther said. "Yes sir, Master McGill, your friend is some fierce warrior, all right."

"Luther, put away that knife," I said.

"Don't make me laugh too hard, now, young Master, or I be liable to crack my ribs and you have another crime that Mr. Lincoln make you pay for. Come on here, Indin skut. Give old Luther some love and maybe I let you be Mistress Boss when Mr. Lincoln come."

I jumped at him. Luther swung his big black left fist like a hammer and knocked me for a flip. I rolled over with straw and dust in my eyes, about to sneeze, and looked at the tiny dots skittering in the light that came in the door. The right side of my face felt frozen. Luther had his hands on Hilda's shoulders and was trying to make her get down on her knees. She was strong but no match for him. He forced her to the ground. I was attempting to haul my addled parts together for another jump at him when Jacob appeared in the doorway. He had his mulberry bow and three arrows.

"That's it, Indin skut," Luther was saying. He turned and saw Jacob and his yellow-white eyes opened wider and his mouth opened and he seemed to be struggling to sober himself.

The first arrow went thang and whump and fong. It tore straight through Luther's chest and stuck into the stable wall, behind him. He looked amazed. Before I could cry out for Jacob to stop it, the second arrow hit Luther higher up, near the collarbone, and drove him back against the wall. The third arrow pinned him there. The knife clattered as it hit the floor.

"And so," said Jacob in Tex-Mex, "that is how this re-solves."

While his mother got up, Jacob fetched the knife from the floor. Luther sagged heavily, broke the arrow, and slid down in a limber heap. Jacob bent over him with the knife.

"No, Jacob, don't scalp him," I said. "You'll have everybody in town after you."

"What is the difference? They will be, regardless," he said.

"No, they won't. I'll tell them how it happened."

"And when Mr. Lincoln comes with his black soldiers?"

"They won't come. We'll beat them."

"I think they will come," said Jacob. He bent over Luther, again but could not get a grip on his grizzly, woolly, sweating, graying hair. "No good," Jacob said, rubbing his hand on his pants-leg. "This scalp is worthless. I would not want it for my first one. But I think I will cut off his pecker."

"Please, Jacob, that will make folks awful mad," I said.

"For you and your mother and father I will not do it," he

said. "Come, Mother, get our things."

"What are you doing?" I said.

"We are leaving here. We are riding to the West to find The People. You say you could explain this to the white men, and possibly so, though from experience I doubt they would wait to listen before they hang me. But when the niggers come they will certainly hang me. That is the right way. So we are leaving. We must take your two best horses. I think whatever value your father got for selling our cattle is enough to repay you. If not, I will repay you myself when I can. You are not going to fight me about this, are you, my friend Peter?"

"I guess not," I said. The truth is, I thought it was kind of thrilling. "I won't tell them where you've gone, but I will tell them this was Luther's fault."

"Perhaps they won't chase me. Good. Now are we going."

I helped them load their blankets, some canned goods, and jugs of water behind their saddles. I gave Jacob a good rope and the old shotgun. After hesitating a moment I also gave him my Dance Brothers & Park pistol, figuring he would need it, and my share of the arrows we had made. I gave them two nose bags and some oats. He didn't thank me, because to an Apache the accepting of a gift implies thanks.

"I have nothing to give you," said Jacob.

"I don't need anything."

"Nothing except this," he said. He opened the little sacred bag that he had tied around his neck on a string of deer sinew and took out a tooth with a hole drilled in it. "This is a lion's tooth. This is very, very powerful magic. As long as you wear this tooth, your enemies cannot slay you. I know that to be the way it is. Killer-of-Enemies has told me." He reached up and took off the religious medal I wore. He unsnapped the silver chain and put the lion's tooth on with the medal. He draped it back around my neck. I looked down at the lion's tooth dangling beside the images of Our Lady of Guadalupe and St. Jude, which were both on one piece of cross-shaped Mexican silver. "You are on the side of all the spirits," Jacob said.

He smiled and we shook hands. I shook hands with Hilda. They ducked under the stable door and rode at a trot toward the river. Jacob turned once and looked back and waved. He did have a wonderful seat on that horse.

7

I have as yet said nothing of my friend Barney Swift, an oversight I will make up for while Excelsior dines on cracked corn. Just now I took Excelsior around to what Ellen and I used to call our barn—a sod, adobe, and wooden structure that for years I have intended to enlarge but now in all probability never will. The barn is sturdy enough to withstand the winters and the high snows along the rim, but it has long been too small for our needs. As I opened the door to the feed bin, rats went scurrying about. I smelled their sharp, acidy odor, and I saw their pellets all over the floor. My cats appear to have gotten fat and lazy. Three of them were asleep in the tack room; the rest are out enjoying the spring afternoon, possibly in track of a rabbit while a perhaps not so tasty dinner loafs in the feed bin. I apologized to Excelsior for leaving him out all night. He did not complain. I think he relishes his role as my watch dog and companion.

I knew Barney Swift since I was about twelve. I met him at the German Free School in a mental arithmetic lesson taught by Miss Mullins, a lady who seemed ancient in her long-sleeve dresses that touched the ground and chokered her neck. Barney's folks had just moved to Austin from Tennessee, arriving with all their possessions wrapped in tarpaulin in two ambulances drawn by four oxen. Old Man Swift was a water-witch, supposedly, with a number of divining rods cut from the forks of sapling willows. The old man went around town with his finest rod until the electricity got him such a shock that he could not move from where he stood but had to yell for Barney to run fetch Mrs. Swift and the ambulances. Once his goods were heaped up on that piece of ground, Old Man Swift went to the courthouse, found out who owned the property, and bought it for ninety-seven dollars. "The rod shot me such a jolt that I was nigh certain we was above a buried cask of gold, and I was afraid the price would go up when word got around," Old Man Swift later told my father.

But what he found was better than gold. It was a pure deep cold mineral spring with a touch of sulphur that gave the Swifts some of the best water a man ever tasted. It was such good water that the old man, claiming to have discovered in it an apothecary shop full of healthful substances, began to sell it by the jug. Swifts Spring Water, as they called it, was a tonic for any ailment from constipation to consumption, and it was said—a tale started, I hear, by Old Man Swift, though nobody proved it one way or the other—that Swifts Spring Water had cured Mrs. Swift of being deaf in her left ear and had healed Aunt Louise Swift of the catarrh. "It's regular elimination that does it," Old Man Swift used to say. "Get rid of the poisons and the body won't tolerate sickness."

The Swifts lived in a tent while they were building their house out of lumber from the mill up by Waterloo. I went over with my mother to take them a crock of vegetable soup and saw Barney, but of course we didn't talk to each other, him being the newest kid in town and me having a reputation as a rowdy. They were digging the well at that time, in fact had hired Big Foot Wallace, the old scout, to help them. It was a pleasure to sit and watch Big Foot Wallace at work and to listen to him tell about the Mexicans and Indians he had killed in his youth. He had been on the Mier Expedition, had drawn a white bean, had given it to a fellow with a family and then had drawn another white bean. Barney and I never could get over that story.

Barney was a towheaded kid, tall as me but not as thick in the chest, and didn't look to be a threat to my title as free-style roughhouse champion of the school. Then in the arithmetic lesson Miss Mullins did a cruel thing. Him being new, she made Barney stand up and recite his full name. He tried to get away with "Barney Swift," but she wouldn't hold for that.

"Your full name," she said.

"That's all anybody ever calls me," he said.

"Your full name," said Miss Mullins.

Red in the face, hearing the titters from the other kids, he finally said very loud: "My name is Barnabas Elihu Swift."

I had to respect him for it.

"Barny-buss," somebody said.

"Elly-hew!"

They all laughed and Miss Mullins rapped on her desk with a peach limb switch.

"Barny-buss!"

"Elly-hew!"

"Swift is what he better be with a name like that," said one lummox who sat on the back row because Miss Mullins said there was no use wasting good space up front on him. That remark was the most intelligent thing I ever heard the lummox utter. He was a big ham-handed boy of fifteen or sixteen, but I happened to know that his full name was Ezekial Columbine Boenker and I didn't see what he had to laugh at.

"Zeke," I said, "An ignoramus like you ought to keep his mouth shut. No matter what you say, it sounds like you're calling pigs."

"McGill," he replied, "you and me is going to fist city."

"Bring your lunch, it's going to be an all-day job trying to whip me," I said, in what passed as repartee at the German Free School.

"Bring your lantern, 'cause it'll last far into the night," said the lummox, not realizing he was using the same rejoinder I had used.

Miss Mullins was flailing the varnish off her desk with that switch and yelling for us to sit down.

"I don't guess I need you to take up for me," Barney said to me. "You want some of me, too?" I said.

"After I finish with this here dummy," said Barney.

"You can't call me no dummy, Elly-hew!" the lummox said. The three of us were marched out behind the privy by Professor Growald, the schoolmaster, and got whelps raised on our tails. Professor Growald, a stout man with an awful temper, broke two canes on us and that made him furious. The lummox sulked and went home, claiming he could use his life for more important pursuits than arithmetic. By that I guess he meant hoeing, plowing, and cedar chopping, which were in truth all he was fit for. He had a sullen, mongrel look to him. When school was out that day I had forgotten the incident, except for a warm feeling in the seat of my britches, but Barney was waiting for me down the road.

"I appreciate what you did," he said.

"It was nothing," said I.

"No, it wasn't nothing, and I'm obliged," Barney said. He kicked up dust with the toe of his shoe. "Well, don't you want to take off your shirt?"

"What for?"

"You might get it tore."

"Now how would I do that?"

"Well, my maw beats me for fighting in my good school clothes, even if I don't get them tore," he said.

"Who you aiming to fight?"

"You, of course," said Barney.

It was an invitation to call him Elly-hew and go to punching. But he was so serious and there was such an expression on his face, as though he would have to be beaten to death before he would quit, and he seemed like a nice fellow, and so I said "Look here, Barney, I got no reason to fight with you."

"You challenged me," he said.

"Forget it."

"You challenged me in front of all them other kids. If we don't have a dust-up they'll think I'm a sissy and I'll have to fight most of them," he said. "I ain't got time for that. I got to help dig the well."

"Nobody will think you're a sissy," I said. "They seen how you stood up to the lummox and to me, too. I can whip all of them. They ain't likely to do any scoffing."

"You sure?" he said.

"Positive," said I.

"In that case," he said, "how about coming home with me and we'll listen to Big Foot Wallace some more?"

"Fine," I said.

"Peter," he said as we went down the road, "I don't mind telling you this is quite a relief."

We were friends from then on.

The summer I met Jacob Gerhardt, or Octavio, Barney was back in Tennessee with his mother. It was some domestic quarrel I never understood. He returned about the time Octavio left town. Barney's mother and father took up with each other again and appeared to do all right, although Barney never had much to say about either of them. But he was a pet of my mother, and often I thought she loved him as much as she did me. After we moved to San Antonio, Barney and I quit seeing each other with any regularity. We were neither of us faithful at letter writing. But we didn't need to write letters or visit a lot to stay close. Whenever I saw him, even if a year had passed, it was the same as if I had seen him an hour before. We didn't need a lot of sparring around conversation but would plunge right in, since we often appeared to be thinking about the same things. Swifts Spring Water went on whitening the eyeballs and uncoating the tongues of Austin, as well as neutralizing acids and ridding the body of bile and waste, and I suppose if you go there today you can buy a bottle of it. I drifted into a number of occupations and adventures. I went to Connecticut to buy rifles and sold them out of a Comanchero wagon from Santa Fe. I made some little pasears across the river to Mexico. I busied myself with one thing or another, and before I realized it two years had gone by since I had seen Barney.

So after I dropped off the white girl in Austin and gave the Rangers a confusing story about the location of the Antelopes, who would have begun moving as soon as they discovered I was gone, I rode on down to San Antonio as I had been thinking of doing. Luckily it was no big problem to dispose of the white girl. She had an aunt and uncle in Austin. Of course everybody set up a fuss. One minute they would treat me like a hero and the next they would look at me suspiciously. Not a one of them offered to repay me for the pony, the gold, and the other items. But maybe that was my fault, as I did not bring it up. It wouldn't have been gentlemanly to say, "Look here, this girl cost me such and such." The girl herself, not understanding Tex-Mex or Comanche or even Signs, had no way of knowing I had bought her from Charlie Otter, though perhaps she did suspect it after watching the fat woman sort out my goods. But she was too happy to be safe with relatives, and at the same time too sad about the loss of her immediate family, and as for the rest, they never let it enter their citified minds that this girl would have been an item for commerce. They figured I had pulled off a daring rescue or that I was a sneaky half-brown devil myself—by then my reputation in Austin was not of the highest order— or maybe her old uncle figured me for a fool. But it was done. In the circumstances, I could not have done less.

When she came to her senses between bouts of weeping and laughing, the white girl was grateful enough. She would kiss me and take on about me as we sat in her aunt's parlor on Guadalupe Street, with a crowd of curious folks hanging around outside, and then she would rush over and give her aunt another hug and then hug her uncle and then come back and hug me again. It was embarrassing. With some sly questions, her aunt established that the girl's virtue was still intact. It was clear that had worried the old lady more than anything else. Finally I got up to go and the girl gave me one last hug and made me promise to keep in touch with her. She was so young then, a baby. Looking down at her big gray-green eyes, wet with tears, and at the little mole on the right side of her throat, and feeling her strong young body as she rose up on tiptoes to kiss my cheek, I did indeed feel like a left-footed brute and hoped it would not take her aunt too long to clear my odor out of the parlor.

"I will write you letters every week," the girl said. "Where shall I send them?"

"I don't exactly have any address," I said. "You'd be as well off if you put my name on the envelope and threw it out the window."

"You don't have a home?" she said. "How horrible! You need a home."

"Yes ma'am," I said, thinking that was about the last thing I needed.

Then I went out and got on my good mare and ignored all the questions from the crowd—I will admit that if I had not been in such a peculiar state of emotion about that girl I might have climbed down and cracked a few heads for those questions—and rode over by our old house on West Pecan Street. We still owned the property and kept up the taxes, but the house was empty and needed paint and somebody had stolen some planks from the shed where my father had built wagons and the yard was grown up with weeds and high grass. It was no good to look at that place. Especially not with the girl's words about me needing a home still fresh in my head. So I rode south to San Antonio.

I went to visit my mother but had rather not say anything about that at the moment. First I checked into the Menger Hotel and got my horse and mules stabled and sat in a tub of hot water until my skin was white and wrinkly. I used up three tubs of hot water. I had the haberdasher come up from downstairs and fit me with a decent-looking suit of clothes and new boots that hurt my feet. I went down to the bar and drank whiskey and smoked cigars. In a while I felt fit again. That girl was still on my mind but I knew I would get over it, as I have got over a number of episodes both before and since. In those days I felt I was all myself and needed nothing but health. When things got to me, well, they sooner or later got out again. And when I felt fit, well, I was sooner or later bound for trouble. My mother said I could no more avoid it than a hog could avoid mud. She said it was bred into me because I was the most human fellow she ever knew.

With the whiskey in my stomach and the cigars stinking pleasantly on my breath, I wandered over to a cafe by the river. There I sat and watched the lights in the oily-looking water and listened to mariachis playing their guitars and singing Mexican cowherder songs. The town had a fragrance about it, spring night perfume. I ate a dinner of beans, rice, tacos, enchiladas, and carne asada—thin slices of beef—heaped over with Mexican red chilies and green jalapeñas, and poured down three or four bottles of Mexican ale. What a joy it was to be alive that night! There were pretty girls on the streets and in the café. At a table across from me was a beauty wearing the high comb and lace mantilla of Andalusia, much as my mother did for dress-up occasions. Her escort was a handsome Spaniard gentleman in a short jacket. They were lively and interested in each other, leaning close to talk so that the lady's old dueña at the next table could not hear them. Watching gave me a vague pang that could hardly have been hunger. Eventually I got up and hired a carriage and driver and had myself transported over to the Vaudeville for some sporting action.

The Vaudeville was a fancy saloon run by politicians and catering to rascals the like of which are seldom gathered under one roof even in the cow towns like Abilene. We were then in what was called the Reconstruction. It brought out the worst in everybody. Texas was full of carpetbaggers and scalawags, and many of the Texans were acting like gun toughs. I stayed away from the towns most of the time, preferring the company of wolves, bears, and Indians to that of fellows like King Fisher who once put up a sign on a highway that said: THIS IS KING FISHER'S ROAD. TAKE THE OTHER. It wasn't that I was scared of King Fisher or doubted I could outdo him in any respect. He was just not interesting and did not concern me, and some of those fellows traveled in bunches and were not above shooting a man from a dark alley and then claiming they had bested him in a fair fight.

I went up to the bar at the Vaudeville and ordered a whiskey. Eight or ten girls were dancing on a stage at the rear. Twice that many painted-up girls were mixing with the crowd, getting drunken cowherders to buy them drinks. There were at least ten poker games going on. Off in other parts of the room were faro games, blackjack, and a roulette wheel. My ears had become accustomed to quieter sounds— the yipping of coyotes, the wind in the mesquite, the yowling and grunting of a Comanche dance—and it took me a few minutes to get used to the loud voices, the piano music, the stomping heels, the whacking of bottles and glasses on the bar and the tables. Many of the cowherders had finished spring roundup and had gone on drives to Kansas or out the Goodnight-Loving Trail to New Mexico Territory, but there were still plenty of them in the Vaudeville; in fact, a surprising number. I was leaning my elbows on the bar, studying the rows of bottles against the mirror, when a soft voice said, "Hidy, Peter."

"Hidy, Ben," I said, seeing him in the mirror.

"Gonna play some cards?"

"Could be," I said.

"Ain't seen you around town lately, but then I been away."

"I've been away some, too."

"Mexico ain't a bad place to go."

"Not too bad," I said.

"Well, we'd be proud to have you sit in with us."

"Might do it, Ben, thanks."

"Admire to buy you a drink."

"Much oblige."

He leaned his elbows on the bar beside me. I offered him a cheroot and he lit it. Ben Thompson was about six feet tall and was slender and hard with pale blue eyes and crow-black hair. He was wearing a tall silk hat and a frock coat. His black mustache was waxed and curled at the corners of his mouth.

If you were to make a list of fellows you would not want to have a dispute with, you would put Ben Thompson at the top. Around Austin and San Antonio there had been other fellows with a mean streak—John Wesley Hardin, Sam Bass, Phil Coe, King Fisher, Heycox for a while, fellows like that—but Ben Thompson was as tough as they came. He was some eight years older than I was and had killed his first man at sixteen, whereas I didn't actually kill a man until I was seventeen. Ben had been in Colonel Baylor's regiment in the war but had killed a sergeant in a duel over a girl and later had done time in the Bull Pen at Austin and in the prison at Huntsville. He had killed three fellows in a fight in Laredo and had gone to Mexico and fought in Maximilian's army until 1867 or so. My mother knew his mother, who used to board paupers in Austin, but I didn't get to know him until about 1868 when he hung around the Austin Exchange eating cherry cobbler and drinking iced lemonade.

"Understand you're in business now," I said.

"Yeah, the Star State Savings Association over in Austin," he said. "You heard of it?"

"Can't say I have."

"I got something coming up that'll interest you more," he said. We're gonna organize the Hope Hook & Ladder Company and get us a new fire truck."

"Fun," I said.

"Want to join?"

"Much oblige, but I won't be around town."

"Still roaming?"

"Yeah."

"You ought to settle down, Peter. I know a nice little girl I'll introduce you to. She's a actress, playing in *The Darling of the Regiment* over at Smith's Opera House right tonight."

"Thanks, man."

"Want to meet her?"

"If the cards are no good," I said.

"Well," said Ben, lifting his glass, "here's to the death of all bluebellies!"

"And their mothers and fathers," I said.

We drank. I couldn't see a pistol anywhere on Ben's person, but it was certain he had at least one, probably in a shoulder holster or stuck in his waistband and covered by the frock coat. I could feel my own Colts nudging against my abdomen. It being my turn now, I bought us a round and we drank.

"I heard you brung in a girl from the Comanches," said Ben.

"True enough."

"Pretty, they say."

"Yep."

"How many dead Indins you leave behind?"

"None."

Ben grinned. "Pete, one of these days you're gonna learn you can't be friends with a Indin. They're gonna take your scalp and have a general rejoicing all over the plains."

"They've tried."

"I've heard," Ben said. "I've heard they were some Meskins tried not long ago, too."

"They did for a fact."

"You find much gold?"

"No."

"Wouldn't be likely to let on, though, if you did."

"Wouldn't be any mistake about it if I had. I'd be buying drinks for the house," I said.

"Uhh huh. You ever look for Tayopa?"

"I looked some for the Tayopa."

"Got any clue where it's at?"

"Yeah, I got a clue. You start somewhere around Hermosillo and work south down the mountain range for about eight hundred miles. It's in there someplace. Beats me exactly where."

"Pete, you're a smart hombre. You ought to settle down."

"People keep telling me that lately."

"Feller just came in," Ben said. "You used to run with him."

I looked around and there was Barney Swift. Every step he took, dust fogged out of his clothes. He was wearing a big Mexican hat with the brim turned up in front and had several days of beard on his face. The heels of his boots hit the floor hard as he walked toward the bar, and his spurs clanked. His leather vest was torn and scratched and he had a bandanna around his neck. But it was very plainly Barney Swift. "Pardon," I said and walked over to Barney.

"Sir," I said to Barney in a disguised voice, "I am in the market to buy myself a nice hog ranch. Could you be so kind…"

"Ain't no such," Barney said without looking around.

"Hawg ranch!" yelled a cowherder standing nearby.

"Please sir," I said, "I am new to your country and I thought perhaps…"

"Hawg ranch! Hawg ranch!" the cowherder yelled in a tone such as was likely to burst the blood from his temples.

"Hawg ranch! Hawg ranch!" yelled others along the bar.

"My dear chap," Barney said to the cowherder who was so aroused, "there is no use abusing my ears."

In the mirror I saw Barney wink.

"My dear chap!" yelled the cowherder. "What kind of a place have I got mahsef into?"

"None that you can't get yourself out of, if you hurry," Barney replied.

"Boys," said the cowherder to two or three others who had come around, "I thunk we was dealing with a couple of geldings, but I see now they is more like muley cows."

"A beer please," Barney said to the bartender.

I looked at the cowherders. None had weapons except for one who had a butcher knife in a scabbard on his belt. I did not want to have to harm anybody because of a little joke.

"Whut you muleys got to say about that?" said the cowherder. They had come around so close that their odor of sweat, leather, and cow dung was getting oppressive to my newly bathed and scrubbed self.

"That you can go to the devil," Barney said and stomped

on the bridge of the cowherder's foot with the high heel of
his left boot. The cowherder jumped up and down and
howled. The bartender reached across the bar and rapped
another cowherder over the head with a bung starter,
knocking the man flat and crushing his straw hat. The two
remaining ones showed their empty hands to prove they
were not bent for trouble and then helped their stricken
companions to a table. I heard Ben Thompson laughing and I
began to laugh and Barney laughed and we shook hands.
Until then I had not even removed my hands from my
pockets, which was just as well.

Barney and I greeted each other warmly. It was not the
style in our part of the country for men to embrace. But I had
too much Spaniard in my blood to keep from it entirely. After
the usual curses and accusations exchanged between men
who love each other too much to say so or to use the polite
and cordial forms of address, we took our drinks to a table.
Barney was sunburnt and grizzled and when he took off his
hat I saw there were cockleburs in his hair.

"Peter," he said, "I never thought I would do it, but I got to
confess. I have become a big-shot cattleman and herder of
cows, and may Jesus bless me and set me straight if I am lying
when I say it has been a disaster."

The story he told was that the previous spring he had
hired out as a hand for roundup and had ridden point on a
cattle drive of three-thousand head bound for Sedalia, one of
the last big herds to go to that point, as more convenient railheads were popping up. The cattle were Texas Longhorns,
wild as antelopes and hard to control. But aside from the
ordinary nightly stompedes and a few brushes with cow
thieves and Indians wanting *wohaws*—which is what Plains
Indians called cattle—the drive had gone off well and the
owner made a large profit. The northern ranges were already
stocking up by then and could offer fatter cattle with shorter
drives, but seeing how well his boss did Barney got the idea
of trying for himself.

In the fall Barney worked for the same man rounding up
summer calves and strays and thinking over the situation. By

February, Barney was in business in the brush country south of San Antonio. He had thought about going out and sooner-ing himself a bunch of mavericks but decided to be completely honest about the affair, so he bought for range delivery all the cattle he could catch in a big area of the brush country and hired two vaqueros to work for him as brush poppers at eight dollars per month each. In February, when the leaves were scant, a man had a better chance of seeing horns in the chaparral. For two months Barney and the vaqueros crashed through the thickets of mesquite, huisache, prickly pears, Spanish dagger, and the rest of that growth that can rip the hide off a man and blind an untrained horse. They would rope a wild cow and tie it with a peal to a mesquite and then come back in a few days, after the beast had supposedly weakened itself, and neck the cow to a gentle ox and take it in to a big brush pen. They had plenty of roping, branding, earmarking, and castrating to do. At the end of two months Barney had five hundred head. His cattle were a mixed bag—yearlings, dogies, steers, bulls, cows, even a few stags. About two hundred of them were prime steers that he hoped to sell in Kansas for forty or fifty dollars a head.

Before he could start his drive, however, he heard the market in Kansas was collapsing. There had been a good corn crop on the northern ranges and fat northern cattle were swarming the railheads, and there was a rumor in the East that Texas cattle were diseased.

Barney was advised to forget his drive. Whoever advised him that didn't know Barney. He went to San Antonio to drink and mull the situation and ran into an Indian agent from Fort Sill. After a couple of days of rowdying with the agent, Barney was given a contract to deliver his beef at the Fort Sill Agency for at least enough to repay his investment, plus a profit for his hard work. With the spring grass coming on, he started his drive. The first day Barney and his vaqueros and their five hundred head covered nearly thirty miles, thinking to wear down their beasts, and then slowed to a steady fifteen miles a day with only minor stompedes and one skirmish with four or five outlaw Kiowas who got off with two horses and six steers.

When Barney got to the Red River, though, he was up against a spring flood. Several herds were crowded on the south bank waiting for the water to abate. All the hands and the cattle were nervous and restless. Barney spent two days in the saddle riding around his herd singing them the Texas Lullaby. Along toward evening of the third day on the Red River, he noticed his cattle looking toward the west and bawling excitedly. He knew they could smell rain fifty miles off. Barney and the vaqueros stayed in the saddle. First there was flash lightning in the west, and then ground lightning began rolling in, and the rain hit. The cattle were lying down one minute and the next minute they were all up and running.

"The fox fire was sparking and glowing on their horns and on our horses' ears and thousands of hoofs were drumming," he told me. "The night was black as the inside of a possum hole except for that fox fire and the lightning bolts that killed two steers outright and set up a stench of burnt hair. I was riding fast as I could go at the left of the head of my herd, trying to turn them to the right and get them to milling. But in a few minutes we were messed up with another herd and they were all crazy mad. At the river they turned right and ran along for half a mile in the rain and thunder and I thought we had them saved. But we came to a kind of bluff above a stream that flows southwest out of the Red and the cattle didn't pause for a second. They went pounding right off that bluff and fell thirty feet into the stream and I went right off with them. I couldn't see the bluff coming any more than the cattle could. But my horse sensed it and put on his brakes fast at the edge of the bluff and I went over his head and hit the water in the midst of hundreds of bawling Longhorns. They had broken legs and broken necks and were climbing each other's backs and drowning each other and tumbling downstream. Luckily I found one big old steer who was a strong swimmer and grabbed his tail and he hauled me out the other side of the stream and then took off. One of my vaqueros had gone off the bluff on his horse and somehow had stayed aboard and was swimming with the cattle, still trying to turn them to shore. The other rode downstream to do what he could. The cattle got into a terrible mill and the vaquero in the water crawled over their backs to the middle to try to break it up, but there was no use. I sat in the mud on the bank without a horse and cried like a baby. By morning they were all gone. Except the dead ones. There were so many dead cows in the river and up and down the stream that I could have walked across on their corpses if I'd had the stomach for it.

"I went back to our camp, where our bed ground had been, and found my good night-running horse still saddled. Pretty soon the two vaqueros came in and we rounded up twenty more of the thirty horses we'd had. I'd never had a chuck wagon or a wagon to carry the calves in but had been living off jerked beef and skillet cornbread. I suppose that was fortunate because somebody's herd had come right through our camp and trampled what few possessions we did have so flat into the mud that the only workable thing I could save was the skillet. I came back here just now, and I tell you, Peter, if you ever hear me say again that I want to be a cowherder, you knock me cold and tie me up until I come to my senses."

"Barney," I said, "why don't you come along and be my partner?"

"In what enterprise?" he asked.

"One thing and another. I figure on heading back to Mexico after this fall's buffalo hunt. I believe I know where an old Jesuit mine is, and if I'm right we can eat off gold plates for the rest of our lives."

"I have never been one to think gold plates improve the taste of beans, but I have never tried it," Barney said.

We had another whiskey and another beer and he said, "Peter, I don't aim to be inquisitive, but how come you didn't bring out this gold on your last trip if you think you know where it is?"

"I've got some information about it now that I didn't have when I was there," I said. "That country is rough for a man to negotiate alone. There were some Indians who didn't like me very much."

"You're getting a name with Indians," said Barney. "Every brown booger I run into has heard of you."

"With the two of us, we'll have a better chance," I said.

Barney looked at me through eyes red from the dust of the trail. "One thing," he said. "I am so broke that a tin plate would look like gold to me. If you will stake me in that poker game over where Ben Thompson is sitting, I'll win enough to pay my share of the trip. Then we're partners."

We shook hands and got up to go to Thompson's table.

8

In the fall of that same year, 1873, I met Charlie Otter and
his Quahadi as I had said I would. I met them at the Double
Mountain Fork of the Brazos near the Caprock. But the herds
had not come that far south yet so we abruptly turned north
toward the Canadian River. I was worried that hide hunters
might be roaming over from Kansas, as I heard it had been a
bad summer for grasshoppers and crops were ruined. Charlie
Otter said we would not be troubled. He believed in the
Medicine Lodge Treaty of six years earlier that prohibited
white hunters from coming south of the Arkansas. I figured
if you had the treaty in your hands it would be good to wrap
bullets in but not worth much else. There were too many
people making money off buffalo hides and too many Indian-
hating landgrabbers who wanted the buffalos destroyed. In
some ways a Comanche's mind is a swamp. He can believe a
dozen incredible and contradictory things before breakfast
and still have room to digest the story of the Creation before
lunch.

We went north in a long file. The men were dressed in
finery and riding their second-best horses, saving the best for

the hunt. The women rode or plodded beside the travois poles. Dogs ran up and down the procession. There was already a nip in the air. The sky toward which we marched had a gray and snowy look. The previous winter had been a hard one and another appeared to be commencing, which should have brought the buffalos south much sooner. Since the slaughter had begun, however, the herds were being even more erratic than usual. So I kept my apprehensions private, being as yet uncertain how Charlie Otter felt about me taking that white girl out of his camp along the Nueces in the spring.

Badthing and No Nose were with us but stayed to themselves and mostly spoke only to me. Badthing was in a sulk because Charlie Otter had brought along a shaman who was a buffalo-finding specialist and had a kit of tricks that he pulled around the fires at night when the Quahadi did their dancing and singing. Badthing told me the shaman, who had come from the Quahadi band of Quanah Parker, was a fraud. He claimed this fellow, Yellow Head, had a bag of peyote buttons that he was using to entice Charlie Otter's patronage. But as Badthing considered himself the fanciest and most mystical medicine man who ever astounded a horse Indian, I put his muttering down to jealousy.

Yellow Head made a rousing show when we crossed the North Palo Duro. He rode his hairy little paint pony through the cottonwoods, willow and hackberry trees along the creek. He peered at the leaves and sniffed the wind and held his sagebrush cap up to the heavens and then clapped it to his ear as if it was a receiver box for The Sure Enough Father's personal telegraph. Badthing snorted and frowned and fiddled with his medicine bag but did not comment. Yellow Head paused at a wild plum tree as though that was a very good thing to discover. Charlie Otter rode on with his head down, mulling about something, and it took the locating of a skunk bush to get his attention. I overheard part of what Yellow Head told him about talking to the skunk bush and learning that it would be a beautiful hunt, but Charlie Otter was no more impressed than I was. Charlie Otter was an unusual man in that he was brave and fierce enough to have become a war chief but wise and old enough to be regarded in council as a civil chief as well. Like most Comanche leaders he went along with the shaman's *hojarasca* but he put scouts out nevertheless. He could have made a good Jesuit.

There was no reason to doubt Yellow Head's prediction. We camped in perfect buffalo country with great flats broken by dry washes and low knolls so that there was plenty of cover for me to shoot from. Bluestem and bear grass grew among the sage and pokeweed. Along the arroyos were a number of wallows about two feet deep and ten feet across. During calving season in late spring, when the buffalos were shedding their old coats, they rolled in mud or dirt to get the flies and mosquitoes off their hides and they would paw out these wallows in places that were likely to be damp such as anywhere near a creek even though the spring rains had gone and the creek was dry. Our camp was on the west side of an arroyo. The herd, if it came, would probably come from the northeast. That direction was upwind from us, a necessity. I have heard hunters claim a buffalo can smell a man at four miles, but I am skeptical of that figure. Two miles would seem to me more accurate.

In the evening after a dinner of dried and powdered buffalo meat mixed up with plums, pecans, apricots, and fat, we finished off the last swallows of corn beer and Yellow Head proposed a buffalo dance. From the bundles that his woman hauled on his travois with his tepee and various equipment, he took a half dozen buffalo skulls, placing four of them about the camp at the four points of the compass and the other two in the middle. Pipes appeared and the air smelled of the pungent grasses and herbs that the Quahadi smoked. In a while there was considerable jollity. The musicians began thumping their buffalo-hide drums and the dancers hopped around the fire wearing buffalo-skull headdresses and the men chanted a buffalo song that had no melody but a strong rhythm. A big round yellow autumn moon came out as if at our request. It was the kind of moon you see nowhere except in West Texas, where there is nothing to interrupt the view, and I lay beside the fire smoking a cigar and feeling that I was very much of the earth and the Human Beings. I felt at that moment that I could, as the Indians say, hear the grass growing and smell the color changing in the mesquite. It was no good to think that the only choices the Human Beings had were to die or to become something else, so I quit thinking about it and went over to sit with Badthing and No Nose.

Badthing was in an ill humor again as he watched Yellow Head prancing in the firelight naked except for his sage cap and with his body painted in curving yellow lines like buffalo horns. No Nose was busy at the occupation she most favored when not traveling or working—chewing nits and lice out of the seams of her clothes. I tried to talk to Badthing but he had no philosophical riddles for me this night. He pulled his calico bonnet down over his head and mumbled and drew symbols in the dirt with a stick. No Nose sighed with a whistle of wind out of her exceptional nasal cavities. After a bit, I slept. I recall that the last thing I saw was that moon and it got me into sentimental notions that are all right for such a night but luckily were gone when I woke.

In the gray dawn an hour before daylight men staggered out of their tepees yawning, scratching, and belching while the women cut pegs for hides, built smokeless dung fires for the coffee I had fetched along as a gift, organized skinning and butchering parties and generally kept as occupied as they knew they had to. Near the ashes of last night's fire Yellow Head had called a meeting of Charlie Otter and several of the more responsible and prestigious warriors. Yellow Head crouched on the ground with a horned toad, spoke some tomfoolery, made a few passes in the air with a buffalo tail medicine stick and let the toad loose. The toad ran a few feet toward the northeast, paused, got prodded by the medicine stick and ran in that same direction out of camp. Yellow Head nodded proudly. Charlie Otter looked around at his counselors, who grunted and went to prepare their bows, lances and what pistols and rifles they owned. Charlie Otter beckoned to me. I joined him at his lodge for coffee.

"The toad magic says a big herd is coming from just that

side of where the sun rises," said Charlie Otter in the first complete Tex-Mex sentence he had uttered to me in days. "Yellow Head says the toad magic does not fail when combined with his own powers which are such that a buffalo will almost rip off his own skin and cut out his own meat for the Human Beings at a mere word from him." Charlie Otter glanced at me. "Never mind what I think of the toad magic," he said. "My scouts have also told me there is a herd approaching. Between them and the toad and the dancing and the skulls somebody should be correct. We will find many buffalos this morning. Now the question is how to kill them. We have discussed this matter in council and here is our decision, though of course we await your opinions with great respect and, ah, anticipation."

Briefly he went through each suggestion of the council. One warrior had wanted a surround in the old style in which the men would encircle the herd, creep close and then attack fast before the herd bolted. Another wanted to drive the herd off the bluff of an arroyo and break their legs, but that was chancy owing to the fact that the buffalos might choose another direction for flight. Knows Nothing held out for a chase with the hunters riding beside the herd and killing with lances and short bows. That idea was rejected because it was dangerous, wasteful, and left the buffalo carcasses strewn over a big area, causing difficulty for the skinners and butchers. Charlie Otter's plan had been the one accepted.

"You, honored friend," he said, choking somewhat on the words, "have been generous enough to offer to hunt with us for a fair share of the hides and meat, even though you are not in the hide business and it is too early in the season for prime robes." Charlie Otter paused to consider the affair once more from all angles and try to guess if I might be up to something. "Well," he said, "we accept your offer and will use your long gun for the benefit of the Human Beings as I am sure you intend."

"I am privileged," I said.

"Hmmm," he said. "All right." He then told me his plan in rough shape, depending for variation on the terrain and the

arrival of the herd. The Quahadi were to get in as close to the
herd as they could, hiding their horses in gullies or whatever
cover offered itself. I was to take my Sharps .50-caliber and
find a choice shooting spot within a couple hundred yards of
the herd. From my stand I would shoot as many buffalos as I
could before the herd began to run. When the running
started, the Quahadi would leap into the chase. With luck and
accurate shooting I could kill perhaps eighty or ninety
buffalos myself and the Quahadi would get thirty or forty
more. That sort of haul was nothing special for a day's
shooting by hide hunters, who left the meat to the wolves,
coyotes, crows, and vultures, but for a band of Quahadi it
meant a winter of luxury and full bellies. I agreed with
Charlie Otter, shared his pipe, finished my coffee—which, as
usual when there was sugar, Charlie Otters fat wife had
sweetened so as to be almost undrinkable—and went to
round up my gear.

At his hut Badthing was testing the pull of a short *bois
d'arc* bow, since the long bow he usually carried would be
worse than useless in a hunt from close quarters on a
running horse. His mood had changed from sullenness to
outright anger and so had improved his conversation. "That
Yellow Head," he said, his nose ring wagging. "Did you notice
how he poked that toad so it would flee in the direction he
wished? If that is proper magic then I am crazy as a Tonto
wine sot."

"You are envious," I said.

"True. But I am no fake. When I do magic it is real magic,
not just tricks. Anybody with the ignorance to defile the
spirits can learn tricks. It takes a genuine wizard like me to
do magic."

"If you have so much magic, make Yellow Head disappear," said No Nose in her whistling, breathy voice.

"I will tell you," Badthing said. "Eagle caught a mouse who
begged to be spared. Eagle replied, 'First you must answer my
question correctly. The question is: Will I spare you?' The
mouse's answer was 'Yes,' which was not true so Eagle ate
him. 'If the answer had been no,' Eagle said, 'that would have

been true, so I would have been obliged to eat him in any case.'"

"I wish you would talk sense," said No Nose.

"Who will make a mouse of Yellow Head?" I said.

"Oh, the spirits," he said. "It is too bad."

"If his is not true toad magic, how does he know where to make the toad run?" I said.

"You don't know anything about tricks," said Badthing. "While my body slept last night I had my ghost watch Yellow Head. When the fires were out he left the camp and rode until he found the buffalo herd. It is moving this way from where he said. He had a hard ride and got back a short time ago. My ghost saw it all."

I could see the braves were ready to leave. Most had stripped down to breechclouts and moccasins despite the chill. Their hair was unadorned and some had it tied back. Their bodies and their ponies were painted with buffalo and hunting signs and some wore in paint their particular vision symbols. Each man had his arrows marked so the skinners could return them. The women of the skinning and butchering party were going out with their horses dragging empty sleds. I wished Badthing good luck and received his blessing, noting over his shoulder that one of his horses was very lathered. As I went to my blankets, Yellow Head was conducting another ceremony. After much pipe smoke and many invokings of supernatural help, he released a raven. The raven circled and then flew to the northeast. That cinched it for most of the hunters. But it was not much of a feat. Ravens nearly always head for a big buffalo herd, as there is much for a bird to feast on in such a vicinity. I once saw a buffalo magician release two doves to fly toward a herd. The night before he had located not only the buffalos but a large pond near the herd. Doves seldom fail to fly to water in the mornings.

I checked my Sharps big .50 with the octagonal barrel and heavy action and breech that are vital if you are going to shoot many overcharged bullets from much range. The evening previous I had cleaned the rifle carefully and had loaded my bottleneck shells, stuffing black powder down to half an inch of the top, putting the rimmer in, tapping it with a hammer, setting the wadding on top of that, putting in a pinch more gunpowder and then the bullet. I had taken to loading a ninety-grain cartridge with up to one hundred and ten grains of powder, but I insisted on doing the loading myself. You don't want an accident or a jamming when you are in a hot stand. I also took along my old Henry rifle, as I intended to join in the chase, and my pistol and Bowie knife for emergencies. Hunting buffalos, even from horseback, can be done without too much risk, but the beasts are quite volatile when finally aroused and an emergency can be on you before you see it coming.

As we were leaving camp a scout came in and told us the herd was about ten miles away having its morning graze in a big flat between a dry arroyo and a long low mesa. Yellow Head didn't bother to brag, he was that arrogant. Badthing didn't bother to listen, he was that angry. Charlie Otter grunted at the scout, looked at the two medicine men and grinned. We rode out and by nine o'clock were in position.

I crawled for forty minutes through the mesquite, sage, and cactus, but I had put leather pads on my knees and elbows and the crawl was not bad except that I kept getting dirt and pebbles inside my pants. I selected a spot behind a sage thicket two hundred yards from the herd, which was in a flat upwind and slightly below me. To the rear of the herd about seven hundred yards from me, the blue shadow of the low mesa the scout had described fell across the hindmost buffalos. The Quahadi were in the arroyo below and one hundred yards to my left. There were thirty of them standing beside their ponies strung along the wash. I laid out my equipment and set up my forked shooting stick so near into the thicket that sage scratched my left cheek. Then I examined the herd, looking for the leader. It was not a truly large herd, not more than four hundred animals, but that was the average. Those herds of fifty thousand or more that the tales are told about were never common in my experience although I did witness a number of them.

The herd was grazing slowly and without alarm. There were a few bulls placed here and there in a loose protective ring, but inside the ring the animals grazed in bunches. The cows and calves grazed in separate bunches from the bulls as a rule, but a few bulls had joined some groups of cows and calves. In the spring the bulls were more attentive. I started with the nearest bunch and decided it had two leaders, a bull and an old cow. I wiped off and adjusted the bone sights on the Sharps and took aim at the cow. There was hardly any windage to think about, which was lucky not only for the shooting but because a herd can spook quickly from no more than the shadow of a blowing cloud.

I shot her through the lungs. As I heard the soft lead smack into her, she took one step backward, spewed blood from her nose and fell over dead. The bull looked up for a second before resuming grazing, but the others paid the dead cow no mind. I had guessed right about the leader. What those buffalos saw was a small puff of smoke and then their leader lay down. They did not connect those events. If the leader had started to run—as they frequently do after a heart shot, sometimes going four or five hundred yards—they all would have run with her and not stopped until she did. I reloaded and shot the bull. At his death two other cows looked up, so I marked them for next as curious beasts can be pesty ones. It was a clean stand. Taking the nearest and then working back, changing that method only for the inquisitive, I killed thirty buffalos and they all fell within a radius of forty yards. They would erupt blood, stumble, and flop over. The bull alone was fourteen hundred pounds and stood six feet high at the shoulder. So there were thirty excellent fall hides, not yet too shaggy with winter hair and worth about sixty dollars to the buyers. And maybe twenty thousand pounds of meat, bone, tallow, sinew, and whatnot for the Quahadi.

As I looked to the next targets, a bunch near the dead ones began bawling. They started coming over to peer and sniff at the dead ones and kept up bawling louder until the bawling spread through the herd. The bawling was a grieving sound, although perhaps I thought that because I had done the killing. I kept on killing until my shoulder hurt and I had to cool the rifle barrel with a kidney of water I had brought from camp. A hot barrel swells and causes bullets to dance. By now there were forty-seven dead ones. The live ones tore the ground with their hoofs, milled around, shook their horns, drooled long strings of saliva and bawled at the blood and death that they could not comprehend.

There are various ideas why buffalos stood to be killed. Most said it was because buffalos were stupid. But I say it was more than that. The smell of blood and gore profoundly disturbed them and they would carry on in some strange mourning ritual, bawling and milling and rolling their eyes sometimes until every last one of them was killed. I say all creatures are fascinated by the presence of much blood and many deaths. We get in a spell over the death stink.

At sixty dead I was working well. My shoulder was numb and the barrel was too hot to touch without gloves. The entire herd was bawling and they had their heads up and would soon run. Through the smoke and stench of black powder I glanced down at the wash and saw that the Quahadi were very restless, also affected by the bawling and the booming and the warming of the sun as it went toward noon. Those brown boogers could smell the blood and wanted to be in on it. I have seen calm decent folk jump off trains and shoot at herds with derringers and other ridiculous weapons and then get sick at the dying. But these Indians had no remorse. They wanted to run and yell and kill and would feel good about it. I estimated I had ten minutes of shooting before one group or the other would break out. But my estimate was wrong.

For a moment I thought it was an echo. That blasting had been at my ear for so long that I thought my head was doing stunts. Then I realized what I was hearing was another buffalo gun. Each gun had a fairly distinctive sound. As I listened again to a flurry of booms I counted four different guns and saw smoke from the blue mesa behind the herd. No animals were falling, which did not surprise me. Anybody who would shoot from that mesa, upwind, and intrude on another man's stand had to be ignorant as well as greedy. But the mischief was done. Amateurs get people hurt. The herd caught the scent of the hunters on the mesa, quit bawling and started running. Shaking their shaggy heads, they took off in a rolling gallop, amazingly fast despite the look of their stride. Hearing the rumbling and the new guns, the Quahadi heeled their ponies up from the wash and raced hollering and screaming after the herd.

The herd was running to my left lengthwise with the mesa but trying to get away from it. Puffs of smoke lay along the mesa like blossoms. I shot for the leaders in an attempt to stop the running, but the range was too great and the beasts were going too fast for my guess. By the time I could adjust, the Quahadi were too close to the herd for me to shoot again. I recognized Charlie Otter's gray pony in the lead. I saw that he and Knows Nothing and a dozen others were racing to cross in front of the herd so that the Indians would be running on either side of it. There was little space for that maneuver. A stumble would leave the warrior in front of the herd, and when a buffalo runs he does it with all his might.

I got up to go for my horse, judging that Four Ravens and the others would make it across the flat to the far side of the herd even though it would be a very tight squeeze. That judgment was based on my opinion that the Comanches are the finest horsemen who ever lived. But I heard the booming again and turned to see the ponies of Charlie Otter and Knows Nothing tumble in front of the herd. The hunters on the mesa had shot them down. Both Quahadi rolled in the dirt and bluestem grass only seconds in front of the lead beasts. I considered a shot at the leaders but decided against it. With the single-shooting Sharps I could fire but once and even if I should get a leader at that range the others would overrun the Quahadi nevertheless. Charlie Otter and Knows Nothing were doomed for certain. I scrambled down the knoll toward where my mare was tied to a mesquite and I knew then that those four hunters on that mesa were doomed, also, and the temper I was in made me relish their demise.

But the disaster on the flat was not the one I expected. Halfway down the knoll I stopped to look again. Charlie Otter had crawled behind the corpse of his pony and by firing with his old pistol at powder-burn range had dropped a big bull about four feet from him. Charlie Otter cuddled against the belly of his horse until they seemed one beast. Sending up a thundering noise and boiling dust, the charging herd split at the fallen bull and flowed around Charlie Otter's dead pony. He disappeared in the dust. I looked for Knows Nothing. He had fallen too far from his pony to get back and had lost his short bow. The herd swept toward him. He crouched to await them. He looked as if he was singing his death song and prepared to fight, no matter how futile it was, using his fists against the buffalos that now pounded onto and across him. In the great fog of dust he went out of sight.

In a moment he reappeared. Fantastic horseman that he was, Knows Nothing had grabbed a buffalo's mane, swung up under the neck of the beast and was riding on the hump with one fist full of hair and the other hand waving joyously in the air. I should not have been so surprised. I had seen him do the same thing as a game with horses. His problem was far from over, for he was vanishing toward the plains in the front rank of more than three hundred hysterical stampeding buffalos. But there was more to think about now than Knows Nothing's predicament.

One of the virtues of the Comanches and most other Indians of the Southwest is their reluctance to leave a fallen comrade who shows the smallest sign of life. The wounded man has a right—the Apaches call it *nah-welh-koht kah-el-kek*—to decide his own fate and if he thinks his situation is hopeless he can demand to be abandoned. But there was no leisure for such speculation in this instance. The fastest horsemen had already overridden the far edge of the herd before they knew Charlie Otter and Knows Nothing were down. The others, however, saw them fall and began at once to unloose arrows toward the leading buffalos, although it was like trying to stop a flash flood by throwing sticks into the water. Two warriors peeled off and rode to pick up

Charlie Otter and Knows Nothing. Picking up a prone man at a full gallop is a common talent for a horse Indian, but in this case Charlie Otter and Knows Nothing were hustling for themselves and the others never did reach them. Both of the rescuing warriors—who I did not identify at the distance—were sideways to the herd and riding hard toward their comrades when the buffalos hit them. I saw one pony flung into the air, come down on the close-packed backs of the herd and then bounce along, kicking and mortally injured. Neither warrior did I see. Both were trompled into jelly.

The Quahadi formed prongs on either side of the herd and proceeded with the hunt. Some were using short, thick lances and some were shooting steel-tipped dogwood arrows with their short bows reinforced with deer sinew for power. The bowmen aimed their arrows behind the short ribs, hoping the shafts would drive forward and down into the lungs or heart, and they rode in so close to the beasts that they often could yank out and reuse arrows that did not penetrate far enough. The lancers used both hands on their weapons, thrusting deep as the wounded animals tried to turn and gore them. Some Quahadi were shooting pistols and three or four had carbines, since a single-shot weapon was no good for that type of action. As they rode they tried to kill paths into the center of the herd where the cows, calves, and yearlings were running, as those provided the choicest meats. I could see Quahadi heads bobbing amidst the herd and there were beasts falling and bawling in the dust. Eventually the Quahadi would work their way out of the herd, unless the herd happened to stampede off a bluff or into an arroyo, in which event the Quahadi in the middle were bound to go along.

As I ran toward my horse I had forgotten about the hunters on the mesa. The dust was thick on the flat in the wake of the herd, but I could see something moving. It was Charlie Otter, standing up, slapping the dust off himself, feeling his bones. Then he went down again. I heard booming from the mesa. The intruders up there were shooting at Charlie Otter. Maybe they were shooting at anything that moved, hoping to get themselves a buffalo by luck. Regardless of their intention, that was no way for a fellow to conduct himself. There was another movement in the dust and I heard hoofs and knew someone had ridden out for Charlie Otter. When I got down to my horse Charlie Otter came in on the back of another warrior's pony. His face and body were covered with dust, blood, and bruises, and his mood was no better than you might suppose.

"We are going to kill them all," he said, glaring at me. "You know how it must be. What do you say?"

"I wouldn't have thought it to be any other way."

That was the truth. Two Comanches were dead and vengeance was inevitable, if not against the hunters on the mesa, then against the first two whites the Quahadi found.

"Good," he said. "You shoot at them from here with your long gun and we will circle the mesa and attack them from behind."

"Begging your pardon, old friend," I said. "Not that I would presume to tell a great warrior how to . . ."

"No speeches now," he said.

"If I shoot at them from here, they'll run. As it is, they think we're chasing buffalos. I suggest we ride down this wash and get them without warning."

"You are right," he said. "They are that stupid."

We set off down the wash with Charlie Otter mounted behind a warrior called Curly who had curly chestnut hair, the result of dubious breeding. We came up out of the wash into a mesquite thicket full of horse flies. The far side of the mesa had an easy slope. We left our horses with a young warrior who was not pleased by the duty and crept up the slope. In my Ute boots I am a quiet mover, which knack has been most helpful in my survival to date. But beside those Antelope People I sounded like a pregnant hog. Our stealth was not entirely necessary. We could hear the hunters from seventy yards away. They were cursing and banging pots and pans and tossing gear into a wagon that we came across the track of. Creeping near and lying on my stomach I parted a mesquite bush and could see the wagon. My, it was a grand one. It had spring seats—which experienced hunters discarded in Indian country so as to sit on the bed of the wagon to get the protection of its sideboards—and water barrels and skillets and coffeepots tied all over it, and there was a grindstone in back covered with a buffalo robe.

There were five men rather than four. One was clearly a skinner they had hired. He was a man of experience and he was afraid. As he watched the others do up their equipment he kept looking in our direction and begging them to hurry. A tall, paunchy fellow with sideburns told him in an English accent to shut up.

"You shouldn't of shot at them bufflers and you sure shouldn't of shot at them Indins," said the skinner.

"It was marvelous fun," said the tall fellow, who was wearing shiny leather boots and a kind of cork helmet that I had never before seen the likes of. "Did you see them scatter? Noble redmen, what? By George, savages are all alike. Cowards every one."

I glanced over at Charlie Otter, whose dirty face had the nastiest look on it I ever saw although he couldn't have understood more than a few words of what the Englishman said. Charlie Otter was not my idea of noble, but he had dignity and pride according to anybody's lights. If he had been a coward he would have been back working with the women. The other hunters began to chatter at each other about what keen fun it had been shooting at buffalos and Indians. The skinner turned his head anxiously as if he could already smell us. So Charlie Otter shot him through the chest with an arrow and he fell threshing and squirming and was lucky, at that.

The others were game. A skinny blond boy who looked and sounded like an Easterner fired his big Sharps .45 at us pointblank as we rushed them, and the kick of it knocked him against the wagon and out cold. A fat boy, not more than seventeen and on vacation from school by the looks of him, swung at Curly with a cooking pot before Curly laid him out with the side of an ax. The tall fellow shouted something I could not discern. It sounded like a regimental battle cry. He began shooting with a revolver at a warrior called Creek Slayer. Creek Slayer also had a revolver and from a distance of thirty feet the two emptied their pistols at each other without either being nicked. In my life I never saw more than a handful of Indians who could shoot a firearm with accuracy. There were many fights the Indians would have won if they hadn't shot high. But I would have expected better of the Englishman, who stood rigid, shouting his weird cry and blasting away until his ammunition was gone, whereupon he did an even weirder thing. He threw down his pistol and raised his hands and said, "I surrender with honor. There's a good sport." Creek Slayer hit him on the head and knocked him into the dirt.

The last member of the party was cannier than the rest. He ran for his horse, shooting back over his shoulder as he went. He was mounted before Charlie Otter put an arrow between his shoulder blades. He came down sideways into a cactus, but his horse got its reins held up in a mesquite and stopped. I would have hated to chase that beast.

So now we had them all. One dead, one dying, and three in assorted degrees of consciousness. I had hoped they would all be killed in a sudden fight, as I could take no pleasure in what was coming next. Charlie Otter scalped the skinner and the one who had run. With his skinning knife he cut circles around the crowns of their heads, got a strong grip on their hair, braced his foot against their foreheads and pulled. It sounded like shotguns when the scalps popped loose. The Englishman with the sideburns was awake and watching. His eyes were wide and yellow and he had a goofy look on his face, as if the blow had addled him.

"Thank the good Lord," he said, looking at me. "A white man, I believe."

I didn't answer, for I had nothing to tell that he would not almost immediately know.

"I am Colonel F—," he said and identified his British unit

as if it could possibly matter to me or to the Quahadi, who were sharpening stakes out of mesquite. "These nice young chaps," he said, indicating the fat boy and the blond boy, both still stunned, "are my nephews from Boston. My sister married a colonist, you see, common chap but decent enough and quite rich. Those others"—he looked at the two scalps that Charlie Otter was rubbing dirt on the fleshy sides of— "were until recently commercial enterprisers who hired out their services to us up on the Cimarron.

Curly and Creek Slayer had finished three stakes.

"I've had ever so much experience in dealing with savages," the colonel said. "I understand that a ransom is required and we are quite willing to pay whatever you ask. Trusting that it will be reasonable, of course, but you seem a reasonable chap to me, my dear man. Didn't I see you last year up in Kansas? I was with Lord T—'s party. Oh, what a gorgeous hunt it was. We killed hundreds of buffalos, littered the plains with them, all in a sporting manner to be sure, on horseback, none of this long-distance potting. We had the most marvelous tintypes made. I've got one on the wall of my mess. They're enormously envy-making. You've no idea how many officers are planning to come to the colonies to hunt buffalos."

He went on and on until at last I said, "You shouldn't have come here."

"Dear man, why ever not? I made inquiries of the Army and they told me it was perfectly legal."

"These Indians think there's a treaty."

"But there is no treaty," he said. "Texas retained its public lands after the Mexican War and the treaty is with the United States, so the treaty does not apply to Texas. We are in Texas, are we not? I have as much right to hunt here as these primitives."

He continued with legalistic babble until I walked away and then he began explaining his rights to Curly, who grinned and nodded as if he understood every bit of it and considered it a whopping joke. The fat boy and the blond boy had revived and stared at me with scared eyes.

"What are you going to do with us, mister?" asked the fat boy.

"Me, nothing," I said.

"You're going to let them kill us," the blond boy said.

"You broke the rules," I said.

"But they're savages," said the fat boy.

I looked away.

"I can't believe they would kill us," said the blond boy. "I'm only sixteen. I didn't shoot at them and I didn't hit any of them. We haven't been here an hour." There were tears on his pale cheeks. "I want to go home. I didn't want to come here. Please let us go home."

Four Quahadi held the colonel down while Curly drove a stake through his abdomen, pinning him to the ground like a bug.

"You're no Christian," said the blond boy. He could not fathom the situation. He had one of those churchgoing attitudes that confers its own order upon things.

Curly castrated the colonel and hung the grisly ornaments on the stake. To another stake they tied the colonel's head so that he would have to look at himself and then they clipped off his eyelids. His hands were tied to the stake near his head. His screaming took on a warbling note.

"Come on, Ronald!" the fat boy said and leaped up and ran. Curly threw his hatchet at him and missed. Creek Slayer pursued the fat boy into the mesquite. It could not be much of a race. The blond boy lost control of himself. Trembling and whimpering, he covered his eyes as he was dragged away from the wagon. I did not watch. As I went to my horse I passed Creek Slayer, who waved the fat boy's scalp at me and laughed. There was more screaming. I smoked a cigar and waited for the Quahadi.

Later I tried to get Charlie Otter to burn the wagon and hide the bodies. This was the sort of incident the Army would use as an excuse to destroy the Quahadi. He would not listen and suffered as a result. But first we went back to the camp. On the way we passed the women skinning buffalos in the flat.

They had rolled the bulls over on their bellies with their legs spraddled but had left the cows on their sides. The women cut the beasts across the neck and brisket and peeled the hides back so as to extract the forequarters at the joints. Then, avoiding the sinews nimbly as surgeons, they made cuts down the spines. Vultures wheeled above on spread wings and there were wolves at the fringe of the flat and coyotes out beyond the wolves. The odor of meat and guts was thick in the heat of the early afternoon. The women grunted and quarreled as they worked. The grass was brushed with blood and around our horses' hoofs rustled hundreds of tiny creatures—mice, rats, insects drawn to the slaughtering ground. Pulling mightily the women tore back the hides and then unjointed and cut out the hindquarters. With the rumps still attached to the backs of the animals, the women would rip up the flanks to the stomachs and take them out with the briskets. The entrails were dug out by hand and the rib steaks were snapped off from the spines. The women wrapped the meat in the hides and loaded them onto packhorses and travois for the trip into camp, where the meat would be sliced and dried and the hides would be pegged, scraped, and tanned. A few of the choice hides would be converted into robes. The Comanches had a use for most every ounce of the beasts—the gall and bile for flavoring, the horns and bones for utensils and ornaments, the hoofs and horns for glue, the stomachs and bladders for bags and canteens. Where a white hunter might feel he was using up an animal if he took sixty pounds of meat out of a fifteen-hundred-pound bull, the Comanches barely left enough for a wolf to lift a lip at.

As we entered camp we heard the mourning of the wives of Beaver Toes and Lodge Maker, the warriors who were killed in the buffalo run. The women wept and lamented and rent their clothes. A Comanche woman's hair is not much to look at anyhow, being all hacked up and dirty compared to the long handsome locks of the men, but these were pulling out their hair or sawing it off with knives and they had rubbed ashes on their faces. The wife of Knows Nothing was there, too, looking sad out of respect but not mourning, so I surmised her husband had survived his ride on the bull's back.

I sat with Charlie Otter before his tepee. He was wearing the Englishman's cork helmet. The pipe went around the circle and we smoked it and some of the men prayed. Although the Comanches had no organized religion, no priests or holy books, they did believe in a life after death and in an encompassing spirit that was involved with the sun. After death a good warrior who had not been scalped—for scalping prevented immortality or rebirth—went to a country beyond the setting sun where the horses were fast and the hunting was fine and there was no war, darkness, or sorrow.

While we smoked, several of the men prepared Beaver Toes and Lodge Maker for burial by washing them, painting their faces red, and closing their eyes with clay. The bodies were dressed in their best clothes, their heads tied to their knees in a sitting position, and the bodies wound in sheets of buffalo hides. The wives, one of whom had torn off her clothes and chopped off the index linger of her right hand, went around giving away the dead warriors' possessions. Curly moaned loudly, claiming the deceased had been his closest friends, and was awarded a horse and a new ax. Of course the names of Lodge Maker and Beaver Toes would never be spoken again, not only because of the risk of offending their ghosts but because it was improper to remind the mourners of their grief.

In a short time the bodies were ready. The bodies were mounted on their best horses and were ridden off toward the burial place flanked by weeping women and followed by a few of the men, including me. We found a dry wash with a sharp crevice and wedged the bodies into the crevice facing east. The two horses were shot and left in the wash along with the favorite bows, lances, and knives of Lodge Maker and Beaver Toes. The ceremony did not take long, as the

Comanches believed—rightly, to my thinking—that such matters should be attended to with feeling but not lingered over. Then we rode back to camp. Ordinarily the camp would be moved at once, but there was too much meat to be cared for and too many hides to be scraped.

Charlie Otter called a council at which all but the younger men would have opportunity to speak in deciding whether to dispense with the scalp dance, the buffalo dance, and the feast in view of the misfortune. I ducked into Badthing's ba-ak, where he was laying out peyote buttons in a cross after the Kiowa fashion. I sat on a drum and watched. In a moment he looked around at me.

"You are concerned about the deaths of the white men?" he said.

"No more than I can help."

"I warned you what would happen if the spirits were defiled," he said. "Now go away while I pray and then I will come out and tell another tale."

A crier went through the camp announcing there would be no dancing or celebration, but there would be feasting. Hams were already hanging in mesquite trees. Humps were being sliced to be fried in tallow. The women roasted tongues over chip fires. When the tongues were done they were served by a woman of virtue to men who sat in a half-circle apart from the women and smoked. That, too, was rushed because of the circumstances. After a happier hunt there would have been dancing until midnight and feasting all the next day. The five women of Beaver Toes and Lodge Maker set up such a racket with their wailing that I had no appetite. Since both men had been young and healthy, the mourning would go on for weeks.

The tepees of Lodge Maker and Beaver Toes were struck and burned. Sitting near the black smoke was Yellow Head, his sage cap gone and his eyes dull. No one went near him until Badthing arose from his tongue dinner and raised his arms. The little Karankawa had put on his silk top hat and his red blouse. As he was standing near the fire, sweat bubbled in the black paint on his face and light glittered from his brass nose ring.

"Once," he said, "Coyote came into the forest saying, 'Make way for the King of Beasts!' 'Where is the King of Beasts?' inquired a hare. 'Right here. I am the King of Beasts,' said Coyote. When the hare merely stared at him, Coyote said, 'I will prove it.' So Coyote danced about on one hind leg with his tail in the air. 'Does that not prove it? Who else but the King of Beasts could dance like that?' said Coyote. By then more hares as well as some birds, possums, beavers, and other animals had gathered. 'I am the King of Beasts,' said Coyote. 'Listen to this.' Coyote began howling in his finest voice. 'Who else but the King of Beasts could sing like that?' said Coyote. The animals cheered. 'March with me through the forest and you will have nothing to fear,' said Coyote. So they marched through the forest crying, 'Make way for the King of Beasts!' They met Bear, who asked, 'Why, where is the King of Beasts?' 'Right there,' a hare replied, pointing at Coyote. 'Well, well, this is quite an honor,' said Bear, stuffing into his mouth all the little animals he could get his paws on, 'I have always wanted to meet the King of Beasts.' Coyote ran away saying, 'What bad luck! I thought it might work!'"

Badthing sat down and lit his pipe. Yellow Head did not look. At length Charlie Otter said to me, "After today all Human Beings will know you are our friend." I made a speech thanking him and when I was through I turned and Yellow Head had disappeared. Badthing stayed in his ba-ak eating peyote and chanting for the next three days while I salted and partially cured two hundred pounds of hams that I could take back to a smokehouse. When I was packing to leave for Austin to pick up Barney Swift and go look for the mine in Chihuahua, Badthing appeared and presented me a gift of a bag of marrow that I could spread like butter on my biscuits. He pronounced he had had a most favorable vision for my journey. I replied that I would need it, and I did.

9

More enters a man's head than he perceives, so we do things that amaze ourselves. A little while ago, after a sleep, I climbed onto the roof of my house and watched the sun go down behind the edge of the desert. Sitting on the roof it occurred to me that I have no idea how many days and nights have passed while I wait for Octavio. The passing of time has become confused in my mind. I would not be surprised if I were told I had been here two days, a week, or if I were told it was only a month since I last saw my mother, for what does it matter? All that I have done is what I am at this moment.

What am I at this moment? As I sat on the roof I noted that I felt jangly, glowing, nauseous. I kept turning my eyes from the sunset to peer down into the valley of Valdez, to look at the sheep in the meadows, at the fast clear river, then up the canyon to the red hue on the snow peaks, then to the south along the wooded plateau, then across the valley to the forested hills, peering as if I were searching, feeling somehow as though I wished to shout. What am I at this moment and, more, what am I becoming? I recall that in the mission I told Father Higgins: "I do not pry too deeply. Things

I cannot understand I do not give much thought to, having all I can cope with to handle the things I do think I can reason out." That was the truth, and must remain so. I must not be anxious. I am thankful that I have my chronicle to sustain me. Otherwise, I suspect I might be talking out loud. I think, in fact, that I occasionally speak these words out loud as I write them, for I hear words spoken and there is no voice here but mine.

I am thinking now of the last visit to my mother. It was in the summer after the poker game with Barney Swift and Ben Thompson at the Vaudeville and before the buffalo hunt with Charlie Otter. She was living in San Antonio then, lives there yet I suppose. Riding out to the mission to see her, I remembered the day she decided to leave Austin. It was a day of terrible events, but it began happily when my father was released from the Bull Pen.

If ever a man was destined to be clapped into the Bull Pen, it was my father. Although he was, as I have said, of divided heart over the War Between the States, he could not tolerate the aftermath. Austin streets were full of carpetbaggers and scums of the worst stripe. In 1865 George Custer camped with the 6th Cavalry along Shoal Creek and was often seen in the town, sitting his saddle foppishly, long golden hair falling over his ears like a woman's. John Wesley Hardin, the gunfighter, was a boy in the town, and the militant, Phil Sheridan, was on the streets. Octavio had been gone for a couple of years and we heard nothing of him. His killing of Luther Freeman had not stirred up a commotion. What was one coon more or less? Barney and I went about our childish games. But daily my father became more morose, less inclined to tend to his wagon-making business even though the demand for new wagons was great and the carpetbaggers had money to spend.

My father never had much small talk. He was liable to go a week without saying a word to anyone except my mother and, at least in my presence, he would mostly only grunt or nod to her. Then he would look up from his work and say, "Do you figure those fellows really know how far it is to the moon by doing arithmetic?" He was skeptical about such matters. Or he would say, "A horse kicked old man Wilbargers nephew and broke his leg. Had to be shot." Or, about the war, "I'd rather kill a fellow from Oklahoma Territory than one from Massachusetts, for I know the one from Oklahoma Territory well enough to know he deserves it." Or, "A man shouldn't have to be what he hates." Between each of these pronouncements two or three days might go by. He never expected an answer and would likely have flailed me if I had dared offer one.

I overheard him have a bad argument with my mother during that period. I couldn't understand exactly what it was about, but I got the impression he wanted her to have another child. That was the only bad argument I ever heard them have.

In the spring of 1866 the Yankee soldiers built the Bull Pen south of their stables and to the west of the tent city they had erected for themselves. They took heavy logs fifteen feet long and planted them upright in the ground to form a stockade some one hundred and fifty feet around. Near the top of the logs on the outside of the fence was a plank walk for the guards to pace on. The Bull Pen had no roof. The prisoners, who were sentenced for offenses from murder to fouling the sidewalk, had to sit on the ground in sun or rain. My father used to invent reasons for riding in the vicinity of Little Shoal Creek and the stake-and-rider fence nearby. He watched the Bull Pen go up. Then he would watch the thirty or forty prisoners a day being escorted into the stockade.

One afternoon—it was searing hot—my father ceased working on a wagon in the big shed and put on his hat. His mustache was limp with sweat and he had got that dogged angry look in his eyes. "For every right there is a committee to discourage a man from using it," he said and taking a horse, not the buggy, rode into town. My mother asked where he had gone but I did not know. "To Dutch John's, I presume," said she. "He has much on his mind." As he went to Dutch John's several times a week, I did not see that it was any serious matter. But late that night Old Man Swift, Barney's father, came over and told us what had happened. My father had been arrested and sentenced to twenty days in the Bull Pen for singing *Dixie* at the top of his voice on Congress Avenue after General Sturgis himself had ordered my father to desist.

We were not allowed to visit him although we did smuggle several packages of food to him by way of a lieutenant who seemed embarrassed that such a noxious erection as the stockade would enter the gaze of such a lovely and aristocratic lady as my mother. Barney and I, of course, made much of it. We hatched a dozen plots for helping my father escape and planned our flight to freedom through the hills. But the summer dragged on and the twenty days were up before our scheming was finished.

To say that my father came out of the Bull Pen unrepentant is to put it feebly. He had allowed his beard to grow. He had not washed. He leaned hard on his crutch as he hobbled through the gate. After kissing my mother on the cheek in an unusual show of affection, he rubbed my head and then looked into my eyes. It was to me an odd moment, for it was like looking into the eyes of a madman and yet I felt that I saw into the depths of the man and he into mine, and what was there could have been love, and we knew that we were father and son and were bound together. There was a feeling that covered the three of us—how can I describe it? As though we three were roped with a mysterious cord, but what tied me to each of them was stronger than what tied them to each other, and we all realized it, and I felt my mother flinch as if from pain and I thought my father would cry out in rage and frustration. Then that feeling vanished, for it was too powerful for us to bear, but the impression of it remained. My father hugged us both. He smelled old, buried, damp, bilious. He hugged us with all his strength, awkwardly, for I was by now as tall as he and his beard crushed into my cheek and my mother's face was mashed against his chest and against my right arm. He hugged us until I could not breathe and the feeling covered us, and then he released us suddenly and stepped back.

He gave my mother a letter that had been written on butcher paper, folded over and sealed with wax. He walked away. We moved to follow but he turned and waved us off with his crutch. My mother tugged at my shirt sleeve. I took her arm and helped her into the buggy. She was silent. As we drove away, he was walking toward the town in the dust and heat.

What happened that afternoon I heard from a number of witnesses.

My father returned to Dutch John's. He had been given the money and the derringer he was carrying when arrested. Witnesses said he entered Dutch John's like a maniac, pounding the floor with his crutch, buying whiskey, singing *Dixie*, making speeches that no one understood. He chased two Yankee soldiers out of the place. Just as the others thought he had calmed, a tall, thin fellow walked into the saloon and my father whooped curses, yanked his derringer out of his belt and fired. A derringer does not deliver a heavy blow from a distance. The tall fellow pulled a Navy revolver from inside his shirt and shot my father in the throat, cutting off, they say, an obscenity. My father fell over backward against the footrail and died with his head in the gutter that runs along the bottom of the bar. The other fellow staggered coughing and choking out to the sidewalk and fell into the horse trough, his blood rising to smear the surface of the water. Both were dead. Nobody in Dutch John's knew the other fellow. They were puzzled as to the source of my father's hostility.

When I heard of my father's death I thought, what a lot of trouble, who will handle this? Then I felt sorry at not having known him better and sorry at not being sorrier. I went to the mortuary and looked at his body. I knew then, for a time, the anguish of mortality. The body lying on that table had been alive. Walking on, I came to the man my father had died fighting, and vice-versa. He looked familiar. In the corner I saw the black Mexican boots with the silver buckles and recognized the man as the Haengebund leader who had killed the Dutchman. I explained it to my mother and to

Barney. Later I told Octavio and found it was he and his renegades who had chased the man out of the hills into Austin.

We buried my father in the little graveyard near the river.
We had opened the letter. All it said was: MY EPETAF—NEVER
MIND. So that was what we carved on his stone:

John Patrick McGill

Born?   Died 1866

Never Mind

After that my mother moved to San Antonio de Bexar
where she had kin. I attended school there and was a good
student. I studied day and night with the priests and the
nuns. I applied myself to my books with a fervor I had not
known was in me. We lived with a cousin in a white mansion
with a red tile roof. My mother went daily to Mass. Candles
were always lighted for my father. My mother wore black and
was seldom without a lace handkerchief on her head. She
was remote from her kin and from me, although she was ever
courteous and gentle. She was driven to Mass in a carriage
with the curtains drawn. She gave her money to the Church.
Her cousin, the head of the house, tried to admonish her but
she hushed him without a word. I think back upon that as a
year of silence. My mother floated through the house in a
long black dress that hid the tiny movement of her feet. Her
expression was serene, her eyes alert. I often had to speak
twice before she understood what I had said. My impression
of that year is of crystal wineglasses, polished wood, the dry
voice of a priest, sung responses, the whiskery sound of satin
in the halls of our house, reading by lantern light, starched
muslin sheets.

It could not last. After a year I awoke one morning,
saddled my best horse, took my father's Henry rifle, some
money and a few supplies and rode West. I left my mother a
note that said I would return when I could. She would know
why I had to go. There was too much of the rowdy in me.

I heard from her a couple of times in the next six years
and wrote her two or three letters, but usually I was in places

where the mail was mounds of Indian message rocks. However, after the poker game in San Antonio I decided to visit her. Maybe that sounds heartless on my part, letting that much time slide past without seeing my mother. But it was not easy traveling where I went and the time did slide by faster than I reckoned and I thought about her some. Would my mother cease to love me because I had not seen her in six years? There is more to us than that.

After the poker game at the Vaudeville, and after the speck of trouble that followed, I got shined up and fancy dressed again in my room at the Menger and rode on my fine Kentucky mare out to the mansion of my mother's cousin. It was a while before the houseman who answered the door recognized me, but when he did the servants took on over me and the family was called in. Over a glass of brandy I was informed that the cousin was dead of congestion. And my mother? They exchanged looks that I did not fathom. She had moved, they said. She was out at San Juan, the old mission. She had been there nearly two years. I finished my brandy, shook hands all around and rode my mare across the San Antonio River to the mission south of town.

The mission is a collection of adobe buildings built inside thick walls in a mesquite flat. Around there begins the chaparral country that goes down to the Mexican border at the Rio Grande. The walls of the mission are so thick that there are rooms inside. For years the mission was a fort as well as a church. The Comanches used to rule that territory and chase the Spaniards and Mexicans about as they saw fit.

I went through the gate of the mission and left my horse with a Mexican boy. There was a cornfield outside the walls. Inside they had a little garden with radishes, onions, beans, and mustang grapes. Priests in brown or black robes were walking around the courtyard. The Franciscans had been thrown out, a beam had fallen from the ceiling of the church and cows looked at me from the granary. As I went toward the sacristy the bells began to ring in the steeple. I inquired for my mother. She had a room, they told me, in the wall at the rear of the courtyard near the granary. I knocked on the door. Sweat got in my eyes when I took off my hat. In a moment the door was opened. Because of the sun I could hardly see the figure inside the darkened room, but I recognized that it was small enough to be my mother. Then I heard her voice and I knew.

"Peter?" she said.

I don't know what made me do it, but I knelt in the dirt at the doorway. When I felt her hand on my shoulder I began to cry. I have cried rarely in my life, but this came upon me without warning. I could smell the muslin of her dress and I cried without feeling foolish. After a bit I ceased crying and, snuffling like a babe, arose, awkward now and foolish feeling as I towered over her, and let her lead me to a chair which I gingerly sat on, not wishing to break it. Her room was no more than a cell. There was a small altar with a silver Christ on a cross in one corner. Two candles burned on the altar as the room's only illumination. There was a cot against one wall, a water pitcher and washbasin on a table, and the chair upon which I hunkered. The floor was packed earth, and the walls were whitewashed adobe. There was a sort of wardrobe in which I suppose she hung her clothes. That was all. Not a one of the comforts among which she had been raised, not one touch of the elegance of her cousin's mansion except for the silver crucifix, not even a hint of the rougher comforts of our home in Austin.

But her face and her bearing reflected a strange pleasure. She sat on the cot as though it were a regal bench. She held herself erect and smiled at me proudly. In the yellow glow of the candles her black hair shone. I noticed that she was barefoot.

"They tell me you are a holy widow," I said. She smiled and I said, "But why have you chosen this? Why do you live like this? You could have much more and be just as devout, it appears to me."

"I wish that I were worthy of becoming a member of the sisterhood," she said, "but I am not, and one must do what one can."

"You are worthy of doing whatever you please," I said.

She smiled again and shook her head and said, "No, Peter. That is not true. Even in being here like this I am selfish, for there is only one way to find sweetness and peace on this earth and that is the way I have chosen."

I began to want a cigar but would not, of course, smoke in her presence.

"Poor Peter," she said. "You don't understand yet. But you will. You are as much a part of me as you are a part of your father, who was never free. He was an agonized soul, just as you are, and he never found his peace until he embraced it. God be merciful." She crossed herself. "I have taken a different and more useful means. The secret to peace is to be used."

"But how are you being used here in this tiny room with no shoes on your feet?" I said.

"I work."

"Couldn't you go back to your cousin's and work?"

"There is purity here. I work in the fields. I work in the hospital. I teach the children. We can never be completely pure, for we were born ruined, but the most purity and the most usefulness are here. It is too simple. You will understand in time."

"I doubt that," I said.

She said, "Would you like a cup of water?"

Before I could reply she poured water from her pitcher into a clay mug and brought it to me. I did not really want it, for it was cool inside the thick walls and I had quit perspiring, but I drank it and recall thinking that if I did not she might get down and try to wash my feet with it—a terrible thought. She padded back to her cot.

"Peter," she said, "deep in each of us is a force, a—I don't know what to call it. A devil? A darkness? A mischief? You see it appear in our maliciousness, our pranks, our evasions. We cannot destroy it because it was bred into us. But we can by the help of God and the strength of our wills keep it down inside ourselves until we are delivered to heaven, where this force cannot live. It does not matter what we call this force as long as we know God's power can help us to overcome it until we are in God's eternal care finally."

"This force," I said, "could be playing a prank on you by keeping you here in this tiny room deprived of the joys of life."

"All the joys of life are here," she said and touched her forehead and her heart. "I have the memory of my husband, and I know of those joys and do miss them, and I have the knowledge of the love of my son. Those are part of the joys but not all. The love of God is the true joy, and that comes only from being useful in God's purpose."

"How can you pretend to know what God's purpose is?" I said.

"I do not pretend. I do know. When you allow yourself to discover it, you will also know. If the world could know how sweet God's love is and how joyous to be defeating the devil. It is the ultimate joy. Oh, it is sweet, Peter." I saw tears in her eyes. "It gives me such joy that I know I do not deserve it."

Well, I thought, the old lady is cracked.

We sat for a while more. My mother did not mention joy or sweetness again, although I could tell it was on her mind. Instead she asked questions about my adventures and I gave vague answers that you might expect somebody to give to his mother. She knew I was lying but she didn't seem to care. Then she stood up and said it was time for her to go to the hospital. Looking down at her small body, her long black hair, her luminous eyes, her smile, I thought oh what a pity. She was a beautiful woman. But I felt as though I had never known her. That feeling made me sad again, but I was through with crying. Who was she, this odd little lady with the bare feet? I bent over clumsily and kissed her. I had intended to kiss her on the lips but on the way down I knew that was wrong and I wound up kissing her in the corner of the left eye. The smell of her hair was like French soap and I thought how remarkable that she could live on a dirt floor and remain so clean. I ducked under the doorjamb and looked back. She was gazing at me but what she saw was behind me someplace.

"Renounce yourself, Peter," she said.

"Yes ma'am," I said, not wishing to pursue the matter, and went to my horse.

10

When I left my mother at the mission in San Antonio, I struck out toward the Double Mountain for the buffalo hunt with Charlie Otter, which adventure I have described. During my absence Barney had time to attend to his affairs and prepare for our expedition. He was high-spirited and ready to go upon my return.

We crossed the river into Mexico in the middle of January. It was one of those clean bright days they often get in the Rio Grande Valley at that time of year. We crossed at Villa Acuña about a hundred and fifty miles west of San Antonio, a ride we made in three days with no incident. We rode through the cactus country veering southwest into the Sierra del Huacha. I insisted on making a wide southerly circle around the Chisos Mountains again, as those same Kiowa Apaches who had reasons for wanting to kill me still had their *ranchería* in that territory. We were, however, well armed and most dangerous ourselves and not overly concerned so long as we maintained caution.

There were four of us—me, Barney Swift, Badthing, and No Nose. I had run into Badthing in Austin. After pondering his vision pertaining to my journey, he had decided to follow and asked to accompany me. I agreed without hesitation. Eccentric and cranky as the little fellow could be, he was nevertheless a wizard of a tracker and woodsman, had a Spanish mule's nose for finding water, could sense danger as keenly as any wild beast and could handle weapons ably enough to be an irritation to our enemies. Barney did not approve at first, as the sight of No Nose's face made him tend to retch, but a couple of days on the trail hardened him to the view and he learned that she was not only a woman of some wit but was a good cook and a hard worker. Badthing had got the idea that even a magician could use a little gold. I was willing to share with him according to his contribution.

To understand where we were going and in what extraordinary surroundings our adventures took place, it is necessary to know something of the geography of Mexico. Moving west from the Gulf of Mexico, the states are in order Tamaulipas, Nuevo León, Coahuila, Chihuahua, and Sonora. The state of Sonora borders on both the New Mexico and Arizona territories and becomes the eastern coast of the Gulf of California. Tamaulipas I do not know much about, as I had few occasions to go that far east and care little for humidity, hurricanes, and mosquitoes, but in a westward-reaching finger of land it has Nuevo Laredo as its primary border town. Monterrey is the largest city in Nuevo León. Near Monterrey rises the great mountain range called the Sierra Madre Oriental which reaches some five hundred miles south toward the Federal District and Mexico City itself. To the west of Nuevo León is Coahuila, whose major cities are Saltillo, Monclova, and Torreón. Coahuila once included Texas. Where we crossed the river at Villa Acuña, across from Del Rio, which is in Texas, we were yet more than one hundred and fifty miles from the western boundary of Coahuila. That boundary is the state of Chihuahua. In Chihuahua are deserts and range lands, high mountains and deep barrancas. To the south of Chihuahua City, a town of political passions, is the mining district of Parral near the northern border of the state of Durango. The mountain range called the Sierra Madre Occidental runs along the western boundary of Chihuahua and on down into Durango and Nayarit for a distance of some six hundred miles, touching also in Sonora and Sinaloa, the latter being on the coast to the south. The two big mountain ranges, then, run roughly down either coast so that the interior of Mexico is a long valley.

In the westerly third of Chihuahua is a land tilt or divide that crosses the town of Creel. Waters to the east of Creel flow to the Gulf of Mexico and waters to the west flow to the Gulf of California or the Pacific. Where we were going, though I did not yet know it, was to Creel and from there south into the barrancas and southwest into the Sierra Madre Occidental. What we were looking for was, as I have said, the Tayopa Mine, but I was willing to settle for much less. Men have searched for the Tayopa Mine for more than a century, since the Jesuits closed it and warned the Indians that to betray its location was to betray God. That notion made sense to the Indians—be they Yaquis, Tarahumares or whatever other breed worked the Tayopa—for they attach supernatural presence to the mountains and do not like white men anyhow. Of finding the Tayopa I had more than a small hope—for reason I will explain—and of finding gold I had no doubt. In another journey I had come across muletas, or surface rock containing iron oxide, in a certain place and by following their hint had been able in a few weeks to carry out part of the gold with which I had ransomed Ellen from Charlie Otter.

Ellen was a cute little rascal. When I went back to Austin after the buffalo hunt to pick up Barney, I decided to visit her. She ran out to greet me when I rode up in front of her aunt and uncle's house on Guadalupe Street. Before I could get off my horse, she had hold of my left leg and was jumping up trying to reach some more of me. Until I saw her I had not realized how much I had been thinking of her, how she had been in my head as I lay by the fire at the buffalo hunt, how she was before my eyes be they open or shut—and not just the vision of her disrobed by the Comanches, although that was a rosy vision that could stick with a man forever. No, she was in my head in many ways. There was the smell of her, faintly sweaty and unperfumed but healthy and of good flesh; the touch, as though there was blood beating in her, feeding her skin, making it alive (altogether too many women feel like rubber); the sound of her voice, clear but girlish; the direct look of her eyes that let me know it was me she was looking at; the way her face split open and showed all her white teeth when she laughed; the way her thick black hair moved in the wind as she ran to me.

It was a cold day in Austin and my mare was blowing frosty breath and I was wearing a sheepskin jacket, but Ellen was shoeless and wore a blue cotton skirt and white cotton blouse, and her little feet crunched in the frozen grass. She kept calling my name—"Peter, Peter"—and grabbing at me and laughing, hardly the welcome I had expected. Last time, when she hugged me in front of her aunt and uncle, her affection was reasonable because of her relief and because I had done something for her. But this time I had figured her to be polite and friendly, little more. White women baffle me as much as they baffle themselves.

When I got down off my horse she leaped up into my arms so that I had to hold her off the ground and she gave me half a dozen kisses. I was trying to look around to see if any neighbors were watching. I was also trying to ask if I might come inside for a few minutes. Evidently I could, for she began kicking her feet and saying to go in by the fire. I got the door open somehow and she dragged me to the sofa and unhitched the snaps on my sheepskin jacket and tossed my hat onto a chair and dug into me with the softest, squirmiest, sweetest, and longest kiss that it had then ever been my delight to experience. I held my breath throughout, not wishing to risk exhaling any gamy odors onto her, and got so dizzy I thought I might fall on my nose. No sooner did she pull back from the kiss than she laughed, although I will swear her eyes were wet, and announced I needed a cup of coffee and she would be back at once. I asked where were her aunt and uncle and she replied it was her lucky day, they were in town and would not return for hours.

I went to the windows and peered through the curtains and saw gray sky and smoke rising from chimneys but no inquisitive old owls peering back. I poked up the fire a bit and warmed my hands. She brought the coffee, bade me sit on the couch and then she knelt and tugged off the tall-barreled cowherder boots that I had worn so that her aunt would not think me a barbarian who always wore Ute moccasins. If the stench of my socks affected her she did not let on but immediately crawled up beside me and kissed me again, gentler, and then sat back and said words that astounded me:

"Peter, I have missed you so much I thought I would die."

Had anybody ever missed me before? A number, certainly, had been concerned as to my whereabouts for one reason or another. And Barney had probably remarked that he would enjoy to see me again. But to have missed me was different. It was so different that I didn't believe her. I remember telling Barney when I was much younger that when I died—we talked about that a lot playing our war games—some people would be curious and some merely interested but none would be so affected that they would actually miss me or feel their own lives altered by my absence. He agreed and said it was the same way with him, and I agreed, and we both felt hurt, but we relished playing the dramatic more then than we did when we were really face-up with events that others consider dramatic.

"Whatever for?" I asked her.

"Because I love you," she said.

That is a prickly word to fool around with. I don't recall that anyone had ever come out and said it to me before, and if they had I would have distrusted them as I now did Ellen. I thought, looking at her, that babies do not know what they are playing with. Loving me was ridiculous and expecting me to believe it implied I was considered a fool.

"What are you doing?" she said as I started to put on my boots.

"Clearing out," I said.

"Are you angry?"

"No, just clearing out."

"Then it's true," she said. "My aunt told me about you, but I thought she was wrong."

Ellen got off the sofa and stood trembling in front of me. Her lips quavered. She clenched her fists. No creature can look madder than a woman of short stature. Tears began coming down her cheeks. The cotton blouse could scarcely contain her bosom. Next thing I knew she was shouting at me.

"I thought she was wrong!" Ellen shouted. "What a pighead I am! Oh, how you must be laughing at me! How stupid I must look to you! All right, then, you scum, go back to your squaws! Oh, I wish you had left me to die among those filthy Indians! That would have been kinder than killing me like this! I should have listened to my aunt!"

"What's this all about?" I said, highly confused.

"My aunt told me you didn't love me! She told me you were nothing but a scum! She warned me! But I thought you loved me like I love you, and now I've made myself silly in your eyes! Go on and clear out, scum! Clear out!"

She ran from the room and came back with a 12-gauge shotgun that was nearly as tall as she.

"Get your other boot on and clear out before I blast you to pieces, you ruffian!" she shouted.

"Wait up," I said.

"So you can make fun of me? Not on your life, lout! I saw that mocking look on your face a minute ago! If I see it again, you'll never see anything else! Coming around here taking advantage of me! I ought to get the sheriff and have you hanged! Then you'd be sorry for breaking my heart, I'll bet! Why did you have to come here anyway? Aren't there enough squaws you can make fun of without picking on a decent girl?"

"Ellen, I guess I love you," I said.

She cocked one hammer on the shotgun and lifted the muzzle to point at my chest.

"I hope you know how to pray, you swine," she said calmly enough that it frightened me.

"I said I guess I love you."

The muzzle shook and her knuckles whitened.

"Don't say you guess you love me," she said. "Either say you love me or clear out."

"But I don't know whether I love you."

"So clear out."

"But if I clear out I might never know."

"You're making fun of me again."

"That gun won't shoot with the safety on," I said.

"You must think my brains rattle!" she shouted.

She aimed the shotgun at the fireplace and squeezed hard with her right index finger and there was silence. She turned the gun toward my chest again.

"All right," she said. "You get up and march over here and show me where the safety is, you lout. And don't forget I can blow you to pieces."

"Why would I want to show you where the safety is?"

"Because I asked you to! You owe that much courtesy after the way you've treated me."

"When I get over there, I might take the shotgun away from you," I said.

"Not if you have the slightest bit of honor, swine."

I stood up and walked slowly toward her, one stockinged foot touching the parlor carpet alternately with one boot, and she never moved the muzzle from my chest.

"It's tricky on these old models," I said. "I'll have to do it for you."

I pushed aside the muzzle and pointed to the tiny catch on the plate below the right hammer.

"Right here," I said, feeling her tremble as I bent over her. "This lever has got to be pushed forward before the gun will shoot."

"It's already pushed forward," she said.

"Yes ma'am. Then you've got to take your finger off the trigger guard and put it on the trigger."

"Oh, Peter, this gun doesn't work anyhow," she said.

She dropped the shotgun and there was a great BLAM in the small parlor and the powder burnt my left arm. I scooped her up and carried her back to the sofa and we kissed for what must have been an hour. It was like becoming something more than what I am. She felt warm and fuzzy. We stayed on the sofa all afternoon. I got up once to carry in more wood from the kitchen. And once I said, "But you're a child."

"I'm not. I'm sixteen," she said.

"I'm going on twenty-four," I said.

"An older man is what I want," she said.

So we stayed on the sofa all afternoon. Once I looked up at the hole in the ceiling. Black bits of fiber hung down around the rim of the hole. Mostly I looked only at her. From one viewpoint it was the most remarkable afternoon of my life, because it was the first I knew I could feel like that.

Eventually, though, I knew it was time to go.

I got my boots on. She ran out of the room, but this time when she came back it was with a bundle wrapped in brown paper and tied with a ribbon.

"These," she said, "are letters I've written to you but didn't know where to send. Take them with you and read one or two a week, as I wrote them, and when you come back I'll have another bundle for you. Peter?"

"Yes?"

"Do you love me now?"

"I guess I do."

"Then I'll be waiting for you," she said.

This episode may sound far-fetched, even absurd, but I am striving in my chronicle to resist embellishments and stay with the truth. Memory being what it is, I may not be accurate in every detail, but that is my intention.

I found Badthing and No Nose sleeping on bags of oats at the livery stable and found Barney at Dutch John's and we went to Mexico.

During the long ride to the border, Barney and I had

ample time to chuckle over the poker game with Ben Thompson. This Thompson did, of course, consider himself a wizard of a poker player and I had no doubt that the other fellows around the table at which Barney sat harbored equally lofty opinions of themselves. Barney, on the other hand, was not a genius with the cards but did have one quality that is to be valued most highly—luck. When he felt that his luck was running right he was nigh to unbeatable. I have always been a strong believer in luck. When the Lady of Fortune is smiling a power has control of the game and you know not only what cards you will draw but what cards await your opponents. Barney had spells during which he was uncanny.

Such a spell occurred early in the game. They were playing five-card stud for the most part, though it was dealer's choice, and Barney won close to $300 in the first hour. Ben Thompson kept a good nature, but some of the other fellows began to grouse. Two in particular were voluble in their complaints. They were the Bowdry brothers from San Marcos, Ike and J.T. They ran a few cows on a little spread down there and had recently fared as poorly on a cattle drive as had Barney. I think it was their total savings they were playing with. At any rate, they acted like it. Toward the end of the first hour another player, a fellow from Huntsville, was in a pot with Barney and Ben Thompson and tried to call for $50.

"Where is the money?" asked Ben.

"I am giving you my note for it," the fellow said.

"Not me you ain't," said Thompson.

"Nor me," Barney said.

"Then I will call with my saddle."

"This game is played with cash money," said Thompson. "Am I correct, Mr. Swift?"

"I have a saddle already," Barney said.

"You are a pair of dirty snakes," said the fellow.

He arose cursing and went to the bar, leaving five in the game.

Barney won the pot with three tens to Thompson's two

pair, queens and jacks, which had been showing while one of
Barney's tens was in the hole.

To me it seemed Thompson should have known Barney
had three tens, else why would Barney have stuck in the face
of queens and jacks showing? Thompson, I suppose, was
paying to find out if Barney could be bluffed. When his luck
was running, Barney could no more be bluffed than an ox
could be taught to sing. But this man Thompson, who had
consorted with Wes Hardin and with the notorious Wild Bill
Heycox up in Abilene when Thompson operated the Bull's
Head Saloon, was a cagey sort who thought he knew what he
was doing.

The Bowdry brothers were grumbling loudly. I do not
mind a man to voice his opinions, but I can't tolerate a
whiner and so determined to sit in the game and look for a
reason to make the Bowdrys shut their mouths. As I have
told earlier, I had been drinking some that night and had
resolved to do up the town, a practice I don't ordinarily favor
but when done I do with gusto. However as I made to sit at
the green cloth, Thompson broke up the game for a moment
to light a cigar and order a round of drinks, explaining he
wanted Barney's luck to cool off and his own to get hot.

Drawing me aside, Thompson said, "I fear there will be
trouble, Peter. The Bowdrys are a bad-tempered lot and that
fellow from Huntsville is mean when drunk and besides
there are at least two others in the bar who wish to kill me."

"Who are they?" I said. Every gunfighter I have ever
known sees potential assassins lurking behind each bush.

"One is a deputy sheriff named Shabay and the other is a
friend of his I have never met. This Shabay is mad at me over
the attentions given me by a certain lady of this town. Also
because I know him to have been one of the leaders of a vigilante mob that hanged four innocent men over in Hill
County."

That sounded very likely. At that time Texas was not only
infested with carpetbaggers and scalawags, as I have said, but
the State Police were for the most part a pack of murdering

rabble, including many bad Negroes. Not even the Rangers were to be trusted. A number of counties were under mob rule by the vigilantes who rode in groups of up to two hundred or more men and were often led by law officers, so that the concept of justice frequently vanished altogether and there was feuding and much blood was let.

"All I ask you to do," said Thompson, "is to stay out of the game but keep your eyes open so that I'll not get a ball through the back of my head."

By so saying he put me on guard against himself as well as against any assassins. I suspected he might want to keep me out of the game so that he could take Barney's money the easier. But after listening again to the ignorant filth spoken by the Bowdry brothers, I decided it was best for me to take up a position against the wall where I could view the room.

The game continued for two more hours. Two players were tapped out and two new ones came in, as the Bowdrys continued losing. At length there was a very good pot on the table with three players in it—Barney, Ben Thompson, and J. T. Bowdry. Barney had two queens and a nine up. Thompson had two aces and a ten. Bowdry had three eights. Bowdry bet $50, Thompson raised $50, and Barney raised another $50, whereupon Bowdry called. Thompson raised another $50, and, as there was a three raise limit, Barney and Bowdry both called. It was the kind of a hand that got the attention of the room. A crowd gathered around the table. I was watching for any movement and also trying to watch the game. Barney dealt the fifth card to Bowdry and it was a ten. "I got your ten, Thompson," said Bowdry.

"There's plenty more," Thompson said.

Sure enough Barney then dealt Thompson a ten. Bowdry cursed. Barney dealt himself a third queen.

"There is a conspiracy here," said Bowdry.

"Are you saying we are cheating?" Thompson said.

"I am saying I will trim you good," said Bowdry, betting $100. Thompson raised him $150.

"Two aces and two tens, so you got a full house with aces

over," said Bowdry. "That won't win this hand, Thompson."

Barney raised $100 and Bowdry's eyes bugged. Thompson kept smiling. "No, by heaven, I will not be run out of this game," Bowdry said. He sent his brother Ike to borrow money. While Ike was gone, Thompson sat smiling and smoking and Barney drank another beer. I was afraid Barney had a full house, queens over nines, and had misguessed Thompson to be bluffing. And Bowdry either had four eights or he was a bigger fool than I thought to stick in the game with a full house, eights over. There was now more than $1000 on the table. A man could get killed for less. Bowdry had one more raise.

When Ike came back, Bowdry licked his lips and began to count out the money. He placed $700 on the table. It was now up to Barney.

"That is quite a lot of money," Barney said, glancing up at me. I made no expression, letting him know I would abide by his decision. "I will call," said Barney and laid out his money.

Now Thompson said, "If it is all right with you fellows, considering what is already at stake here, I would like to suggest one more raise."

"Three is the limit," Bowdry said.

"I know. But I am greedy."

"By heaven, so am I," said Bowdry. "If you want one more raise, that is all right with me."

They looked at Barney, who was staring at Thompson's cards. Now I had started to wonder at Thompson's sanity.

"Well," Barney said slowly, "if you want to change the rule for this one hand, I suppose I have no objection."

"Are you certain?" said Thompson.

"Yes sir, I am certain."

"In that case," said Thompson, smiling, "I declare myself out of the hand, gentlemen."

"You ain't even going to call?" said Bowdry.

"No, I am not."

"I'll be tied and whipped!" Bowdry said. He laughed with relief. "We ought to make you stay in the game since you brought up the extra raise."

"I merely suggested it," said Thompson. "I didn't agree to it."

"By heaven, this man did," Bowdry said, pointing at Barney. Bowdry slapped more money on the table and said, "This is tap town for me, but I raise you three hundred dollars."

"Called," Barney replied.

As he spoke I looked up toward some red velvet drapes that covered a small stage above and to the right of the bar. I saw the tubes of a shotgun poking from the drapes. "Watch out, Thompson!" I cried. He ducked beneath the table and the crowd scattered. The shotgun disappeared. I told him what I had seen and he quickly went toward the rear of the room. Bowdry was beside himself.

"I got four eights," Bowdry said. "What you got? What you got?"

"Four queens," said Barney.

Bowdry fell back into his chair and watched Barney turn over the four queens. I thought Bowdry was going to have a heart seizure. Then in a very hoarse voice Bowdry said, "You couldn't have four queens. I seen the case queen in my brother's discards. We'll ask him if he didn't have it."

"He didn't have it," Barney said. "Here it is right here."

"No, he had it. You must of quick-switched on me when your friend yelled. It was a trick," said J. T. Bowdry.

"I had it," Ike Bowdry said. "I had it in the hole."

"Look in the discards," somebody said.

"You won't find it among the discards," said Barney.

"Because you took it out!" J.T. said.

Barney grinned and stuffed his pockets with money. As I was standing against the wall behind the Bowdry brothers, they made no move to stop him. When he was finished he said, "Appreciate the game," and went to the bar. The Bowdrys left the saloon. I joined Barney.

"Thanks, Hermano," Barney said. "That was a good idea giving me a chance to turn over the table. But I had the queens.

"That was no inspiration of mine," I said. "I did see a shotgun."

"Odds are we will again before the night is over," said Barney. Ben Thompson came back through the room, looking very cold of eye.

"Much obliged, McGill," he said.

"Did you find the fellow?" I asked.

"He was gone," said Thompson. He looked at Barney. "One day, friend, we will have ourselves a real game."

"Suits me," Barney said. He was still dusty from the trail and had begun to look tired. I suggested we return to the Menger Hotel. Thompson said he would go with us, as he had decided to clear out of town for a bit. We had not gone more than fifty feet from the Vaudeville until Thompson stopped. Facing us was a dark side street where crates of merchandise were stacked up before some closed shops. "I don't like this," Thompson said. I didn't like it either. My danger signal was flagging me to stop.

"Well, we can't stand here all night," Barney said.

"Go on if you wish, but I'm not crossing that street," said Thompson.

Barney, whose only fault was that he never feared anything, started across the street and I went after him, thinking to pull him back, but before I could get to him a voice assailed us from the night, shouting: "Put up your hands." We complied.

"Now throw your money onto the ground. We're taking back what you stole from us," said the voice, which we recognized as J. T. Bowdry's.

"I'm not going to do it," Barney said.

J. T. Bowdry stepped out from behind the crates with a shotgun aimed at us. Ike Bowdry came out beside him with a pistol. I could tell that Barney was itching to draw his pistol which he wore in a holster. There has been much made of the fast draw, and truly some men were very fast indeed, but the man never lived who could outdraw the hammer of a shotgun that was already pointed at him.

"These fellows are making me very hot," Barney said.

"Throw down the money right now or I am going to kill you, you cheating so and so," said J. T. Bowdry.

Barney was sweating and fidgeting. I told him to throw down the money, but he was frozen stubborn. "Hermano, this is my money and I ain't giving it to thieves," he said. He meant it.

"One last time," said J. T. Bowdry.

I figured they would shoot Barney first, since his pistol was showing and my weapons were concealed. The moment they fired I would dive to the ground and roll toward the horse trough and if I made it I would kill them both. But I didn't need to. Another voice sounded from the darkness, saying: "You Bowdry brothers drop those guns or you will not live one more second."

It was Thompson, who had crept down the side street against the wall. Thompson was one of the best shots I ever saw, maybe better than Wes Hardin, and there was no doubt in any of our minds that he would as soon kill the Bowdrys as smoke a cigar.

Cursing, they did what he requested. Barney by now was purely outraged. Thompson came out of the shadows, grinning.

"I never before picked a fight with a man simply to chastise him," Barney said. "But I figured you fellows have started this, and the Lord knows how badly in need of chastisement you are. Let the ball begin."

He took off his gun belt and called J. T. Bowdry to him. I made a move toward Ike, but Barney called me off, saying he wanted them for himself. J. T. Bowdry did not endure long. Barney clubbed a fist to the side of his jaw and Bowdry went down with his jaw broken and blood and teeth coming out of his mouth. Barney gave him two kicks to the ribs and summoned Ike. To my surprise Ike proved quite game. He was a wiry man with a big mustache and an almost bald head and he could move about fairly fancy. Barney knocked him down eight or ten times but allowed him to get up again, which he did only to fall once more. After a few minutes Ike

Bowdry's own mother would not have known him. He would lie on the ground groaning and bleeding and finally would pull himself to his feet and rush at Barney, swinging wildly, and Barney would step aside and crash a fist into his face or stomach and beat him down again in order to repeat the procedure. At length, Ike rose no more. Barney went over to give him the jump, which is to leap into the air and descend on Ike's body with the heels of cowherder boots, a process that cracks the ribs and stoves up the organs to a considerable degree. But Barney thought better of it, not wishing to go to jail for causing Ike's death. So we thanked Thompson for his help.

"Ben Thompson always repays a favor," Thompson said, tucking away his pistol inside his frock coat.

We heard later that he had a shoot out in the Vaudeville and won it by ricocheting a bullet off the wall and around a corner to hit a man he couldn't see, but I wouldn't testify to that.

This was in the summer of 1873. August, I think it was.

In January of 1874 we went into Mexico and rode without trouble to Chihuahua City, where we stocked up on provisions and I went to visit an old Indian I had known from the days when I was taking Apache scalps. He was a Tarahumare named James Santiago. He came from near a little Jesuit mission town called Sisoguichi which is in the Sierra del Tarahumare—a piece of the Sierra Madre Occidental—near the headwaters of the Rio Conchos. James Santiago had a Catholic upbringing of sorts, so that his religious ideas were all mixed. He was a devoted peyote eater and a fine little man. I had happened along one afternoon as a half-dozen Apaches were having sport with James Santiago and his three wives. They had tied Santiago to an agave cactus and were taking turns with his women while one Apache kept Santiago's children herded together with the goats. There was always a good market for selling children as slaves.

With my Henry, I killed all six Apaches. That was no remarkable accomplishment. I had excellent cover and concealment. They were absolutely unprepared to be

144

attacked. When I came down from the rocks to take the Apache hair, the wives untied Santiago and the Tarahumares clustered around me chattering with both gratitude and fear, as they could not be entirely sure I would not like their hair, also. Many of the scalp hunters sold the hair of Mexicans, mestizos, Opanas, Tarahumares, or whatnot as well as the hair of Apaches until the authorities caught onto the game. But I never did that.

Poor Santiago looked like a porcupine and was in great pain. However, he had dignity and did not flinch as his wives worked the spines from his hide. When they were finished and I had tied the scalps onto hoops of cactus fiber for drying. I gave Santiago a drink of brandy and he invited me to his cave for a meal of pinole. We sat in the cave and ate the corn mush mixed with goat's milk and drank tesguino and at last he told me, in Spanish, since I could at that time not speak one word of Raramuri, the Tarahumare language, what he proposed to do.

Santiago was going to tell me where Tayopa was.

The trouble with that was, he did not exactly know. He had heard as a boy the location of the lost mine. His father, a chief, had told him and had showed him an old Jesuit map, he said. But the map had vanished. Santiago told me as best he could where the mine was, with the result that I later spent several harrowing months in western Chihuahua and eastern Sonora and did find an amount of gold, though I earned additional at other pursuits. Santiago promised to find the map for me and somehow get word to me in Austin. I did not take that promise very seriously.

But when I got back to Austin after spiriting Ellen away from Charlie Otter, there was a letter. It had been written by a priest and sent to me at Dutch John's. The letter said that the Apaches had again come after Santiago and had captured his children and had killed one of his wives, but he had escaped and gone to Chihuahua City. And, he said, he had the document I wanted. Though it did not say so in the letter, I assumed the document was the map to Tayopa.

11

What can Octavio be up to? He has no right to bore me. I am not hungry, I cannot sleep. I do nothing but consult with Excelsior and come back to work on this chronicle. The tracking of time is past all regaining. The oil for the lamp is running low. The wind came up a few hours ago. I had lit the lamp but I had stupidly neglected to turn down the wick. The glass was badly scorched. I went at once to wipe it with a cloth and when I returned the wind had blown out the lamp and I had to repeat the dreary business over again.

But why would that matter? My temper must be getting short. Not one of my neighbors along the rim has stopped by to see me, though they must have seen my smoke and know that I am here. Perhaps they sense that one who faces death must do it without companionship.

With little urging tonight I would abandon this project and leave the Fathers Higgins and Mulligan, their mission and the pueblo to whatever mercies Octavio can discover in himself. No one can be protected forever. I certainly am not.

I could, of course, leave this country. I am sure Octavio has me watched, but I am as clever as he and more clever than anyone who is with him. I could take that chance. Or I could take my rifle and my knife and slip out of the house tonight and go after Octavio once more and if I fail and the mission and the pueblo are blown to the ground I would not know it.

But I sit. He is coming, he is inevitable, and he does not tell me when. My eyes grow red, my beard thickens, I stink. Have I begun to rot already? I put myself up here like a goat at an altar and I have waited for Octavio for a time I can't even reckon, and that should be enough.

It is a ridiculous affair.

Higgins and Mulligan and the rest will die sooner or later, by some hand or other, no matter what I do.

But my word has been given. Octavio may relent. I may out-argue him. There may be a miracle. I hold with none of that, but I wait. If at the mission and the pueblo they think they are depending on me, then they are, whether they are or not.

I must keep working at my chronicle. It occupies me. It fills my mind and drives Octavio out. My life to me now is nothing but what is in my mind, and in reliving it this way am I not as good as reliving it in the flesh? So I am lucky then. I am living twice.

I look back at this morning's pages, which I keep in an iron box in the event Octavio should suddenly fire the house, and see that I was talking of Mexico. We must have been an odd-looking caravan the day we rode into Chihuahua City to seek out James Santiago and his map to Tayopa. Barney and I were not only rank from the trail but were big, unshaven, heavily armed and were also Texans, a circumstance not calculated to make us welcome. Behind us rode Badthing on a mule. The little Karankawa was wearing the Englishman's cork helmet, which he had somehow got out of Charlie Otter, and a scarlet jacket buttoned up the back. No Nose, that amazing woman, was mounted on a burro. We could hear her breathing above the scraping and jangling of our harness and equipment. Burros are strange creatures. They are very tough, intelligent, and strong. I once saw a panther attack a burro. The burro promptly flopped onto his back and began kicking out with all four legs, the sharp hoofs knocking chunks of flesh out of the startled cat, the burro meanwhile making a fierce cry, and it was not long before the panther knew he had picked on the wrong opponent and limped off into the brush.

But burros can be the most obstinate of beasts. As we came to the plaza in front of the great Cathedral of Chihuahua, No Nose's burro stopped. She got off and pulled and tugged and swatted, but the burro would not go another foot. Badthing sat proudly as he could on his mule, looking straight ahead, while a crowd of Mexicans came around laughing at the noseless woman and the immobile burro. After some minutes of this, Barney and I left them to find a hotel. My good Kentucky mare, White Foot, was going a bit lame, so I left her with a blacksmith to be reshod with rawhide. Barney and I got a room for ourselves and accommodations in the stable for Badthing and No Nose. Then we strolled the square. It was a cool, fine evening with an apricot-colored light around the towers of the cathedral. We sat on a bench and watched the young girls and boys promenade around the plaza with the girls walking in one direction and the boys in the other so that ever so often their eyes could meet. There were trees in the plaza and some pleasant grass. No Nose was still pleading with that burro in her whistling voice. Badthing had not moved. At last Barney put his mind to the problem. Deciding the halt had been caused by the sight of some object the burro did not like—perhaps even the cathedral itself—Barney walked over and wrapped his coat around the burro's eyes. At once the beast broke wind and then plodded along. The Mexicans laughed very much.

Barney and I each bathed in a tub in our room, with No Nose carrying in buckets of hot water to pour over us. We went to a restaurant for a big dinner of beef, refried beans, chili peppers, tortillas, and beer. The Chihuahua beef was tough and gamy, the kind of wild cattle beef that turns a man strong, not the tender, well-pastured, tasteless beef of the Midwest that has no blood to it. I like my beef fairly rare. Barney, like all cowherders who observe the condition of some of the beef they sell, preferred his well cooked. Those who say you can cook the flavor out of a steak are either bad cooks or never had any of that good Chihuahua beef smothered in red and green chilies.

Afterward I opened and read the first of the packet of letters Ellen had given me. She was not the best speller or grammarian I have ever encountered, and her penmanship was accomplished in a tiny, back-slanted hand. But the letter touched me greatly. She thanked me for having saved her from the Comanches, apologizing for having called me names, sent the regards of her aunt and uncle and inquired after my health. She wound it up by saying, Your Friend, Ellen C. Baggett. I realized that I had not known what her last name was, and I got to brooding over what the "C" might stand for (it came to me that it might stand for Charlene, which sensing later proved correct) and then I got to brooding about little Ellen herself, and I got to feeling uncomfortable and sticky, filled with a strange desire, and I began to pace up and down the restaurant while the Mexicans looked at me as though an imbecile had wandered into their midst, and Barney sat there grinning.

So I left him in the restaurant and went to seek out James Santiago at the address that had been in the letter. After a good deal of prowling dark streets among the smells of Mexican cooking, I found the house near the cathedral. It was a small adobe house with a blanket for a door and with only half a roof. I knocked on the wall, chipping off pieces of mud. A frightened woman peeked out but at the sound of my voice James Santiago called for me to enter. I stepped into the lantern light and he rose to greet me. He looked much older than I had remembered. He introduced me to a woman he said was his cousin and then he shooed all the women, children, and chickens out of the room, gave me a mug of corn beer and bade me sit on a rawhide chair that was the house's finest furnishing. We spoke to each other in Spanish, being elaborately polite. Finally he opened an old trunk in the corner, took out a deerskin bag, took out of that a wooden box, took out of that another deerskin bag and out of that he carefully unfolded a piece of paper.

This was the story he told:

Many many years ago there was a mine called Tayopa. The priests operated the mine and the Indians worked as slaves. The priests had a dispute with their Spanish king and as a result closed up Tayopa, covered the mine shafts and buried a great quantity of gold and treasures beneath the mission church at Tayopa. After warning the Indians never to disclose the location of the mine, at the risk of eternal damnation, some of the priests left the country. The others were preparing to leave and kept a few Indians, mostly Tarahumares, around to do the last bit of work. One of the Indians who stayed was James Santiago's grandfather, or so he called him, for he could have meant great-great-great-grandfather and it would have been all the same to James Santiago. When the priest's soldiers marched off, the Apaches who had been hiding in the mountains attacked Tayopa. They killed the priests and what Indians they could catch. The Apaches finished the destruction of Tayopa. They tore down the church and burned everything that would light. Then they ran off. One of the survivors was James Santiago's relative. Being a man of some piety, he went back to Tayopa with the idea of burying the priests in the Christian methods they had preached (he very well may have gone back to see what remained to steal, was my thought). But their bodies were so hacked up that he decided to leave them to the buzzards, who by now had descended upon Tayopa like a black cloud. However, he did find this paper on the body of the chief priest. Examining it, Santiago's relative recognized the paper as a map to Tayopa. He kept the map. He moved into the mountains, begat his family and wandered the barrancas the rest of his life. Because of the priest's threat of damnation, he did not reveal the map to anyone until he was dying. At that time, he told his eldest son. In that way, the map was passed down through the generations. All of Santiago's grandfathers were poor men, nomads, and none ever tried to find the gold although they often lived within a few miles of it, for it was not only unlucky but would have required very hard work. James Santiago's father had told him where the map was hidden in a burial cave in the side of a cliff. But Santiago had had no use for the map until he felt he owed me a debt. And here was the map in my hands.

I had heard similar tales about Tayopa and had seen similar maps. There were drunken Indians all over Chihuahua, Sonora, Sinaloa, and Durango offering to sell maps to Tayopa. But it was impossible to resist the excitement of Santiago's story. What if it were true?

The paper was dated 1627. That was early enough, though the dates of Tayopa were uncertain. My hands trembled as I studied the map in the lantern light. Then I saw something that excited me more. Most tales placed Tayopa near a lake at the headwaters of the Yaqui River. Others placed it hundreds of miles away, down in Durango or Sinaloa or other locations. But this one, though the names on the map were of ancient sites no longer used or so-called, seemed to place Tayopa in an entirely different location.

"This," Santiago told me, pointing with his finger to a large barranca, or canyon, "is the place of the cooing dove."

The Tarahumares, when they felt it necessary to name a place, used the name of an event, an animal, or a bird. The Raramuri word for cooing dove is *uriki*. By the look of the winding of the river, the barranca he pointed to could have been the place we now call Urique.

Some two hundred miles to the southwest of Chihuahua City is the barranca country. There are five great canyons of tremendous depth and breadth where there may be snow on the canyon rim and tropical foliage with orange trees and monkeys on the canyon floor. How many side canyons, lesser barrancas, there may be, no one knows. The Urique River flows northwest to form the Barranca del Cobre and then turns at a place called the Divisadero and flows southwest to form Urique Canyon. South of there lie other great canyons, Batopilas and the rest, and several mines, like the old silver mine at La Bufa. If it were true that the barranca on the map were Urique, then the lost mine of Tayopa was in a side canyon that leads into Urique. The trouble was that there are many side canyons that lead into Urique and it was likely that the map would not be accurate. The map showed a burro road that came up out of Urique so that the gold could be packed to the Rio Verde and thence to the Rio Fuerte. The road would have been obliterated by the centuries, but perhaps we could locate it. On the map was one mountain peak clearly shown as being at the entrance to the canyon of Tayopa. The peak was not named. But there was a straight line drawn, running northeast to another peak some miles away.

"This," said Santiago, pointing to the latter peak, "is the place of the eagles."

The Place of the Eagles, I knew, was what the Tarahumares called a little valley surrounded by sheer rock walls. In the valley was an old church that had been abandoned by the Jesuits. The valley was the place now called Cusarare. From Cusarare we could sight the peak that guarded Tayopa. It was not much to go on, but we had nothing better.

Returning to the hotel, I had the feeling I was being followed down one of the twisty streets. I turned a corner and hid in the shadows. I could hear no footsteps around the corner. I got out my Colts and cocked the hammer. That tiny sound was quite audible in the night, despite the barking of the dogs in the neighborhood. I heard a small scuffling noise, as though my stalker had suddenly stopped. Ducking down where no head would be expected, I peeked around the corner to see a figure disappear between two houses. It was dark and I saw him for only an instant, but I thought I saw lamp light shine on one white pebble of an eye.

I mused about that as I went through the patio to the room I shared with Barney. There were others in the world with a gotch eye. If the man had been Octavio, why had he not approached? We were as yet friends, so far as I knew. I decided I must be wrong and tried to put the idea out of my mind, though it kept creeping back even as I was showing the map to Barney, who was highly excited. The next morning we were up before daylight. As the sun began to throw shadows from the cathedral, our odd little procession set out for Cusarare.

12

What grand country that is down there! The only places I have ever been happy are in the hills of central Texas, up here in the Sangre de Cristo Mountains of Taos and Santa Fe and in the mountains of Mexico. Our ride out from Chihuahua City took us through the sorts of country that I prefer. First we rode through a land that is like central Texas—hilly, full of meadows and pastures, with a wide clear sky where hawks float. We saw children herding sheep and goats. There were many of the small black Spanish cattle that have Longhorn blood in them. We passed several ruined haciendas. Revolutions had all but wiped out the grandees. The country was in political chaos, with large sections lorded over by Indians and bandits. The governors of the states lacked the strength to enforce what authority they had. The federal government, in Mexico City, had its own problems and was pretty useless in dealing with remote areas. We were a thousand miles, more or less, from Mexico City, and the way between lay blocked by mountains, deserts, and hooligans of the lowest type.

Leaving the Texas-like country, we entered a land that is

more like northern New Mexico Territory—high, mountainous, with castle rocks and purple peaks rising above the pines. And going on from there we at last approached the barranca country. The mountains in the barranca country are not overly high, seldom beyond 10,000 feet above sea level. What makes them so dramatic is the plunge into the barrancas. You can look at a mountain that seems nothing special until you round it and descend into the barranca and then look up again and cannot find the peak, lost in the clouds two miles above you.

We went along with some caution. We had brought a mozo to guide us to the town of Creel, which is near Cusarare. The mozo trotted ahead of our horses, mules, and burros. He was a Tarahumare, and so the twenty-five miles a day that we covered was merely a pleasant job to him. No Nose had begun to complain of feeling ill. Her eyes were indeed red and her flesh was hot to the touch, but she found some jakuri roots and made a tea and seemed to improve. Barney, Badthing, and I took turns scouting out front. There had been a number of Apache heads on poles before the prison in Chihuahua City. The Apaches were being frisky and we did not wish them to catch us.

We had one close turn some miles from the town of Sisoguichi. I was on scout and was coming up to the Rio Conchos, where we intended to get water, when I got a warning from my instincts. I dismounted, hid White Foot in some brush and crawled to a bluff above the river. There below me were a dozen Indians of some motley band. Several were Lipans. A few looked like Yaquis, and two wore sombreros. They were a party of bandits, bathing and drinking. Their sentinel was on the bluff opposite me. I did not dare move.

As I lay there, a mere fifty feet from them, I suddenly felt a tickling on my right forearm. As it was a warm day, I had taken off my jacket and rolled up my sleeves. When I looked down, I saw a wicked gray scorpion common in Chihuahua had crawled upon my arm and was inspecting me. Any motion to brush him off might have alerted the sentinel on the other bluff. I lay sweating and watching as the scorpion calmly and with what I would almost swear was amusement lifted his stinger tail, curved it down and shot agony into my arm. The gray devil stung me until he was satisfied. I looked into his eyes. I lay and bit my lips for what seemed an hour. When at last he was finished, he crawled off into the grass. My arm throbbed as the poison rushed through my veins. My arm began to swell and turn blue. I was very glad when those Indians mounted their runty ponies and rode north. I could barely make it back to our little group. No Nose and Badthing wrapped my arm in a hot prickly pear poultice. I spent a feverish night but was ready for traveling the next morning.

After some slow and delicate moving, made so by No Nose's recurring illness, we reached Creel. There we decided to keep our mozo. He was called Valentín and was quiet and a tireless worker. We stayed one night in Creel to get fresh supplies, though it was dangerous there. The news of our arrival was bound to spread through the territory and reach Apache ears. But we could not hope to keep our presence forever secret and considered ourselves lucky to have come that far without detection.

From Creel we went southeasterly to Cusarare and reached the place in half a day. For hours we lay on a cliff above the village and watched for sign. The little stream called the Rio Cusarare ran through the valley below. We saw Tarahumares moving about their cave dwellings and crude huts, tending their goats. The old Jesuit church with its broken-down walls sat silent in the middle of the valley. Once late in the afternoon we heard Tarahumare drums thumping from the mountains beyond, but our mozo assured us the drums were only part of a peyote ritual and had nothing to do with us. Although I had seen Apaches near Sisoguichi, these Tarahumares did not seem concerned. They were, after all, too poor for the Apaches to bother robbing them and in January too scrawny from hunger to bring much as slaves.

We tried to pick out the mountain from which we could see the peak that guarded the canyon of Tayopa. There was no outstanding mountain. The cliffs around Cusarare were of uniform height, with an occasional high knob where eagles nested. Studying the map, Barney decided that we should go down to the church. From there, it was his idea we could look up in the general direction the map would indicate and could spot the viewing point. It made sense to me that the map would be so oriented. Once we found the viewing point, we could turn our map to match up roughly with the landmarks and should be able to pick out the proper peak, though reaching it would no doubt be a difficult matter.

At dusk we descended to Cusarare. The Tarahumares who saw us paid no heed. We opened the door of the church and took our animals inside. Father Higgins would not approve of that, I am sure, but we had to have our animals out of sight. The night was becoming cold, as happens in the high country. Inside the church we could build a fire. We quartered our animals near the altar and took them out one by one to drink from the Rio Cusarare. There were many old paintings, peeling and dusty, hanging from the walls of the church. They seemed almost alive and moving in the shadows from our little fire. But there was nothing else of value in the church. Any altarpieces, crucifixes, or cloths had long before been looted.

We put Badthing and his wife, who had become rather sullen and sluggish, into the bell tower as lookouts and settled down. I read the third of Ellen's letters that night. It was more tender, less formal, than the first two. The mind can do wonders with desiring. She still did not speak of love, but she signed it sincerely rather than your friend. I began to muse upon becoming rich and marrying her. I would ride up to her uncle's house in a carriage like the one that belonged to my mother's cousin in San Antonio. Her aunt would be overwhelmed. The neighbors would come to watch. No ruffian, this McGill. I slept well.

Before daylight, Barney woke me. He had been outside for his morning ritual, balking at performing such an act inside a church. He had heard horses and, peering over the stone wall, of the church, had seen several riders at the river.

"It was too dark to be sure, Hermano," he told me, "but I think they are Apaches."

Almost at once, Badthing came scrambling down the ladder from the bell tower.

"Eight of them," Badthing said in Tex-Mex. "My woman was sick again and I was washing her face and did not see them approach. They don't know we are here yet."

Taking my Henry, I slipped out of the church and kept into the darkness along the wall and crawled to a tumbled mound of stones in a field of gourds to the south of the church. From there I could see them clearly. They gave me quite a shock.

I had expected the same band of Apaches I had seen on the Rio Conchos. But these were different. And I knew them as surely as they would know me. They were warriors from a big family of Kiowa Apaches that had a *ranchería* in the Chisos Mountains—the very coons I had circled wide to avoid, the very ones who had sworn to kill me because of the six scalps I had taken from their kin who were torturing old James Santiago. Now this was a disgusting turn of affairs. I watched them filling their buffalo paunch water bags in the river. They were tall, graceful for the most part, with long black hair. They wore headdresses of crow feathers, owl feathers, and cow horns. They carried lances and bows and wore their arrows in quivers of Mexican leather. I knew that most of the warriors in that family—it was not uncommon for a large family of Kiowas or Kiowa Apaches to live together in a private place, intermarrying brothers with sisters-in-law and so forth until they were a numerous mob of brothers, sisters, uncles, cousins, fathers, mothers, and whatnot—were members of the Crazy Dogs Society, a pretty high-up warrior organization. Some were even Koisenkos, sworn never to retreat. Once that family had joined two other families to form a band of a couple hundred, but they had broken up after a battle with the Rangers and some cowherders near Presidio, and this family had gone into the Chisos Mountains and established a stronghold that nobody had ever tried to penetrate.

From the indolent way that they loafed about the stream, it was clear they had not been informed of our presence. It was possible they would water up and go off. They must have been inside the church on dozens of other raids and would know there was nothing of value there. I could hear them laughing. The sun began to appear over the rim of the valley. My breath blew white in the morning as I lay among the gourds and rocks. Two warriors had a wrestling match beside the river, each trying to dunk the other in the cold water. Both wound up drenched. I lay there, wanting coffee and a cigar, and studied them. They had no firearms, which was a good thing. They had about twenty horses and mules with them but little booty that I could see. Tied to the back of one mule was a silver candelabra, stolen from Lord knows what church or hacienda. Otherwise, their expedition had produced nothing of obvious worth.

Three warriors stripped off their shirts and leggings and marched naked up and down the stream, waving their arms and calling for the Tarahumare maidens to come down from their caves. The others laughed. The three climbed into the cold water and bathed. Two more squatted on the bank in view of all the Tarahumares and did their morning easement and called out strange clattering yells to the valley walls. But none appeared in a mean or warlike humor. In time, I found myself getting tired of watching them. An hour after sunup, they mounted. They rode in a circle around the valley, shouting challenges up to the caves, and then went up a trail to the west and rode out of the valley, heading toward a blue ridge that was marked with a cross, as the Tarahumares do to protect travelers from the devils. I lay there until they were out of sight and then, relieved, got up and went into the church. Barney came in, too. He had been lying behind the stone wall west of the church. Badthing had been in the tower. Valentín had been sitting on the altar. No Nose was lying on a blanket in the corner with her teeth clicking.

"Thought we were in for a fracas," Barney said. "I sure wanted breakfast first."

No Nose was in no condition to cook, so Barney handled that chore. The woman had a fever and her eyes were teary. Her skin, seemed miscolored, but it was hard to tell, as she was of a darkly uncertain complexion anyhow and had been much exposed to weather. Badthing assured us she would be all right, that she was in the time of life when a woman is subject to these minor ills. We sent him back to the bell tower to keep watch. After breakfast of bacon, beans, and biscuits we all felt better, though No Nose could eat little. Barney and I went out to the church yard with our map. We lined it up the way it had to be, with the line pointing into Cusarare. We decided the viewpoint we wanted was on the valley wall to the north. We searched and debated and at last settled on a high bald rock near the valley entrance. If there had been a higher mountain there once, it could have fallen. There were rocks and rubble below it, indications of an old landslide. We packed up, put No Nose astride a mule and went up a steep trail on the north wall, seeing a few Tarahumares—the men in diapers, shirts, and headbands, the women in long dresses with shawls—who came out of their caves to stare at us.

It was well past noon before we reached the bald rock. We approached it through a stand of pines and cedars. Once there, we were hardly better off. Looking to the southwest, we saw ridge after ridge, several marked with crosses, with canyons between, and a few mountains that reared up but none higher than the others. We all got interested in the project, except for No Nose, who lay down and wrapped herself in her blanket. Finally Barney and I agreed that we had to decide on something. Valentín came up with the information that he had heard of gold being near a certain mountain that he pointed out, although he informed us he would under no circumstances go there. The mountain he pointed out looked like an alligator lying against the sky. With his compass, Barney took a reading on the alligator's nose. He wrote down some computations to keep us straight in our journey and drew lines between our current location and the nose of the alligator if that was truly it on the map. We determined to set out at once, rather than spending another night in the church. The problem was whether No Nose could travel.

Thinking about her, I heard an odd snorting cry and

turned to see that we were trapped.

The eight Kiowa Apaches, two of whom held No Nose by the arms, were behind us and we had only the cliff to the front. Preoccupied as we were with our map and our dream of gold, we had laid our rifles on the ground some feet away. Not that the rifles would have got us anything but death, for the Kiowa Apaches had arrows fitted to bow strings and were aiming at us. The arrow devoted to me had an iron tip made from a barrel hoop, and I recall thinking that wounds from such arrows almost always got infected.

"Well, well, this is a very sorry deal," Barney said.

The leader of this troop of cretins had put on a long sash that showed he was a Koisenko. He was almighty pleased with himself. Doubtless, he had not grinned much in his life, for the act seemed to stretch his face out of shape. He stepped forward, muttered some guttural rubbish, and the two coons who were holding No Nose tossed her over the cliff.

"Mother Mary," Barney said.

No Nose cried out sharply once. Then the cry broke as her body bounced off a rock. The leader looked at Badthing, who had not moved. In near perfect Spanish, the leader said:

"I have heard of your magical powers, dwarf. Call your woman back to life. Fly her through the air and plant her feet on this earth in front of me, and I will worship you and make you rich."

Badthing cleared his throat. His emotions must have been quite strong. "What is done is done," he said. "I would not ask the spirits to undo it. However, I will ask them special favors pertaining to you, to assure that all your children are crippled, your mother is blind, your wives have lung fever, and the dogs eat your face."

The leader laughed. "I thought you were a fake," he said. He turned to me. "I have heard of you, also," he said. "The Enemy"—by which he meant the Comanches—call you No-Die. They say they have shot arrows into your heart and have stabbed you and beaten you with clubs, and yet you live. They say they have cut you into little pieces, and you re-formed yourself, like an earthworm. They say you are now a particular enemy of our Forest People and have cursed us as you did the Honey Eaters, who are shamed. They say you are to be feared. None of this I believe. But we will find out. You killed my brothers and cousins. So we will see if you can die."

They gathered up all our weapons, including those on our bodies. One of the coons covered us with my Henry rifle. The leader, the Koisenko, motioned for us to stand away from the cliff. The other six arranged themselves in a corridor leading to the cliff, three on each side, facing each other in a staggered pattern.

"It appears," Barney said, "that we are to have the privilege of running the gauntlet and if we survive that we have the joy of falling off the cliff."

"Some fine reward," said Badthing.

Valentín began to sing his death song. As I understood little Raramuri, I don't know what he was saying. Most likely it was the same theme as the death songs of other bands, telling the gods he was on his way. The death songs are beautiful. Myself, I was thinking that I had bought my ticket to glory. Ellen's letters were in the pocket of my jacket. So long, little lady, they have called in my note, I was thinking. Valentín kept up his chanting prayer. But there were no prayers from the rest of us. All of my Catholic upbringing, all those hours of listening to the priests, all the songs, the liturgy, the kneeling, the candles, all that had to have been crowding into my mind from somewhere. I could feel it, but it felt below, or outside of, what was happening at the moment, rather like a platform upon which I was standing, and my head was clear, and if God wouldn't have me it was too late to go begging.

"I'm first," I said to the Koisenko. "If I live, you spare the others."

"No, first we practice," he said.

He pushed Valentín. The brave little rascal ran forward at once into the corridor. The coons were armed with clubs and axes. The fourth blow dropped him. His head was bleeding.

He crawled, rose, was felled again. He got up and they beat him down. He seemed finished. They smashed his head. He got up and stumbled to the end of the corridor. The brute at the end raised an ax to hit him with the blade. With a shout, Valentín grabbed the big fellow and toppled him off the cliff. We heard them both yelling as they crashed into the boulders below. That Valentín had courage. He was only a mozo.

The Koisenko was most displeased. He was very big for an Indian. He was at least six feet two and weighed about one hundred and seventy-five pounds. He was my equal in height, but I had maybe twenty pounds of weight on him. One of my own greatest failings has been the tendency to think before I react. That can be a grievous failing on the frontier, where the slightest pause can be fatal. I have seen men die because for a second or two they wondered if their enemies truly would kill them, and so they reasoned it out and fell dying as the truth finally soaked in. The thing to do is to strike when threatened and never assume you are being bluffed. I did not think the Koisenko was bluffing, but in judging what would be our best alternative I missed it. I should have struck the moment Valentín dragged the coon off the cliff. We could have made a better fight of it. Now, however, I determined to make a fight of it rather than to die under a beating, as I was sure the Koisenko would not spare Barney or Badthing regardless. At least the coons had put down their bows and only one had a rifle and it was no cinch he knew how to shoot it.

"You are a Koisenko," I said to the leader. "Or so your sash proclaims. I say that to me you look like a cowardly pervert. I say if you are a Koisenko you will stand up to me individually. I say if you don't do that, you are a woman. I say you are afraid to fight me."

To my amazement, the Koisenko laughed.

"I am fearless," he said. "Everybody knows that. But being fearless does not make me an idiot. Why should I fight you? Already you are my prisoner and I am very shortly going to kill you. Fighting you is unnecessary."

He looked around at his troop. He was smiling at my

feeble goad. But his men were not smiling. They were looking at their chief with expressions of disappointment and disapproval. It was his turn to be astonished. I could see him thinking what a lot of trouble it would cause him when they told around the *ranchería* that he had refused to fight me. Thus are leaders brought low. "Very well, then," he said. "I will do the job myself."

So saying, he leaped at me with a butcher knife. The fact that I was unarmed did not bother him in the least; I had got myself into this, he figured, and was receiving better than I deserved. But I had not expected honorable conduct and was prepared. When he leaped, I sprang aside and tripped him. He turned as he fell. I grabbed the knife wrist in both hands as with his left hand he gouged for my eyes. I concerned myself with the knife while I twisted my head from his fingers. It was an old knife with GREEN RIVER stamped on the blade near the hilt. Mountain men from the Rockies to the Sierras often carry that make of knife. From it, they get their phrase, "Going to Green River," which means a chore performed to the fullest.

Now this Koisenko was not only strong, he was slippery. He had coated himself with bear grease against the cold, and it was difficult to hold him. He was threshing about and trying to bite off my nose. I turned a bit and gave him a knee that made him sick. Then I quickly jabbed a thumb into his right eye and as quickly returned both hands to his wrist, which I lifted and cracked over a rock. I felt the bone break. The Koisenko howled. I reached for the knife. But he was faster. With his left hand, he recovered the blade and drove it at me, ripping my jacket but not my flesh. I clutched his left wrist with both hands. He clubbed me with his right, despite it being broken and dangling. I found I could hold his left wrist with my right hand. My own left being freed, I used it for other purposes, such as to gouge and choke. When at last I felt his strength leaving, I snatched the knife from him and sank it into his throat. He coughed and his bowels went off and that was how I killed the big Koisenko.

We still were far from saved, with six of the Kiowa Apaches left. I got up, ready for whatever encounter awaited, I thought, but I was not at all ready. For when I rose, with the bloody knife and whirled to meet a charge or a lance or bullet, instead I saw the mutilated, grinning face of Octavio.

He had come out of the pines and cedars behind us, just as had the Kiowa Apaches. This knob was becoming a veritable way-station for travelers. With Octavio were about a dozen warriors of various sorts—Lipans, Yaquis, some mestizos, sierra Indians I could not readily identify. But I did pick them out as the Indians I had seen at the Rio Conchos the day I was stung by the scorpion. Clearly, Octavio had been following me perhaps all the way from Chihuahua City.

"My old friend," he said in English, walking toward me with his hand extended.

The Kiowa Apaches, having thrown down their weapons, gaped as we shook hands with the one vigorous shake he had learned from the Dutchman.

Octavio reached out, unbuttoned the top two buttons of my shirt, and lifted out the chain around my neck.

"You still wear it," he said. "The lion's tooth. It has protected you."

He frowned. "But what is this?" he said. seeing the medal of the Virgin of Guadalupe and St. Jude. "The Great Painted Lady and the Bearded One? Companions for a lion? I would have thought you would have discarded them. No wonder your magic is so notorious."

"All things are one," I said, giving him an opportunity to go on talking.

But instead he looked at Barney, nodded at Badthing and looked at the Kiowa Apaches. Meanwhile, I was looking at Octavio. The name Gotch Eye certainly fitted him. His left eye was like a pebble from a stream bed, and the scar plowed through the eyelid and eyebrow, disfiguring both. Otherwise, Octavio, or Jacob Charles Gerhardt, had turned out quite handsome. He was nearly as tall as I and very impressive of build. He was dressed utterly in the Lipan style, with no

remainder of his Dutchman upbringing. His black hair was
cut off even with the top of his left ear, but on the right side
it grew long and was folded up and tied with a string. Still, it
fell to his shoulder and was studded with feathers and trinkets. There were eight earrings in his left ear (I wonder
should that manner of ornament, though not unusual among
Lipans, have made his name Octaviano?). He wore high-top
moccasin boots, buckskin leggings, a red loincloth, a buckskin tunic with fringe and beads, and had a red and blue
Mexican blanket wrapped around his shoulders. Beneath the
blankets were crossed belts of bullets. At his waist he had a
butcher knife and a Smith & Wesson pistol. Cradled in his
arms was a new Winchester Model 1873, a really fine,
dependable, and deadly rifle for fast moving and close
fighting, as I gathered was Octavio's way.

Viewing the fellow, I was struck at once by what a
mixture he was of the noble and the beast. His face was
haughty, arrogant, intelligent, or would have had those qualities were it not for that hideous eyeball glistening from its
furrow. His voice was resonant, his body splendid, but his
costume barbarous. (Thinking back, though, was my own
costume less barbarous? I was wearing Ute boots, buckskin
trousers, wool shirt, neckerchief, long underwear, wide-
brimmed hat, fleece-lined buckskin jacket with fringes and
beads and had not shaved in a week.) He had been actually
tender when he lifted out my lion's tooth and religious medal
for inspection, and the smile on his mouth and in his eyes
had been genuine, and now, looking at the Kiowa Apaches,
he was a different being: without a decent emotion.

He ordered his crew to seize the Kiowa Apaches, who put
up a ruckus. Three of them were killed quicker than immediately. The other three Kiowa Apaches were stripped naked
and tied upside down to pine trees. A mestizo with black
mustaches and a big sombrero brought cones and sticks. The
Kiowa Apaches looked very doleful. The mestizo built fires
beneath each prisoner's head. Soon their hair was burning
with an unwholesome stench. In a while the fires burned
into the tops of their skulls, roasting their brains. They could

not be blamed for screaming. Octavio's crew squatted and smoked and laughed. Barney and I went over and sat at the edge of the cliff, looking down at the bodies of No Nose, Valentín, and the big Kiowa Apache and out at the blue ridges and the alligator shaped mountain where our bonanza might be. Octavio came over and knelt beside us. I gave him a cigar.

"I suppose you think this is excessive," he said, meaning the treatment of the prisoners.

"They were getting ready to do much the same to us," I said.

"Well, I've had many disputes with them over who belongs in these mountains, and I want this word to get back to their *ranchería*," said Octavio. "Also, my men enjoy it and I don't mind." He glanced at Barney. "I know of you," said Octavio.

"You're Jacob Gerhardt," Barney said. "I thought I knew of you."

"Barney Swift."

"Yes," said Octavio, shaking Barney's hand. To me Octavio said, "It was you, then, that I saw in Chihuahua City. I wasn't sure until a few hours ago. We were trailing these miserable creatures after I heard in the city that they were raiding. We almost attacked them at the river this morning, but they rode off too soon. We waited for them at the notch but they turned back and as we followed we saw you climbing the rocks. Unfortunately we couldn't get here in time to save that one's woman. Maybe he can get a new one who is more handsome."

We sat quietly for a moment, watching Badthing, who stood with his arms upraised.

"I hear many many things about you," Octavio said to me. "You are becoming famous among all People. The tales they tell about you are wonderful. I heard from some Comancheros that you turn yourself into an owl and fly to heaven to converse with The Sure Enough Father. They say you have the magic of the priests as well as of The People. They say you have the magic of all The People, from up on the Platte to the jungles far below this place even. They say no mystery is denied you."

"I can't help what they say," I said. "You know me. You know I have no magic."

"It is possible that you have magic and don't understand it," he said.

"We're alive, anyhow," said Barney. "Seems like magic to me, I don't mind admitting."

Octavio laughed. "And what are you doing in these sierras?" he said. "This is a dangerous area even for a man-god."

"Poking around," I said.

He laughed again.

"I know what you are after," Octavio said. "Since it was you I saw in the city, then it was you who came out of James Santiago's house. It is said that James Santiago's grandfather had the map to Tayopa. James Santiago is in your debt, I have heard. So you have the map. Now we are partners. A great idea, isn't it? You have the map and I have the men to see that you remain alive to reach the mine."

"It is said that it is very unlucky for one of The People to seek the mine," I said.

"I believe all things," said Octavio. "The priests said whoever of The People sought the mine would die. I believe that. The People say the same thing. I believe that also. We all die eventually. I believe in all magic and all gods, in the priests and The Sure Enough Father, in the Little People, in the Owl Spirits, in the Sacred Snakes, in the Peyote Lady, in the Turtle Ghosts, in the mysteries of the Kiva. I believe it all, Peter Hermano. So we will go get the gold together, eh, old friend."

"Looks like it," I said.

13

No Nose was not entirely dead when we reached her, but she could not speak and soon died while two of Octavio's bandits were carrying her out of the rocks. Although she was, I think, of Kiowa origin, she was buried with a Karankawa ceremony, not that it could matter to her. Badthing painted himself up as a Coma, or Karankawa shaman, and prayed to Pichini and Mel, two principal gods of his faith. He smoked two pipes of hemp and danced a mitote that I suspect was of his own invention.

Octavio watched the ceremony with patience and amusement. We left No Nose's body in a tree for the vultures, as Badthing evidently did not believe she would arrive in the other world without her parts, except of course for her nose. We had to help Badthing onto a mule afterward. He babbled and sang for hours as we picked our route generally westward toward the snout of the alligator. Turning northwest and later heading south, due to the terrain, we went down a deep and narrow canyon past the falls at Baseachic, which looked to me higher than the famous ones at Niagara, and on into unknown country.

I will not detail that journey except to say that it turned off very cold. It snowed and we had more climbing and descending to do than I like to recall. Several of Octavio's bandits got frightened and ugly-tempered. We lost three animals and one man on the hazardous trails. Once we were following a narrow trail and came to a place where it had been destroyed by a landslide. Looking down, we could see the canyon floor a mile below. There was no room to turn around, so we had to back up, a process that consumed a day and further irritated the bandits. But Octavio does not run his band as the usual Indian chief does, listening to arguments and speeches and trying to decide what is best for the group. Octavio runs his band as its king.

The night of the turn-around we camped on a high shelf with some shelter from the wind and snow. The wind was tearing through the pines and the snow was snowing up at us from lower down the canyon. Barney and I were wearing fleece-lined coats and were wrapped in blankets and furs. We squatted with Badthing beside a low dung fire, trying to boil coffee. We had melted water for our livestock and had given them about the last of our corn in nose bags. I put a fur around White Foot to protect her as much as possible. Barney did the same for his horse, Bill, a big brindle. Badthing told us a story about the Little People. He claimed to be in frequent contact with them. He said they would hurt no one unless crossed. Barney said he had heard reports of a spirit—he thought it was Karankawa but wasn't sure—called Badthing that supposedly showed up at somebody's house and pulled off the occupants' arms. He asked if our Badthing knew of the other.

"Indeed, indeed," said Badthing in Tex-Mex. What Barney couldn't get, I translated. "He is one of the ancients, a bearded spirit who does not eat but does pull out the intestines of his hosts. He takes out a small bit of the intestine and cooks it. Then for fun he cuts off an arm, not tearing it but slicing it off with a sharp flint. However it is merely a game. Later he restores the arm to health, leaving only the scars. He lifts houses and drops them with a crash. He lives near the great water around Galveston. He is no Karankawa but is Avavare located. I am not called for him. I am called for my own vision, which is considerable. I know the secrets of life, you see. I know what all flesh, earth, air, and water is made of. I know what causes fires and light. I know what the stars are. I know who the important gods are and how to go safely through this life."

"How does that get you called Badthing?" asked Barney. "My true name cannot be repeated," the little Karankawa said.

"I am called Badthing due to being mistaken for the very Avavare spirit you mentioned, though as you can see I have no beard and am in fact quite handsome. That they call me Badthing does no harm and sometimes helps. But my true name must remain unspoken."

"What, then, are these secrets of life you possess?" said Octavio, sliding in beside our fire.

We each took a cup of coffee, enjoying the heat on our hands. Octavio's gotch eye looked very eerie, almost devilish, in the firelight with the snow flakes shining on his blanket and blowing around our lean-to shelter and his eight earrings dangling from his left ear. Badthing was almost invisible inside a buffalo robe; about all we could see was his chin beneath the cork helmet he had got from Charlie Otter.

"I can't tell you everything," Badthing said. "But a night like this is good for talking. I will tell you the Worm Truth and the Truth of the Geranjé."

"This promises to be a pleasant discussion," said Octavio.

The two savages settled deeper into their robes and blankets. I took out the butt of a cigar I had been saving and began to chew it, letting the strong bitter juices mingle with the black bitter coffee. Barney was smiling and there was ice on his hat.

"The Worm Truth," Badthing said, "is just what it says. The truth is that all of the world, all of the earth, the air, the flesh, and the water is made of tiny worms that have been put together by The Sure Enough Father."

"The Sure Enough Father whose son is Our Jesus Christ?" asked Octavio.

"The same. But Our Jesus Christ is merely one of His sons or spirits and not a major one at that," Badthing said.

"My belief exactly," said Octavio. "What do you think, Peter Hermano?"

"I don't think about it much," I said.

"To proceed," said Badthing, "these tiny, tiny worms make up all of the world that we know except for fire, the spirits and the Self Ghost. The stars and the heavens are tiny worms. This hand I hold up before you, this flesh, it is tiny worms. Cut it off and bury it in the earth, and it reverts. The worms rearrange themselves to become sometimes larger worms, sometimes smaller as dust. We foolishly think the worms are eating the flesh when they are merely becoming themselves once more. This snow is tiny water worms borne about by air worms traveling fast to become wind. But this fire is a non-worm. Fire is a releasing of the Self Ghost that is in all things. When we burn a piece of wood, we do not burn the wood at all. We release the Self Ghost of the wood, and the worms that made up the hardness and look of the wood and were held together by the Self Ghost then become what we know as ashes although they are still worms waiting for another shape. Thus fire is one way of releasing the Self Ghost. Fire is light. The light that comes from the sun, the stars, the moon is great Self Ghost light. The Sure Enough Father is all Self Ghost. He is Self Ghost in its entirety. He forms the worms into shape and He exhibits Himself as light."

"When you die without being burned, is your Self Ghost trapped among the worms?" asked Octavio.

"No. The Self Ghost is freed by death and returned to The Sure Enough Father which, as I have said, is Self Ghost in its entirety. The spirits who are part of The Sure Enough Father detach themselves and form into wormless beings to appear to us. Often, you will notice, they have a weird light about them. That is The Sure Enough Father shining. The Sure Enough Father is all Self Ghost and also all wisdom. From all wisdom comes the Geranjé."

Badthing paused for a moment to be sure we were listening.

"Each of us has a Geranjé that appears to us in various forms throughout our lives," he said. "The Geranjé is a guiding spirit that tries to tell us what to do and is more effective the more we listen. If we refuse to listen because the wisdom of our Self Ghost has become entangled in other matters, the Geranjé becomes less and less visible and noisy and eventually gives us up. But if we listen, he becomes more visible and louder. He may appear as an owl, a tiny man, a gust of wind in the leaves, an overheard voice. He appears and tells us. I have heard the priests talk of angels who appear to their holy men. What are angels but Geranjés in winged form, usually glowing with light? A Geranjé appeared to my dead wife in the form of a balky burro. She would not listen. She came despite the warning. She died."

"If all life, or I mean if the soul, is Self Ghost or The Sure Enough Father or whatever you call it," Barney said, "then what happens to bad, wicked people when they die?"

"They join The Sure Enough Father," said Badthing.

"Same as the good people?" Barney asked, and Badthing nodded. "You Christians are peculiar," said Octavio. "If The Sure Enough Father is exactly as you say He is, then no wonder He cannot come to your aid when you call Him. He is too busy keeping score on who was wicked and who was good. I have seen in the stores that the more ledgers you keep, the more ledgers must be kept; they multiply each other. The Sure Enough Father could not save Our Jesus Christ on the cross because The Sure Enough Father was still a thousand years behind on keeping his ledgers and deciding who to send to hell and who to heaven. I would hate to think how far behind He is now. Eh, McGill? Stir your mind. Think about it."

"I hope He doesn't catch up any time soon," I said.

"Me too," said Barney. "I ain't anxious to be judged."

"Why do you pray to Pichini and Mel?" Octavio asked Badthing.

"When you are a representative of The Sure Enough Father,

as they are, you have magnificent powers of strength and wisdom," said Badthing. "They can lend those powers to me."

"Your schemes sound reasonable enough," Octavio said.

"Some things I say I also believe," Badthing said.

This was our conversation as well as I remember it. We spoke no more on the subject at the time because we were interrupted. A particularly wretched-looking scalawag ducked into our lean-to. He was a dark, squatty fellow wrapped in a blanket. When he talked his words came out in a lisp, as he had several teeth missing here and there somewhat like a fence that has had pickets kicked out by a horse. His nose was flat, seeming to have no gristle left in it. I knew him to be called Eagle Dancer. He was Octavio's lackey and shaman.

"Colorado says he is leaving," said Eagle Dancer.

"Bring him to me," Octavio said.

Octavio sat quietly, thoughtful, in the firelight while the snow pelted around us and the wind tore through the pines. Barney reboiled the coffee, which already tasted strong enough to dissolve a belt buckle. In a few minutes we heard scuffling, crunching noises and the big mestizo, Colorado, squatted before us. He was so called because of his red hair. It is impossible to guess how many different blood strains flowed in him. I would say he was a quadroon at the very least. There were a half-dozen more figures squatting in a semicircle behind Colorado. We could see them only as dark shapes against the snow.

"I wish to go home, *jefe*," said Colorado.

"As we are about to get rich?" Octavio said.

"Ah, *jefe*, I do not believe that," said Colorado. "These mountains are full of treachery. Walls fall down and trails disappear. I hear ghosts singing. I hear many dead men crying. I hear my grandfather's voice telling me not to search for the gold. I think of a warm, sunny place. I think of my women. I think of mescal to drink. I think of tortillas and green chilies to eat. I think of dancing and fighting. I do not want that gold. I want to go home."

"How do the others behind you feel?" Octavio said.

"*Jefe*, you must ask them yourself. What I do has nothing to do with them," said Colorado.

"Very well, then. I wish you a happy journey," Octavio said.

"A thousand thanks, *jefe*."

"You have far to go. You must be on your way," said Octavio. From beneath Octavio's blanket came an explosion and a crack of fire. People who have never seen a bullet hit a man do not understand what it does to him. The bullet hits very hard. It does not merely pierce a neat hole and go on its way. Imagine a rock that is thrown at your head hard enough to tear through your skull. A bullet is a piece of lead that hits that hard, spinning, tearing out bits of bone, spewing forth pieces of brain. When the bullet hit Colorado there was a loud spat; his head flew back and red and gray nuggets showered the area. The pistol was still smoking and we could smell the burnt powder. At once there was a loud click as Octavio cocked the pistol again.

"Divide up his possessions. Dancer, you see to that," Octavio said. "The rest of you get some sleep. We have work to do tomorrow."

The dark shapes faded away in the snow. Octavio finished his coffee and tossed the cup onto the ground. "Good night, my friends," he said and curled up in his blankets and pulled a buffalo robe over himself and went to sleep beside our fire.

In the morning we set out again. The blizzard abated and by the following day we had a different problem. The sun came out and we had to travel in extremely dangerous slush. A pack burro went off a trail and fell nearly a mile, its body bouncing off the rocks, its cargo scattering in the gorge. With frequent stops to consult James Santiago's map, we made it to the alligator's snout. We searched carefully but could find no trace of the old burro road, nor could we locate any sign of an old church. Octavio examined the map for a long while. He caught an old Tarahumare and questioned him about the presence of a side canyon such as the one we wanted. The old man knew nothing or was too frightened to talk, and so we let him go.

It was Barney who made the discovery. He got off a snap shot at a buck that was running along the canyon floor beside a stream bed. The animal fell badly wounded. As Barney approached, the buck leaped up and disappeared into the side of a cliff. Following the animal's blood drippings, Barney found an astonishing doorway in the cliff. The doorway was so disguised by a tall, partition-like rock, that it was invisible at a distance of more than six feet and even that close all but impossible to see unless viewed at an angle.

Behind the doorway was a steep narrow canyon. Poking about at the canyon entrance, we found some nicks and ruts cut into the rock. It was my idea that those markings were the remains of the burro road, carved by the sharp hoofs of burros carrying heavy bags of ore. We were all very excited.

Octavio did not like the situation. Desirous of the gold though he was, he kept looking up that steep defile that was tangled with brush and boulders, and I could see that he was arguing with himself. Most of his men had crowded around to peer at the markings in the rock. They agreed the markings could have been made by the hoofs of many burros. The markings made them eager to proceed in search of the mine. Finally Octavio took me aside.

"I will tell you what I am thinking," he said. "I have examined your map and have studied these cuts in the rock, and I believe we are close to Tayopa. But I do not like the look of this canyon. The sides are too near and the top too high. If you look up, you will see much snow on the rim. You will see many boulders up there. You will see the sky is a mere slot. Suppose it is true that this mine is a sacred place, guarded by spirits. This is a perfect location for them to ambush us."

"But you don't believe spirits are guarding this mine," I said.

"Why not? They might be. Also it is very possible the spirits could have taken the form of some Tarahumares, if you understand what I mean. From up on that rim they could damage us greatly."

"We could climb to the rim and explore the canyon that way."

"I doubt it," said Octavio. "The canyon is too deep and too brushy. From the rim, way up yonder, we would be able to see nothing. If the old church and its treasure vaults are on the canyon floor, they would be hidden from above. Even the mines—of which I have heard there are a dozen—and their slag heaps would be hidden. The canyon must open into a valley if it would support a church and a mine. Even so, it might be so far to climb down into the valley that we could never do it."

"The cautious way would be to travel along the rim and see if there is a valley ahead. Maybe we could get down into such a valley and explore. It would take longer but would be the safer way," I said.

"Ah," Octavio said, sighing deeply, "I have not become famous by taking the cautious way. Besides, these men are eager and I must give them excitement. And," he said, wiping his face with a red neckerchief, "I feel strange. I feel it necessary to conclude this adventure and go home."

So saying, he took his pony's reins and began to lead the beast into the canyon. I started to suggest that in wisdom we should send two scouts up on either side of the rim to follow our progress from above. But the bandits were plunging into the defile behind their leader, and Badthing was right behind them. Barney was looking at me. I recall very well that his eyes that day seemed unnaturally blue and bright, like polished turquoise.

"Well?" he said.

"I guess we'll go in and get that gold," I said.

"You think this fellow Gerhardt will let us keep our share?"

"Even if I didn't, we wouldn't have much choice," I said.

We had not gone fifty yards up the canyon before we were blocked by boulders. Chopping pines to use as levers, we managed to move some of the boulders and continue. I noticed Octavio looking up toward the rim, from whence the boulders had probably come in a rockslide. However, there was little evidence of a large rockslide at that point. I expressed to Octavio the thought that the boulders had been washed down the canyon by a flood. He agreed that it was possible and pointed out to me that with the melting snow we were quite likely to find ourselves suddenly in the path of a torrent of water that would be rolling down this narrow canyon from some high mountain country that we had not even guessed at; even now the flash flood could be a few miles away, sweeping toward us, pushing boulders and timbers with it. Could I hear the rumbling? At my expression, Octavio laughed. "They don't need spirits to guard this place. The earth has guarded it already," he said.

Beyond the boulders we came to a deep cold pool with ice floating in it. Bending to drink, one of Octavio's men let out a cry. He held up a bit of something he had found beside the pool. "What do you think?" Octavio asked me.

"I think it is the hammer of a Spanish pistol," I said.

"A very old Spanish pistol. This proves nothing. A Spanish soldier could easily have gotten lost in these barrancas. But this is a more hopeful sign than if we had not found it," said Octavio.

In the course of the day I doubt that we made more than a mile up the canyon. In places it became so narrow that I wondered if we could go farther. At one place it widened into a pleasant little glen. When night came we slept among the rocks. We were cold and wet. Thinking about the possibility of a flood, I climbed high into the rocks before I slept.

About the middle of the second day in the canyon, we saw smoke on the rim. It is a practice among the Tarahumares to build fires in the forest; they think that by burning acres of timber, they can cause rain. But with the snow there was no need for rain. Also it was not likely that this thin gray column of smoke was a cooking fire. The Tarahumares may lack their Apache cousins' sense about woodcraft, but they would never build such a cooking or heating fire with bandits in the area.

Octavio's thinking was the same as mine.

"Signal smoke," he said.

His men were looking at the rim and muttering. Several were shaking their heads. As we watched, another smoke rose on the other rim of the canyon to our left. Then a third appeared behind us. The canyon ahead was not only narrow, but the rim on either side was extremely heavy with boulders, fallen timbers and mounds of snow. It looked almost as if material had been piled up to build a bridge. More likely, of course, the material was for an ambush. But it was deeply covered with banks of snow and my first impression was that it would be difficult to dislodge.

"There is only one thing to do," Octavio said. "I will scout ahead to see if there is a valley where we might be safer. I feel we are near the mine and with luck could rush through this tight place before they could crush us. At worst, we must know whether to turn back."

The rest of us moved to the walls of the canyon beneath whatever overhang we could find. Octavio gave the reins of his pony to Eagle Dancer. Taking his rifle, the Lipan crept around a boulder and was gone. A fourth smoke came up, this also to our rear. We waited for Octavio to return. Most eyes were on the canyon ramparts, but we also watched to front and back. I had a feeling we might never leave this canyon.

From Barney's face I could tell we were of the same intimation, but he grinned when he saw me looking at him. Badthing bent his ear to the ground, knocking off his cork helmet. He was disturbed. The dozen bandits had disported among the rocks. They all seemed to be trembling, listening, watching, smelling, aware of danger they could not identify.

Directly ahead of the boulder around which Octavio had disappeared was a growth of skinny pines that shone wetly. A red madroño tree had somehow got mixed up in the pines, and I kept my eyes on it, watching for it to move. The smokes trailed up above us and the canyon had become very still, even hushed. I could hear myself breathing and again began to want a cigar. I lined up the sight of my Henry rifle on the madroño tree and peered down the V-notch to the left of the tree as it faced me, as that was the side a right-handed rifleman's head would appear from. In shifting my position I knocked loose a few pebbles that rolled down to the rocky floor of the stream bed. The bandits looked around at me.

"The earth is moving," Badthing whispered. I shook my head.

"It is moving," he said. "Far off."

Just then there was a stirring of the pines and a crown of black hair showed around the edge of the boulder, to be followed at once by a brown face with a white pebble of an eye. I tried to read Octavio's expression as he loped toward us in a crouch. He motioned for the bandits to keep their positions. Kneeling in the stream bed just below me, he looked up with his one good black eye. He seemed most agitated, both pleased and frightened.

"I think we have found it," he said. "Half a mile ahead the canyon widens and forms a shelf on either side of this arroyo. On one shelf I saw what looks to be the ruins of a large building. Only stones and pieces of foundation are left, but it could be the church. There are heaps of what could be slag on the shelves. Three other canyons come into this one from the west and there look to be trails and maybe digging in them."

"What about the smokes?" I asked.

"I saw no one. I feel them, but I think they must be feeble or they would have attacked us by now." He frowned. "But I have heard a rumbling far up this canyon to the west. It is a bad sound. We are on the west slope of the high divide, so that all waters should be flowing from behind us toward the sea. But ahead of us the ground is much higher than we are. It is not unknown for the snow waters to come down to the east from the high mountains before turning below and flowing west again."

"That is what has worried me," I said.

"I think that is what is happening," he said. He looked at the pack animals tied back among the brush. I hate to leave the supplies here, but I fear we must try to climb up these walls for safety. I am afraid the waters are coming down from higher up this canyon as well as from the other three canyons."

By now we could definitely feel the earth moving, as Badthing had warned. In the distance, high up, sounding strange in the thin cold air, suddenly came a thundering sound, steady and increasing.

"That is it!" Octavio shouted. "No time to go back! Climb! Climb!"

I looked down at White Foot. The beautiful Kentucky mare was tied to a blackened dead limb. I couldn't abandon her. I slid down from my perch in the canyon wall and ran to her. I heard Octavio yelling for me to come back. The thundering was coming closer and even the cliffs had begun to shake. Pulling my Bowie knife, I slashed the reins loose. With the flat of my hand, I spanked White Foot on the flank and sent her off down the canyon away from the impending flood. Rocks had begun to fall around me. I was bumped and, turning, saw Octavio yanking at the pack on one of the burros. "Idiot!" he shouted at me. I went for the canyon wall, clawing up it, holding the Henry in one hand, grabbing at roots and rocks that came loose in my grip, tumbling rubble down into the canyon. Octavio ran forward in the stream bed, toward the thundering that was now so loud I could not make out what he was yelling. Gasping, I paused and looked down. Octavio had taken a shotgun and a handful of shells from the pack. He aimed calmly up at the heavy snowbanks on the canyon rim and began shooting. The shotgun boomed amidst the thunder.

After three or four shots, there came another sound—the deep grumble of shifting earth. The heavy snowbanks began to slide down into the canyon from either rim, carrying along the timbers and boulders. Octavio kept shooting. The slide grew, tearing out part of the canyon walls, tons of earth and rock and wood falling into the defile with the avalanche of snow. The noise was deafening. I was high enough that I could see over the boulder. I could see the shelves Octavio had spoken of and I thought I could see white stone that might be the church foundation, but I wasn't sure. Then from all four canyons at once came the water. It was a high brown tide, pushing trees and rocks with it, smashing against the canyon walls. The thundering flood came out of the four canyons into the small valley, rising above the stream bed and flowing over the white stones, rising onto the ledges, dissipating for a few seconds as the flood spread out to the valley walls, gathering strength and then moving down again in a wider brown flow, deeper and quieter but larger in volume, being pushed along by the steady torrents pouring down from the canyons.

Octavio's avalanche had filled the defile to a depth of some thirty feet and was still falling. The Lipan had just begun to climb when the water, narrowing again as it came from the valley into the canyon, rammed into his dam. There was a tremendous battering noise. The canyon wall against my body trembled like a frightened horse. Octavio was coming up the wall like a monkey, but, looking down, I saw several of his bandits coming up much more slowly, as though they were sick and had been debilitated by the journey. The dam was saving them, holding back the flood as they labored up through the rocks.

There was a blow on my shoulder. A fist-sized rock bounded down into the canyon. I thought little of it until another rock of similar size struck near my face, throwing chips into my eyes. Looking up, I saw a small brown man with another rock held above his head with both hands. I fired one-handed with my Henry. I missed him but he also missed me. I tried to shout a warning but the flood water pounding at the increasing dam was too loud for me to be heard. I found a niche and looked across to the other wall, where Barney and Badthing were climbing. They were about ten feet below the rim. Above them were several small figures wearing tunics but barelegged in the snow. They had bows and arrows and wooden swords and were throwing rocks down at the climbers who were near helpless as they clung to the cliff. One bandit had reached the rampart with his hands and was trying to throw a leg over onto the top ground, but a Tarahumare was prodding at him with a wooden sword, about to fling him backward off the cliff. Steadying myself as much as I could, I shot the Tarahumare with my Henry rifle. Working the lever on my rifle almost unseated me and pitched me down. Without lifting the rifle, I snapped off another shot that again missed but did have the gratifying effect of scattering the coons. They rushed off into the pines and rocks, tromping through the snow. The bandit who had been at the rim clambered over and grinned at me and I saw the cretinish face of Eagle Dancer. Had I known him as well at the time as I do now, I would have delighted in seeing the Tarahumare lob him into space.

My shots dissuaded the Indians above me as well as those across. As I carefully poked my eyes above the rim, I saw their tracks in the snow. They had fled. As guardians of the Tayopa mine, if indeed that was their duty, they had not been outstandingly efficient. But they had not been needed. The brown waters had covered the mine site (I refer to it as being the mine, for that is how I have thought of it since, wrongly or no) as thoroughly as if the old Jesuits had sent the flood from heaven.

All of us had reached the rim and comparative safety when the dam broke. With a shattering explosion, boulders burst into the air and timbers flew like matchsticks, and the brown water soared over the top of the dam, ripping a deep crack in it, rapidly eroding its sides. The water with its debris poured down into the narrow valley and went racing on toward its destination. Most of our terrified animals had torn themselves loose from their peggings and had started to run down the canyon, but the brown water swept over them. We saw them bobbing and tumbling like little boats, threshing and straining to keep their heads above water, the mules and burros sinking first beneath the weights of their packs, then the ponies and horses going down, some with their skulls smashed against the rocks. Two or three were still afloat when they went out of sight down the canyon. I think White Foot, a fine and nimble beast burdened only with saddle and saddlebags, might have escaped from the canyon. However, I never saw her again. I hope the Tarahumares did not eat her. I have seen how they will kill a horse, in times of starvation, by thrusting a sharp stick into the animal's neck and bleeding it to death, of course catching the blood in clay vessels. I also hope they did not turn her into a plow beast to haul their wooden plows through their rocky corn patches. I prefer to think she broke free and survived the bears, wolves, mountain lions, and Indians, and the cold winters and dry summers and is living wild yet, but I know what the chances are.

Octavio sent several of his bandits into the pines to be certain the Tarahumares had gone. Then he and I sat and looked at the flood waters. We were bruised and muddy and soaked to the flesh. Vultures floated overhead, already aware of the dead Indian on the opposite bank. Octavio was the first to speak.

"So much for the gold," he said.

"After the water recedes we can get down to the ruins easily enough," I said.

"Peter Hermano," he said, grinning at me with his awful white-eyed look, "it is winter in a barren place and we have no food, no blankets, no animals and only the ammunition that is in our belts. We can't wait for anything. We must start home. The gold is not worth staying here and dying for. If the elements did not kill us, the Tarahumares would, eventually, when we are weak."

"Then we will come back," said I.

"Maybe," he said. "The thing we must concentrate on is to get to my *ranchería* alive. It will be difficult."

We sat for a moment. "You know, of course, that the map was in my saddle pocket," I said, and he nodded. He lowered his head, his shoulders shook and he looked up laughing.

For the sake of any who may find this journal and be interested, I will draw the map from memory. But it must be kept in mind that I am no cartographer, and the adventure I have just described happened nine years ago. I have forgotten the ancient names, and so have used the names I know.

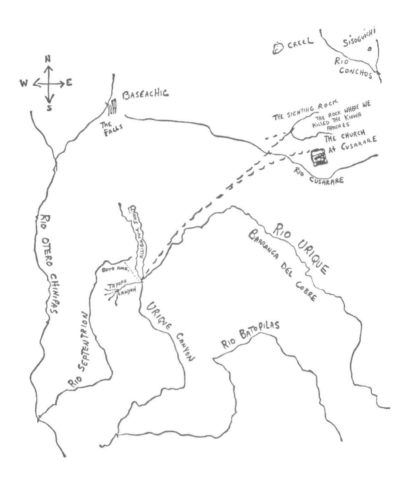

14

Today I mounted Excelsior and rode east along the rim a few miles to the settlement called Arroyo Seco. I bought supplies in the store and asked the storekeeper, Moreles, if he knew how long I had been isolated in my house. Moreles looked at me oddly and said it had been about two weeks since I had left the mission. I could tell he wanted to ask questions but would not. The soda crackers in his barrel were stale and sodden. I spent the last of my money, buying enough beans and flour and coffee for me and oats for Excelsior to provide victuals for at least two more weeks. Then Excelsior and I came slowly back along the rim, looking down at Valdez, at the sheep and the pole fences and the Hondo River, swollen with snow water, flowing toward the Rio Grande. Behind us the Sacred Mountains were white and we could see white among the pines up the Hondo Valley. Off to the west the sky was blue and yellow and we could see the black of the gorge and then the vast range of the prairie on to the distant mountains. Several men were working in the irrigation ditch at the farm of Justo, a neighbor. They were all neighbors, and I recognized them. We waved to each other. They bent back to their work, cleaning out the ditch, and I rode on.

Now I am at my journal again. Looking back at the map I drew last night, I see there may be errors in it. The scale seems all off to me. But I have no reference work to check the rivers and barrancas. It is of little importance. Circumstances being what they are, I doubt this chronicle will ever be found. There is, though, always the hope. Would I write it otherwise?

The map again interests me. Looking at it, I recall vividly the flood and the climb up from the narrow canyon. As our group was split, we had to backtrack for miles to find a place where we could cross the brown waters, below the canyon, and rejoin. We were in poor condition. We walked to Creel, being stealthy, fearing more Kiowa Apaches might come down from the Chisos Mountains and fall upon us. Outside Creel, on the road to Sisoguichi, there was a hacienda that Octavio knew of. We snaked up to the place in the night, not wishing to fight if we could avoid it but merely wanting to steal horses. About two dozen vaqueros worked that ranchero. Octavio had an Apache's contempt of them as fighting men, although I had not; however, he saw the wisdom of exercising cunning in this instance. We poisoned the dogs and got into the corral without detection. The moonlight was so bright that the night seemed a pale dusk. Barney led several bandits into the tack room to carry out saddles, bridles, and blankets. They made off with a half-dozen saddles, which was plenty, since most of the bandits, being coons, preferred a blanket or a rawhide stretched over wooden forks rather than the big Mexican leather seats. *Sillas*, they called them. Chairs.

But a fracas resulted. As I was opening the gate to the main corral, a vaquero yelled and began shooting. There was great confusion. Shapes ran this way and that, and gunfire flashed. I got the gate open after a bullet had knocked the latch out of my hands, stinging me. We ran off the entire remuda, catching horses and swinging up on them as they came through the gate. Rifles and pistols were blasting every-place. No one was hurt. We met at our rendezvous point, each cut out and roped up an extra horse, and then rode for Creel. We hit the town hard before a warning could get out. In the moonlight, with the noise of our hoofs, the roosters became addled and began crowing. Dogs were barking. Mexicans and Indians were shouting. Running toward what I thought was the back door of a general store, I fell over a trough into a mess of muddy slop and heard pigs grunting and squealing. The pigs went into the street to join the milling about. I got up, cursing, and with pistol drawn kicked open the door. Instead of a store, I burst into the bedroom of a startled Mexican lady who had been entertaining a lover by lantern light. Both were nude as plucked hens. The man leaped up with his hands raised and implored me not to kill him, and I understood that he thought I was her husband. The woman lay atop a down comfort, the lantern light on her white flesh, her long black hair fanned over the pillows. She gave out a screech and began praying. A crucifix hung on the wall at the head of the bed and the other walls were covered with paintings of various Madonnas and there was an altar in one corner. In one swift glance at the woman, I thought of Ellen. Putting that thought out of mind, I ordered the woman to get up. I forced her and the man to kneel in the corner—accidentally, by the altar—while I snatched the comfort off the bed and, catching up the four corners of it to make a sack, filled it with foodstuffs from the kitchen. While in the kitchen I heard them praying, their voices together, his high and hers low. They were fortunate it was I who had come in and not one of Octavio's murderous coons. Even so, I was sorely tempted. Coming out of the kitchen, I went over and grabbed her by the hair with my pistol hand and hauled her to her feet and started to kiss her, but there was something distasteful about the scene, with the man cowering naked at the altar and the woman with strands of her hair wrapped around my fist and the rest of it falling to her buttocks, and I thought again about Ellen and about the unread letters that also had been in the saddle pocket on White Foot, and I let the woman go. Besides, she had great swatches of hair under her arms. They were still praying when I left.

We galloped down the main street of Creel, shooting into the houses to discourage the residents from pursuit. We headed out due north, by the star, veered east, doubled back, rode down a stream and turned northwest. We rode all night, changed horses, rode all the next day, covering more than one hundred miles, rested a few hours, rode the remainder of that night, and by mid-afternoon were approaching Octavio's *ranchería*.

There were sentinels up in the rocks. We were in some very rough country, somewhere south of Juárez. As we climbed up the trail, I looked back and saw dust devils whirling across the desert below. Scrubby pines grew among the rocks. There were pin oaks and thorn bushes and gnarled dry twisty growths, but the path up was mostly bare rock, much of it black bad country rock, and I wondered how Octavio's band could survive in such a location. When we came into the hollow where the camp was, I saw a spring miraculously pouring from a cleft, and some little patches of grass.

By this time, at least half the bandit-warriors were ill. They were sneezing, coughing, dribbling mucous from their noses. They had been getting steadily worse during the ride and when we arrived in the camping ground several of them were so weak they fell off their horses and had to be carried into their wickiups. It was no mystery to me how a man could have got sick. We had been frozen, soaked, starved, and exhausted. The only mystery to me was why we all did not have pneumonia.

Looking around, I saw that while Octavio's renegades were composed of all types of coons and breeds, the band was predominately Lipan. The Lipan women who were singing and dancing a welcome wore doeskin smocks with the hair and tail hanging down the back, except for the widows and unmarried women, who wore nothing but loincloths, and had rubbed their bare breasts with sage and evergreen to make their nipples stick out. The women who were not Lipan seemed to be mostly Mexican captives, dressed in cotton and calico or doeskin, but they danced also and slapped their thighs. All the women wore tin and brass ornaments, necklaces, bracelets, and the like. The Lipan men who had stayed behind as guards had their hair cut off on the left sides of their heads, as did Octavio, and wore feathers, trinkets, and earrings. The women ran up with bowls of corn beer and with what looked to be sotol flour ash cakes. Boys took our horses and led them off. I estimated there were some forty fighting men in the camp and perhaps twenty children and close to one hundred women.

Octavio put Barney and me into a wickiup that we shared with four women, two of them widows and two unmarried. We rested and then went out and sat around the fires for the story telling and drinking and eating. Eight of the twelve bandits who had been with us were seriously sick by the finish of dinner. Eagle Dancer put on a grotesque headmask made of an eagle with wings outstretched and danced and shook eagle claw rattles. We smoked a long clay pipe, passing it around. It had hemp in it, and Barney and I got to feeling quite giddy. We watched Eagle Dancer dance in and out of the wickiup of each ill warrior. He would chant and then plunge a flint knife into the ground behind the warriors' beds. We thought it was funny but tried not to laugh aloud. Badthing had lost all his fine costumes save for a cavalry tunic that he wore with his cork helmet and his nose ring. He got very wobbly on hemp and corn beer but showed good sense to tell no stories or interfere with Eagle Dancer. The women who had been assigned us were most attentive. They shoved food into our mouths, poured beer for us, rubbed our aching limbs, stroked our heads, took us into the wickiup and poured hot water into curled-up beefhides and bathed us. In some ways, those Ipa-people know how life ought to be lived.

One of our women was Mexican, a captive who had been the wife of a warrior and was now a widow. With her, I could converse. I know a smattering of Apache words in several dialects, but the Apache language is such that the tone of a word is vital to its meaning and a mispronounced word can say the opposite of what you intend, and so it is dangerous to speak. After I had bathed and was wrapped in a blanket, a messenger came to fetch me, saying Octavio wanted me. Barney was lying back on a pallet that was made of grass covered with a hide, fur-side up, and two bare women were tickling his pink skin with feathers and were putting a pipe to his mouth and keeping the beer bowl filled. "Peter," he said to me as I went out, "if anybody ever asks you what happened to old Barney Swift, you tell them he finally got what he deserved."

Octavio had me steered into his wickiup, which was about seven feet high and eight feet across, made of bent willow poles tied together with yucca leaves and fibers and covered with hides. He wore a loose tunic and had removed his earrings. I sat and we smoked and after a while he beckoned to a beautiful girl who was nursing a baby on a blanket nearby. Her black hair was caught in a brooch of silver and dropped between her shoulder blades in a single shiny rope. The baby was a fat little brown rascal with black buttons for eyes, like the eyes of a doll I had once seen somewhere but couldn't recall where.

"This is my favorite wife," Octavio said to me. "Her name is Dove Speaks. This child is my only son. He is very strong. Look how strong he is."

"He looks very strong," I said, and Octavio was pleased.

"My other wives are nothing to me," he said. "They know it. They know I have feeling for Dove Speaks, and I have feeling for my son. I have feeling for them as I never had for any person, not even my mother, not even the one we saw hanged, not even the great warrior who I did not know, not even you or your mother or father or not even myself."

We smoked some more. The baby had not been named yet. It is a Lipan custom to wait until there is some name that strikes a fancy or is really pertinent to the child. I looked at the woman, whose eyes were lowered to the suckling babe. She was truly lovely, with a thin, delicate face, Spanish blood in her. The idea of her husband having other wives would not rankle her. A Lipan man will not cohabit with his wife from the onset of her pregnancy until she is through nursing the child at the age of two, meaning there is a period of nearly three years when they do not partake of each other, and a man must do something, so it is better to have more wives, though Ellen would not have viewed it that way. Also the women outnumbered the men enough to go around several times over.

"She and my son are all I want on this earth," said Octavio.

"Why don't you take them up to New Mexico Territory?" I said. "You could settle on a reservation and they would be safe and not worried about you being killed on a raid."

"I am wanted by the Rangers for killing that nigger," said Octavio.

"That is forgotten," I said.

"Then there are a hundred other reasons they could want me," he said. "And I would never go live in a pen with The People who have given up. I could not do it. That is all."

"Well," I said, "it's your affair."

"You are my friend," he said. "Now we go sweat."

Eagle Dancer had built a new sweat wickiup in a secluded corner of the compound. The Apaches hold, and I agree, that sweating is very healthful for mind and body. Octavio and I crawled into the sweat house through the east-facing door, shoving aside the heavy hide covering. First, though, I dropped my blanket beside the door and stood naked while Octavio pulled his tunic over his head. He has the most powerful muscles of any man I ever saw, though his movements are quick and light. He looked at me and with one index finger touched the lion's tooth and the Virgin of Guadalupe and the Jude that I had around my neck. Carefully, I hung the medallion and the tooth on a branch and we entered the sweat house. Eagle Dancer gave us each a mug of mesquite bean tea prepared with the mystic four beans. We rubbed our heads with sage and our bodies with juniper and sat beside the pit while Eagle Dancer brought four hot stones to put in it. Then he brought water and poured it over the stones and there was a hiss and the steam came up. When the sweat got tickly, we scratched ourselves with twigs. After a bit, the stones were changed and fresh steam clouded us.

"I am bothered," Octavio said. "I have too many sick men. What do you think is wrong with them? Eagle Dancer tells me they are cursed because I have brought you and Barney Swift here. I don't believe that. But what is wrong?"

"They have had too much of the cold and too little food and sleep," I said.

"No, they are tough. That is not it. I am bothered."

But I'd had too much cold and not enough sleep, myself, and I began to drowse. Octavio woke me when our steam was over. We stepped outside to be rubbed. I returned to my wickiup where the women were waiting, and I slept very warm that night.

Despite the obvious comforts, I would not have slept so well had I known what we were in for. It was Badthing who roused me and asked me to go with him. Grumbling, I got up and dressed and followed him across the compound to the wickiup of one of the sick bandits. Several people had gathered outside. The sun was up, but the wickiup was in shadow from the rocks and it was cold.

The tiny Karankawa pushed through the people at the entrance and we went inside. There, Eagle Dancer, in his regalia as shaman, was on his knees beside the sick man's bed. Octavio's white eye turned toward me. The sick man groaned. Eagle Dancer was chanting and tossing powder into the air in an annoying way. Being so newly risen, I felt like clouting him. The sick man was shaking with a chill. His eyes were red and puffy.

"See this," Octavio said, pulling down the blanket that had been around the sick man's nose.

On the man's face were several half-moon groupings of rose-red spots.

He had measles.

"He brought the sickness! He brought the sickness!" Eagle Dancer said, pointing at me.

I ignored him. "The others?" I said.

"Three have the spots. All have chills and fever," said Octavio.

"He brought the sickness!" Eagle Dancer said, his voice muffled beneath the mask.

"I think I will kill you," I told him.

"It is better that we should cure these men," said Octavio in a very cold tone.

Measles are bad and difficult at any time, with the threat of death or blindness, but to these renegades up in this desolate mountain stronghold an epidemic of measles could be a disaster, I realized.

I don't know what to do. I am no doctor," I said to Octavio. "You remember my mother kept us quiet in a dark room and gave us medicines to break the fever."

"I remember nothing," Octavio said. "I want these men cured."

We worked hard on them. We kept their wickiups dark and kept them on their pallets, plying them with herb poultices and hot teas and Eagle Dancer's infernal rattle. For a time we moved all the sick men into the same wickiup, but the sickest began to rave with fever and we had to separate them. I established a quarantine, though I was certain it was useless, as the sick men had mingled freely with the others during the dancing and the feast of return. To make matters worse, a cold rain began to fall. The compound became a great slosh. The wood got wet. The wickiups leaked. Some of the sick men got pneumonia. More than half the residents of the stronghold were sneezing and wheezing and feverish. On the advice of Eagle Dancer, Octavio called for a peyote ceremony.

"Your people come along and each tells us the only way we can know Our Jesus Christ and go to heaven is the way he does it, even though your people don't agree how it is done." Octavio said to me. "Either they are all wrong or they know no more about the Great Mystery than we do. Suppose Our Jesus Christ has come back this time as peyote to help the poor People? When he came as a white man, you murdered him. Your shamen admit that. Through the peyote, is it not possible we get the Holy Ghost, as you call it? Is it not possible that the Holy Ghost can cause miraculous cures?"

I went along with the plan, reasoning that it could do no harm and would at least take our minds off our misfortune.

To begin with, they tore down a wickiup and built a new one on the same spot, under a tent cover of hides, in order to have the ground as dry as possible. A religious ceremony such as this required a new structure. There were to be twelve of us in the ceremony, not counting Cedar Man or Drummer Man. Barney was invited, but Badthing was not. A Mexican called Titcheestoque had a large bag of mescal buttons that he said he had got in trade with the Carrizo Indians up in Texas. Perhaps they were especially good buttons, else I fail to understand why he would have bothered, as the turnip-shaped cactus grows all along the Rio Grande and there are, that I know of, more than two dozen different types of plants in the area that can be smoked or chewed to produce a dreamlike effect. Of them all, the mescal button seems to be the favorite, and its use is widening among the Indians today. There is a story that the Tarahumares first learned of it from a race of giants in the Sierra Madre Occidental and passed it on to the Apaches who in turn gave the secret to the Comanches and Kiowas. I have heard that the great Comanche chief Quanah, a leader of the Quahadi, says that when he chews mescal he sees the face of Jesus.

The Lipans have a word for the mescal button that sounds like *Wok-Wave*. I am uncertain of the spelling, but I heard it repeated often that afternoon as I sat in my wickiup and watched the peyote place being built in the rain. The men who were to take part in the ceremony did no work. At dusk, with the cold rain still falling, our women procured bone combs and combed our hair—mine and Barney's—parting it in the middle and painting it with a straight red line made from ocher clay. I explained to Barney that the red line stood for the Peyote Road, as the coons call it, or the straight and narrow path that leads to salvation. An hour or so after dark, the women bathed us and we dressed in the finest garments that could be produced. We wore paint, buckskins and feathers, being indiscernible from Indians ourselves. As we waited to be summoned to the ceremony, Badthing crawled into the wickiup. He wanted to talk to me, and we went off to whisper.

"I have been thinking," he said. "There will be deaths here. There will be anger. Soon Octavio and the others will realize where the red spots came from. I have thought, and I know. They came from my woman, who is now gone. This was the sickness she had."

"Might be right," I said.

"Yes," he said. "I might be right. When you are in the ceremony, ask Peyote Chief to give a blessing to Badthing, who will need it. Though I know all the spirits and the secrets of life and death, though I know of the Self Ghost and the Worm Theory, I will use any blessing I can get. I have had a visitation from a shining one. I am in danger." He held up his right palm, upon which had been painted a lightning sign. I held up my palm and we touched. "The owl and the lion meet," he said. "The lightning and the mountain. You ask in my behalf, and my spirits will protect you. That is what I say."

He crawled out of the wickiup. After a while, Eagle Dancer came to get us.

We entered through an east-facing door and sat upon bunches of sage in a circle around the fire hole, which was dug in a V toward the door. We rose and walked once around the fire hole, led by Eagle Dancer, and sat down again. The odor of sage was mixed with the smoke and made my eyes water. Eagle Dancer sat opposite the door, looking toward it. Cedar Man, whose duties were to tend the fire and keep the incense burning, sat beside the door. Drummer Man sat to the left of Eagle Dancer. Octavio, his face painted fiercely, sat to the south of the circle. I was at the north and Barney beside me. We sat cross-legged. In the center of the circle, by the fire hole, was a big round mescal button that Eagle Dancer addressed as Peyote Chief.

Bowing his head, as in a Christian prayer, Eagle Dancer

intoned, "Oh, Comforter, which is the Holy Ghost, whom the Father will send in my name, he shall teach you all things, and bring all things to your remembrance, whatsoever I have said unto you." He said it in Spanish and it struck me as familiar, no doubt something he picked up from the priests.

Eagle Dancer passed around Titcheestoque's bag of buttons. Watching the others, I saw we were to take four each. I placed mine between my knees, picked the downy tufts from the middle of one button, put it in my mouth and began to chew the bitter, pulpy bean. I could hear the crackling of the sage and sticks burning in the fire hole and the crunching as each man chewed his peyote button. When the button had become a paste, I took it from my mouth, rolled it into a ball, passed it through the fire three times and swallowed it, massaging my throat to get it down. Each man thus ate his four buttons quickly.

Now Eagle Dancer picked up a gourd rattle and sang a small song, almost a lullaby, his voice crooning and soothing as Drummer Man tapped on his drum and all of us stared fixedly at Peyote Chief. I had a spasm in my stomach and began to feel nauseated. Beside me, Barney turned and vomited over his shoulder. That was considered very bad form and I tried to keep mine down but could not and soon duplicated Barney's act. My eyes dimmed with the effect of the vomiting. But none heeded. Eagle Dancer sang his song four times and passed his rattle to the left. The next man began to sing. The songs were in assorted languages and dialects—Apache, Comanche, Spanish, Tex-Mex, Yaqui, and so forth. I saw one man in the circle pull his blanket over his head. It was strange. I had thought of him as a very scurvy-looking individual, with a long scar on his cheek and villainous eyes, but when I looked again his face seemed quite pleasant, radiant even, with the blanket over his head and his eyes looking out softly as the eyes of a Madonna. The nausea had passed and I realized, somewhat surprised, that the mescal had taken over.

At first it was just an increasing of sensations and the

discovery that things were different. The inside of the wickiup had moved, the circle had shifted a few feet and the figures in it were outlined in blurred gold. I began to get a nervous tingling feeling. I looked at Eagle Dancer and he was ridiculous. I looked at his feathers, his paint, his eagle gear, and he looked to me like some fat bedraggled barnyard chicken, ludicrous, and I laughed. Some others looked around at me. It took them hours to move their heads. By then I was swelling up, about to burst, with golden tingling. My heart swelled up and I thought, well, I feel too good, if this doesn't stop in a moment my heart will explode and I'll die, too bad.

More sticks and sage fell on the fire. The hiss was gigantic and flames shot to the ceiling, showering us with firefly sparks. I found the rattle in my hand. It was my turn to sing. I sang a lullaby mother had sung to me when I was a child, except I didn't listen to the words but instead saw them as they came out of my mouth and floated around the wickiup, twisting and darting or soaring, depending on how my voice wanted to move them. I caught a burning spark in my palm and watched it glow, thinking of the Self Ghost coming out, until it died. They took the rattle from me. WHOOM WHOOM WHOOM I felt, with every beating of my heart, my blood churning through my veins and arteries, WHOOM WHOOM WHOOM, even thinking about it now I can feel similar. I pulled a blanket around my head until only my eyes showed. I stared at Peyote Chief. Beside me I was aware that Barney was rocking back and forth, keening, sorrowing maybe, but I didn't care.

At midnight (I found out later) we paused. Cedar Man left the wickiup. I heard an eagle scream four times. Cedar Man came in with a bucket of water which he gave to Eagle Dancer along with an eaglebone whistle. Eagle Dancer sang a song and blew four times on the whistle. He made a cross in the bucket of water with the whistle. He dipped an eagle feather fan in the water and flicked drops onto us around the circle. Those who felt so moved began to pray for the sick. After each prayer, Eagle Dancer blew on the whistle. We drank from the bucket. The bag of mescal buttons was passed

around and I took four more and ate them, not getting nauseated this time. A clay pipe filled with hemp went around the
circle. We prayed as we puffed it.

Well, now, you take the highest mountain goat atop the
highest mountain in the Rockies, far above the timberline, far
up in the clouds, perched in a crag where he can see down
through gaps in the clouds the whole laid-out pattern of the
earth, with the brown and green laid out there, and turning
he can see down and out in the distance the sun sparkling off
the water of the great ocean, and to north and south he can
see the brown humps of the lesser mountains, and looking
up only slightly he sees direct the brilliance of the sun so
close, and that was where I was for a while, except I was
several feet above that mountain goat and controlled the
entire affair. From there I began the descent. The WHOOM
WHOOM WHOOM came back and I felt myself fighting a
terrible fracas, as if a river was washing over me and carrying
me off and I swam against it, believing I would perish if I
didn't. I went under water. I was under green water with blue
shapes floating past. Then I went on down into a red place.
Devils were there. I was dead. I quit fighting. I saw my
mother in her lace mantilla, her eyes peering at me without
recognition as she walked slowly by me, not noticing me,
walking somewhere slowly. I saw a man with a long
mustache that I took to be my father but upon closer inspection found out was a Chinaman. The red place dissolved and
I had the greatest peace. Everything was good. I wanted to
reach out and hold hands with Barney and with the murderer
on the other side, making the entire circle hold hands, as
though that would be important. I knew there was unity if
we would seek it. I knew I had died and it was all right, it was
all the same. I knew that vanity caused all the trouble and
made life what it is, and I had lost my vanity and had died but
yet was living somehow, I don't know how, but I knew it. I
knew I was part of a great wheel, only part, but each part was
important and still unimportant compared to the whole
wheel, that it was the flowing force of something I could not
comprehend but had to join in, and pettiness was the danger,

and I felt a thousand little vanity bugs fly off of me, and I resolved that they were gone forever, and then I must have lost my wits.

When I aroused, sunlight was shining through the doorway. Drummer Man was drumming and Eagle Dancer was singing. It was a noisy, stirring song, calculated to rouse us dreamers and jerk us back. At its finish, women handed in four pots that were lined up between the fire and the doorway. Eagle Dancer sang another song, repeating it four times. Then Drummer Man pulled the skin head off his drum. The drum, water bucket, rattle and fan were passed around the circle, each man sipping from the bucket, and placed outside the doorway. The men of the circle began to laugh. The four pots were passed around. They contained corn, sweet beef, hash beef, and fruit. I have never eaten food that tasted so exquisite. They began to pull down the wickiup. The rain had quit, though it was still cold and muddy. We got up and went to Octavio's wickiup for a jolly feast, with much laughing and joke telling. After the feast, as the party was breaking up, we received the news that two men had died in the night.

"You see," Octavio told me. "It makes no difference what you believe. None of it is any good. The Sure Enough Father does not listen, regardless how you ask."

Barney and I went back to our wickiup and slept until dark, when we were roused by the sad drumming and mourning and the sound of rain on the hides above our heads. I went out to look for Badthing, but he had disappeared. He had slipped off on foot. They tracked him for a while. That was a wise thing for him to do.

15

The next two weeks were very bad. The cold rain fell off and on and a cold wind blew through the camp. Nine men and seven women died, as much from exposure and poor diet as from the measles, but measles got the credit. The drumming and mourning never ceased. Each morning there was a procession going down through the rocks along the muddy path with a corpse wrapped in a blanket. Despite the Lipan belief, Octavio refused to move away from the *ranchería*. He said they were not strong enough to risk both the weather and their enemies. There was a theological dispute, but Eagle Dancer sided with his chief. To compromise, Octavio ordered that the corpses be taken far down into the desert so the spirits could not find their way back to the stronghold. Barney suggested that we slip out, as Badthing had done. But the bandits watched us day and night, always with rifles cocked. According to Octavio, we were not prisoners. It was clear that we were.

"This is starting to spook me, Peter," Barney told me one morning. "Tonight I'm going to make a try at leaving this place."

By that night, however, it was too late. Octavio's wife, Dove Speaks, and his child had been ill for two days. Though they were kept warm and dry and got the best care possible, Dove Speaks died in the afternoon. One of the other wives took the child from her arms. Cuddling it, she found that the baby was blind. Perhaps it had been too close to the fire. Whatever the reason, there was no doubt the infant could not see beads dangling in front of its pretty little fat face.

Octavio took the child himself. He walked with it out into the rain. He held the child at arm's length up to the dark, pouring heavens, and there was thunder and lightning in the west. The rain streamed down Octavio's face. His white pebble-eye looked up unblinking into the rain. Because of the thunder, I could not hear what he said. I saw him holding up the small wet bundle and I could see his lips moving. Then he swept his arms down and dashed his son's head against a rock.

A great crying went up around the camp from each wickiup. Octavio walked back to his wickiup with the small bundle and placed it atop the body of his dead wife and folded them up in a buffalo robe. He sat down beside the fire and smeared his face with ashes. Little gargles came out of him. Raindrops flowed from his hair down his cheeks and dripped sizzling into the fire. There was a weeping, chanting noise all around the camp, like animals talking in the gray cold day.

"Peter," Barney said, "they are going to kill us."

"I don't think they will," I said.

"I know they will," he said. "I felt death."

We went to our wickiup. Our women ran out of it when we came in. Barney got down on his knees and scrabbled through his possessions, looking for his pistol, but it was not there. My Henry, my pistol, my derringer, and my Bowie knife were missing. We looked at each other. Rain blew in as the flap lifted. In came Eagle Dancer and four bandits. They squatted and looked at us, rain dripping off their ponchos, and I knew Barney was right.

The mourning for Dove Speaks and the infant lasted three

days, during which time Barney and I were confined to the wickiup. We talked to each other a lot. I felt toward him as I would have toward my brother. We talked about the old school days in Austin. We talked about the poker game with Ben Thompson. We talked about Barney's cattle drive and vowed to try it together when we got free. There was some reserve between us, as there must always be, but we got closer even than we had ever been and unbent all our secrets. I told him about Ellen and planned a wedding with Barney as best man. That was the first time I had actually faced the prospect of marrying the girl. We would have the wedding in Austin and throw a fandango at Dutch John's and shoot up the place and punch a lot of noses and drink all the whiskey in the county. It was great fun to talk about.

When the weather broke, they came and got us. They tied our arms and delivered me to Octavio's wickiup. They stripped Barney naked and turned him over to the women. I could hear them screeching outside. I struggled to go out, but the bandits held me. They threw me down at Octavio's feet. He was sitting on a rug and had probably been there all through the mourning period, as in a trance. I think he did not know me until my shouts and curses made him open his eyes.

"Let him go!" I said.

"They demand him," said Octavio.

"You're the chief," I said. "You know he's innocent."

Octavio closed his one eye for a time while the cries and screeches outside grew louder. Then he opened his eye again and said, "No, I think he is not innocent. I think Eagle Dancer is right. I think you brought the sickness."

Most of the rest of this I will skip over, as I do not like to write of it. They beat me some and dragged me out to watch part of what they did to Barney. The women hacked him up with knives. They ripped him with flints. At Eagle Dancer's direction, they made him stand on a rock and curse God. They made him deny Christ. Eagle Dancer was very keen on that, thinking it would please Octavio, but the chief stayed inside his wickiup and I do not know if he heard it. I must stress in this journal, for whatever good it may do him if there is an afterlife, that the creature who performed thus on the rock was not Barney Swift but was instead a bloody hunk of meat and agonized nerves with no mind left, merely a quivering thing, not Barney Swift at all.

At last they carried this hunk of meat over to a sharp stake that had been set in the ground. The stake was about four feet high. They lifted up the meat, sat it on the stake and then let it slide slowly down. That procedure took some time. Even now I can hear the thin high wail that came from the meat. Toward the end, Eagle Dancer pushed down on the meat so that the stake near came out the top of it, and the wail ceased. Many of the people ate little pieces of the meat, for that is powerful medicine.

I had another audience with Octavio. I cursed him until I was exhausted. Every few minutes Eagle Dancer would hit me with a club and knock me down. I lost several teeth in this way. When I finally realized that this was getting me no place except toward the grave, I shut up. Octavio, who looked much older, still sat cross-legged on his rug as he spoke.

"You are dangerous," he said to me. "You have brought the sickness. You will destroy The People. We are friends no more. I must kill you. But I owe you my life from many years ago. I will let you leave this place and will give you a chance to escape. Then I will hunt you down and kill you. I swear that, McGill. You are too dangerous to The People."

I, of course, made a similar threat to him, calling him a one-eyed coon and promising him a highly painful departure from this life, which resulted in Eagle Dancer attempting to beat my brains out. At last they took me outside and sat me on a burro. I must have been a pathetic, ludicrous sight, with my long legs dragging on the ground and my head beaten and bloody and my body shaking in the cold. They gave me my Henry rifle because Octavio remembered it had belonged to my father, but it was empty of cartridges. They gave me my

Bowie knife and nothing else. They whacked the burro with a rawhide lariat, and I could hear the coons laughing and cat-calling as we started down the path out of the stronghold, with me clinging to the burro's neck, wondering if I could hold to my consciousness as well.

16

A sandstorm saved me. The storm blew up from the northwest. I saw it coming as a huge orange cloud that covered the
sun. Hours before it reached me, my nostrils were clogged
with it. Despite the difficulty, I kept going through the storm,
knowing it would cover my tracks. I was certain Octavio
would come after me. Without tracks to follow, he would
have to guess at my destination. The obvious place for me to
go was to Juárez, thence across the Rio Grande to El Paso.
Octavio would figure I would turn off to confuse him, maybe
back toward Ojinaga and Presidio, maybe toward any of
several little border towns. So I took a chance and continued
straight toward Juárez, or straight near as I could reckon as I
hunched over on my burro with my legs drawn up and my
torn shirt around my head, the sand stinging my body and
dimming my eyes.

I was very lucky. I arrived in Juárez almost starved and
expiring of thirst, but I was alive. I sold the burro for a dollar,
which I spent on a steak dinner. That night I sneaked around
behind a hotel where the wash was hanging and outfitted
myself with a nice new shirt. I slept in a stable and awoke in

the straw hearing chickens clucking below me. The door banged open and an old coon in a high-peaked black hat peered up at me with no curiosity, as though he found a desperate scoundrel in the loft every morning. After wandering the streets of El Paso all day, I found work as a bull-whacker on a freight train going to Santa Fe. It was to be a large train guarded by four squads of Cavalry, which meant there was nothing to fear from Octavio. Where I wanted to go was back to Austin, as I had quite a yearning to see Ellen C. Baggett, but I had no money and no horse and did not want her or her relatives to set eyes on me in such a condition.

We arrived in Santa Fe without adventure. Taking my pay, meager though it was, I sat in a monte game at a gambling house operated by Señora Arias. The town was full of freighters and a number of mountain men had come down from the high country to sell furs and pelts and squander their money, which I was glad to make as easy for them as I could. The game of monte, so called because of the mountain of cards that is left after dealing, is played with a Spanish deck with suits of Clubs, Swords, Suns, and Cups, and the cards came into my hands as though my mother's Spaniard ancestors were controlling my fortune. I played all through that first night and walked out in the morning richer by nearly one thousand dollars.

From a distance, then, the town of Santa Fe looked like a wall of dirt and clay that rose up from the desert at the edge of the mountains. The houses were connected, so that children ran along the rooftops where grass grew. Inside the wall were pleasant patios. I walked along the street past the black-haired women, their cheeks and lips rouged, their faces white with flour-paste powder, rebozos over their shoulders, their dresses low-cut at the breast, their ankles showing. I found a boardinghouse that had been whitewashed with mica and looked presentable. A lady who was painted up with algeria showed me a room that had whitewashed adobe walls, covered to shoulder height with calico to protect clothing from the gypsum that easily rubbed off. There was a Spanish fireplace in the corner, built so that the logs stood on end, and the bed had a goose-feather mattress and an eiderdown quilt. After the way I had been living, that room seemed grand as a king's bedchamber. I rented it, ordered some decent clothes and paid for both in advance. That was fortunate, for after sleeping all day I returned to the monte game at Señora Arias's and lost all but the fifty dollars I had stashed in my room. A mountain man called Poulsen put up a display that night of destroying the establishment.

Whooping, stomping his moccasins on the floor, Poulsen whipped off his beaver hat, let his blond hair fall to his shoulders and danced up and down beside the bar, proclaiming in mountain man speech that he was the issue of a coupling between a cougar and an alligator, that he used skunk musk for toilet scent, picked his teeth with a live porcupine, could chew up a keg of nails and spit bullets a mile and a half. He said he took a fourteen-foot grizzly bear to the governor's ball and waltzed all night and the first eight bears that tried to cut in he kicked to death without missing a step. He said God crossed the street to keep out of his way. He said he had saved a wagon train from the Utes by using his pecker as a bridge across the Yellowstone River and that later the same instrument had been employed as a flagpole at Fort Kearny. He said he had laid waste to armies, was the scourge of the Mormons, swallowed whole buffalos when hungry, had been personally complimented by the Queen of England on his beautiful singing voice, and so forth. "This chile," he yelled, "in life a puzzle, in death a mystery!" When he paused for breath, two ladies who worked in the place ambled past and he followed them up the stairs. Señora Arias kept dealing. I saw that scene repeated a score of times. Poulsen, himself, did it eight straight nights and then went back into the mountains for more furs.

I went to work for Señora Arias, who was a nice lady from an old Santa Fe family, not at all the rock-hearted wench that gambling ladies are made out to be (and usually are), and settled into a routine, though going to see Ellen Baggett was still uppermost in my mind. Between what I earned at Señora Arias's, and what I made on my own at other houses in Santa

Fe, where gambling is a favorite sport, I began to accumulate quite a pile, by my standards. In the fall we had a big fiesta where they burned a statue of Gloom and everybody was drunk and riotous for three days. Christmas came and the plaza was covered with snow and the buildings were outlined with rows of candles. I heard several times of Octavio. His bandits were raiding as they pleased in West Texas, northern Mexico, and southern New Mexico, though they were never reported north of Albuquerque. One dispatch in the *New Mexican* said "This murderous savage called Octavio has a blind eye that looks like an onion." There was talk of taking the 9th Cavalry and the 15th Infantry out of Santa Fe to chase Octavio in the south. I went to Fort Marcy, which was no fort but merely a garrison below the north hill, to volunteer as a Cavalry scout. It was in my thoughts at all times to go and kill Octavio for what he had allowed his coons to do to Barney Swift, but I had not determined to try it alone. To me, the death of Barney was no trivial deprivation. I knew I would encounter Octavio sooner or later, and it seemed a good idea to have the Cavalry with me, although sometimes the Cavalry was less help than a troop of empty saddles would have been.

The citizens of Santa Fe became aroused and petitioned the Governor of New Mexico Territory to request the Army to stay where it was, as there were supposed to be plenty of soldiers in the south to protect the towns and settlements there. The commander at Fort Marcy let me out of my pledge, promising to send for me if he ever did pursue the renegade. In the three or four days that I lounged about the Marcy garrison, I met and was in the company of Crazy Face Wiggins, the famous half-breed scout, a White Mountain Apache on his mother's side and, near as I could tell, an ape on his father's. He was a thick, squatty devil with very long arms and short legs, built somewhat like Eagle Dancer but more powerful. Had he been hairy, I would have felt inclined to capture him and sell him to the St. Louis Zoo. Crazy Face Wiggins had an interesting philosophy. He was forever abandoning his troop or patrol and going off alone to slaughter some Navajo or Zuñi or Hopi or Pueblo Indian who, I am sure, could have been blamed for some crime or other were his history examined long and carefully enough. Crazy Face was such a good scout, however, that he was always forgiven, though constant fines took all his pay. "I don't care about that," he told me when I asked if the fines weren't annoying. "I don't worry about ghosts, either. When they're dead, they're done with. I like to kill is all. But I don't like to kill the Army way. A sheep-brain captain is liable to get me murdered in a fool charge if I stay next to him. I'd rather do it on my own. When I'm killing, I'm getting close to finding out what makes folks tick. I like to watch the life go out of them." As he talked, he would get excited and pace up and down in his gibbon-like manner, fingertips almost dragging in the dirt. "You get a fellow down and start cutting on him—oh, my— and you can see him dying. There's one moment when you can just about grab hold the life as it leaves him. You can near get your hands on it. Oh my! Yes, one day I will." He said he kept on as a scout, rather than devoting his entire time to his hobby, because the Army assured him of a meal when he felt like it. Later he went with Custer, I hear, with the well known Major Reno, but I did not see his name in the published lists of the dead after that fracas. He's probably still out there somewhere.

That was a grand period in Santa Fe. I was there in June of 1875 when Lamy got promoted to Archbishop and the bands played at the ceremonies at the rear of St. Michael's College. If I was not gambling or doing some odd jobs for Señora Arias, I often hung about the bar at the Bank Exchange Hotel, for the talk there was of a lively nature though the decorations were a bit too female for my taste. Whenever the indoor life began to depress me, I would camp in the mountains for a few days. A man needs to be in the mountains now and then to remind himself of his true size. There was one place up in the Sangre de Cristo where I could camp in a meadow and above me ridges rising through clouds looked like ships on a gray-white sea. But mostly I stayed in the town. It was a woolly place. The calabozo was usually full. I have, here in my house, a poster that I took off a wall only last spring, as I needed the paper for bullet-making during my quest but never got around to using it.

The poster says:

NOTICE!

To thieves, thugs, fakirs & Bunko Steerers, among whom are J. J. Harlin alias "Off Wheeler," Saw Dust Charlie, Wm Hedges, Billy the Kid, Billy Mullen, Little Jack, The Cuter, Pock-Marked Kid and about twenty others. If found within the limits of this city after 10 o'clock P.M. on this night you will be invited to attend a *Grand Neck Tie Party*, expense of which will be borne by about 100 substantial citizens.

I got that poster in Las Vegas, a little town in the Pecos Mountains, in New Mexico Territory, close enough to Santa Fe to speak for the capitol. Many desperadoes came and went at Santa Fe. The trade was good. The gambling was heated. There were many fandangos. The mountain men would dance like Indians, howling, whirling, doing little shuffles and hop-steps, and would kidnap a few women and knife a few *pelados* and otherwise enjoy themselves. We had some of the more formal *bailes*, to one of which, at the governor's palace, I had the pleasure of escorting Señora Arias and smoking a cheroot with the governor himself. That was in 1876, on the occasion of the 6th Cavalry replacing the 9th. By then I was about ready to leave Santa Fe. I had purchased this land on the plateau rim north of Fernandez and the Taos pueblo, and I had my pile built up, and my mind was turning steadily toward the hills of Austin and the girl who I hoped was waiting there.

17

I journeyed to Austin by way of Kansas City, St. Louis, Little Rock, and Fort Worth. It was pleasing to be home again. I came down among the cedar hills and the clear streams with a feeling of great nostalgia. At once I rode out to the house of Ellen C. Baggett's aunt and uncle. In my agitated state, I had been knocking on the door for several minutes before I realized the house was empty. I peered through the windows and saw that the furniture was covered with dust-cloths. A neighbor came across the road with the information that the aunt and uncle had gone to the East for some purpose and had taken the girl with them. The neighbor seemed hard put to keep from grinning at me, and then I noted I still had a bouquet of flowers in my hand. Disgustedly, I flung the flowers to the ground, mounted my new-bought Tennessee horse and rode off in the mood to do up the town.

Perhaps my temper was inconsiderate, as I had not talked to Ellen Baggett in nearly three years and had never written her a letter. But she had promised to wait, or so it seemed to me, and had gone back on her word. I was by this time twenty-six years old. I had sewed a generous amount of wild oats, as the expression goes, and would not have been loathe to try settling down, had she been there.

Bursting into Dutch John's, I ordered drinks for the house and, when recognized, shook hands all around. I had been thinking to visit Barney Swift's parents, but I no longer felt like it, and what could I have told them that they would have wanted to hear? From Santa Fe I had written a note to inform them Barney had been killed by Indians in Mexico. Would the details of his death, the description of him up croaking on that rock, have eased the loss for his family? I thought not.

However, several questions about Barney were asked me in Dutch John's. I replied that he had, in fact, been killed by Jacob Charles Gerhardt, who was remembered by some locally. They were amazed to learn Gerhardt was now the infamous Octavio or Gotch Eye. Immediately there was shouting of organizing a vigilante band to seek out Octavio and hang him. The idea struck me as fitting, but I did not wish to ride with a group made up mostly of amateurs, as they are too dangerous. I made no definite comment. During the afternoon the customers at Dutch John's worked themselves to a high pitch, organizing their lynch crew, naming officers, discussing equipment and procedures, vowing to be off at dawn. The sun, I knew, would find them drunk and asleep, and a number of obstacles to the hanging project would arise by the morrow, and they would be still talking about it for months.

Some people curse their limitations. I have always been grateful for mine, as it is awesome to consider how much trouble I might have got into were there no boundary to my strength or imagination. That afternoon in Dutch John's is an example. We tossed coins at a spittoon. We shot out the lights. We chased women. We marched up and down the streets and frightened the citizens. I rode my thoroughbred into the saloon and sat with one leg hooked over the saddle horn, drinking, while the horse caused several messes. I had a fight with an old acquaintance. The sheriff came and asked me kindly if I would tarry around town no longer than necessary. We took the trousers off a scalawag who had claimed to see merit in the Reconstruction and ran him down Congress Avenue, along the new sidewalk in front of the Hancock store and into the lobby of the Sutor Hotel, where he treed and was forced to perform oratory in his shirttails. We did all of that, and more, while I was yet weary from the road and depressed from the idea of losing Ellen Baggett. Had I been fit and truly boisterous, rather than tired and in a sour humor, no doubt it would have been jail for me before that party ended.

However, the funning began to pall on me after a while and I fell to brooding. I was standing at the bar with my foot on the rail, looking down at the gutter at approximately the spot where my father's head had laid when he died there. Looking down past the toe of my Ute moccasin-boot, a new pair of which I had bought in Santa Fe, I fancied I could see a blotch of blood spreading into the gutter amidst the cigar butts, paper scraps, and spittle. Such a vision contributed to my morose air. I was about to go to the stable and fetch my horse and set out upon some aimless wandering when the bartender said, "Hey there, Peter, we got a batch of letters for you." He produced a box from the manager's office. In it were fifty-odd letters from Ellen Baggett, the most recent dated only a month back.

I retired to my room at the St. Charles Hotel and pored over the letters with eager heart. For the first year she had written twice a month, the early letters warm with friend-ship and regard. For the year of 1875, by which time I was in Santa Fe, her letters totaled more than a dozen. One mentioned having heard of Barney's death. She said she knew I was in Santa Fe but did not write me there because she had no address, nor did she know how long I would stay. For 1876, the letters were less frequent and a tone of exasper-ation crept in, as she had received no word from me and had begun to wonder seriously about her future, since she was eighteen years old and ready for a woman's responsibility. The latest letter, dated in September, made my blood leap. In it she informed me she was going off to Baltimore, Maryland, to attend Mrs. Merrilee Pritchett's School for Young Ladies. That was at the urging of her aunt. Ellen Baggett said she

would be a student at Mrs. Pritchett's for two years, at the
end of which time, not having had any communication from
me, she would marry an Eastern gentleman, as her education
would have so prepared her, and would raise a large family
and live a life of gentility and style, not regretting one jot
having missed a life among cockleburs, dust storms,
murderous savages, smelly goats, drouths, blowflies, ticks,
cactus, mesquite, cedar, empty spaces, water wells, outdoor
toilets (to have mentioned such a topic meant she was
growing steadily more angry as she wrote), lawlessness, hard
work, fear, loneliness, profane men, and the other things I
seemed to like so well. Now then, I thought, that was not fair.
I have never been partial to goats, hard work, or fear. As for
profane men, I have always tried to stay in touch with the
nobler emotions.

I took a look at myself in the glass, examining the new
scars of the past three years. Fortunately, the missing teeth
were along the jawbones so that while eating Texas beefsteak
was not the delight it once had been, my smile was not
impaired. I sat on the bed and drank from a jug of bourbon
whiskey and thought about Ellen C. Baggett. The rosiness of
her, the sweetness of her touch, and the flattery of her devo-
tion were quite nice to think about. I still could not get
entirely over the notion that anybody who loved me must
have something wrong with them, but in Ellen's case I could
place the blame on the ignorance of youth and that would
not be a bad mark against her personality.

Considering her as a wife, as I had shocked myself by realizing I had begun to do, called for more careful thought than
whether or not she was rosy, sweet, and devoted. A wife had
to be a good worker, first thing. She had to be cheerful and
smile often. She had to be middling pretty. (I had observed
that a man who married a woman purely for her beauty was
soon in more trouble than he could handle, for a beautiful
woman, unless she is a holy lady like my mother, sets up
strife, and if she has beauty and little else, she forces her man
to try to maintain the position of number one in her affec-
tions at all times, which is a strain and leads to conduct of the

worst sort.) Of course, a man would not want to marry a woman unless he could be proud of her for something or other, for her homemaking or her bright and entertaining manner or her ability to crochet, etc. Ellen had several good qualities, plus a great deal of spunk. I found her very cozy to be alone with and I could imagine how I would swagger when escorting her to a dance. Also she had, as far as I knew, virtue. I admire and respect a really good and virtuous man or woman who behaves slightly less well than my mother thinks people should behave, and at odd times in my life I have dreamed of being able to be virtuous, but that is hard to explain to those I have associated with.

At the end of several hours of reading Ellen's letters, contemplating courses of action and drinking from the jug of bourbon, I arose, put on my coat, packed my new cloth bag, paid my hotel bill and went to the stable. There I arranged for storage of my horse and my weapons save for my derringer, Colts pistol, and Bowie knife—a minimal assortment for a wayfarer. I walked over to the stage line. In those days the trip by stage from Austin to Dallas took nearly four days and cost ten cents a mile, or about twenty dollars. The new Houston & Texas Central Railroad was nearly as cheap and more than twice as fast, depending on the number of break-downs. So I went to the station and purchased a ticket. Meanwhile, I had bought another jug of bourbon and was nipping at it liberally. Had I not bought that bourbon, I cannot say in all truthfulness that I would have done what I did next, though probably I would. In any event, I got aboard the rail-road train and set forth for Baltimore, Maryland, to locate Mrs. Merrilee Pritchett's School for Young Ladies.

18

The railroads are a curse. They are laying iron tracks across the grasslands. They are bringing noise, filth, fire, and ash. Most distressing of all, they are spreading white men throughout the country. When taken individually, white men can be very decent. Some, like Barney Swift, are as fine as ever a human could be. But when encountered in the mass, white men are sorry rascals, indeed. Their prominent characteristics are greed, selfishness, arrogance, scurrility, impatience, vanity, and deceitfulness. In the mass, they are a rabble that swarms like termites, gnawing up all that is beautiful and reducing it to their own insignificant dimension. They have not the independence of the brown Indian, the joy of the Mexican or the strength of the Negro. For the main part, their ancestors were not even of good stock in their homelands. Yet they conquer, as rabble inevitably must. And I am a white man, willingly or not, though I sometimes feel that I am descended from Irish kings and Spanish nobility and have the spirit of a coon.

From Dallas I rode the Texas & Pacific over to Longview and thence continued to Memphis, Nashville, Charleston,

Washington, D.C., and Baltimore. It was a journey recalled for the cinders in my eyes, the soot on my face, the continual jouncing and the poor food which caused me to drink more than is beneficial to the liver. I arrived in Baltimore at twilight, got a room at a hotel near the railroad station and inquired the location of Mrs. Pritchett's School. Nobody in that neighborhood could tell me, so I bathed, had dinner and slept and the next morning went to a newspaper office. As I was still wearing my Ute boots and broad-brimmed beaver hat, and the handle of my Bowie knife caused a noticeable projection in my frock coat, though I had left my Colts in my room and had concealed my derringer in my waistband, the editor at the newspaper became excited at my appearance.

In that year the newspapers had devoted an unnatural amount of their toil to the frontier. Scarcely did I pick up a newspaper in Santa Fe, Austin, or on my journey to Baltimore that I did not read of some great adventure of daredevil deeds. It was difficult to tell which had agitated the authors most—the so-called "last stand" of the fool Custer, in June; or the killing of Bill Heycox by Jack McCall in Deadwood Gulch in August. While riding the train I had read a book called *Perils of the Frontier* about Kit Carson and had perused Frank Starr's *The Fighting Trapper; Or, Kit Carson to the Rescue*, which cost me ten cents and was overpriced. On the cover of that paper book, Carson was depicted killing two coons by stabbing one in the chest and one in the back simultaneously. The literature likewise informed me Carson was the terror of bullies, killed mountain lions barehanded, leaped his horse off high cliffs, rescued white women from the Apaches, caused panic among hordes of savages by his presence, was the chum of royalty and could shoot the eye out of a wild turkey at five hundred yards. That seemed to me a furious lot of activity for a fellow who stood about five-feet-six-inches, weighed about one hundred and thirty-five pounds, was stoop-shouldered, had red hair and blue eyes and seldom spoke. I saw Carson on two occasions when I was a young buffalo hunter and of course he lived in Taos with some other famous mountain men like the Bents and

Ceran St. Vrain, but that was before I moved there, and Carson was now dead some eight years or so.

More amazing was what the newspapers and magazines were printing about Jim Heycox, or Haycox, or Hickock, who had taken the name Wild Bill, as it was a popular name at the time among a certain element and was also favored along with the name Buffalo Bill by Heycox's friend, Cody, who I saw him with in New Mexico Territory in the late 1860s. *Harper's Magazine* printed several stories about Hickock's physique, glowing curls, marksmanship, and derring-do. What I recalled was Ben Thompson had told me Heycox was a grafter who surrounded himself with scoundrels, thugs, petty thieves, and other low types. But Thompson was not on the most cordial terms with Heycox, who had killed Thompson's friend, Phil Coe, by shooting him in the stomach in the Bull's Head Saloon in Abilene. The young Wes Hardin had recently fooled Heycox with the Border Shift, I had heard. Hardin had held his pistols out to Heycox butt first, then had spun them and got the drop, resulting in much laughter. I am not sure I believe that tale any more than the rest of the romances involving Heycox.

(But what flabbergasted me most were the stories that appeared in subsequent years concerning a boy I knew around Santa Fe by the name of Henry Antrim, later Henry McCarty or William Bonny. He was called Kid because he looked like one, being a runt in size and youthful in features. During the Lincoln County troubles, the papers referred to him as Billy the Kid. I suppose he was dangerous if he got the drop, as any murderer is. Now, at this writing, the Kid has joined Carson and Heycox in the grave.)

The newspaper office was an untidy place. People rushed about through the small room between the desks and the spikes that were cluttered with paper. I noted that some of them stopped and stared at me as I spoke to the editor. I thought they were funny-looking, also, but had the manners not to show it. The editor was a small fellow with a green eyeshade on his head and clips at his biceps to keep his cuffs up out of the ink, I suppose. He looked to me like a gambler in the manner of dress, though a cheap sort of gambler and probably a poor one. He couldn't understand what I wanted. Instead of telling me where Mrs. Merrilee Pritchett's School for Young Ladies was, he began asking me questions. Where was I from? Texas. Was that a real Bowie knife sticking out of my coat? Certainly. What was my name? I told him, politely. People were gathering. I was getting irritated. He started questioning me about life on the frontier.

"Sir," I said, "I am not here to lecture on life on the frontier so you can fill your newspaper with the usual bosh about that topic."

"What bosh?" said he.

"Those wild deeds you print."

"You mean they don't happen?"

"They are greatly exaggerated," I said.

"Have you ever killed an Indian?"

"Well, of course," I said.

I heard people gasp. As I looked around the room, their faces were moronic with awe. Nearest I can describe them was they had the same expression that was on Barney Swift's face the first time he saw an albino.

"Hundreds?" said the editor, writing on a piece of paper.

"No."

"Dozens?"

"I suppose dozens, yes."

Another gasp. This was ridiculous. I repeated that I wished to locate the school and informed the editor that I wanted to find Ellen Baggett, an acquaintance from Austin. He wrote down her name. I assumed his memory was faulty. And where did I meet her? he wanted to know.

"In a Comanche camp. She was a prisoner." I saw the looks on their faces. "But not for long," I said. "I got her out of there before the first night."

"You rescued this girl from the Comanches?"

"Well, yes, I took her away from them. What would you have done?"

Activity had ceased. People crowded in so close that it

was becoming stuffy.

"Could I see that knife?" asked a young man.

After warning him to beware of the keenness of the blade, I gave it to him. He took it in his right hand and the weight of it slammed his hand down onto the editor's desk. "My God," the young man said.

"Have you ever scalped anybody?" a woman asked.

I nodded. "With this knife?" she asked. When I nodded again, the young man jerked his hand back and left the knife on the desk. I returned it to its scabbard. From all sides came questions. I answered graciously as I could. Yes, I had seen Carson and Heycox and Custer, though I was not personally acquainted. Yes, I had fought Apaches and Comanches. No, I had never fought Cheyenne or Sioux. Yes, I thought Apaches were the best fighters and would have been better had they been truly interested in horses, as the Comanches were. Yes, I thought the Indians were doomed to lose, not only because of the white man's overwhelming advantage in numbers and equipment but also because the Indians had no political unity. Yes, when the Indians united, as a few of them did against Custer, they were formidable, but they hardly ever got together on anything. No, you did not cut off a man's head when you scalped him; you only lifted a circle of flesh and hair from his crown. Yes, I had killed buffalos. No, I did not consider it a risky proposition or a sport to brag about. We went on in this vein for a while, and finally I allowed my impatience to become obvious.

"Ah, but you must be off to fetch your young lady," the editor said.

The gentleman supplied me with a carriage and two of his employees to drive it. He insisted, saying one was a good driver and the other knew the way. They stacked a large box in the front of the carriage and we rolled off through the streets of Baltimore. Mrs. Pritchett's School was in a red two-story house that looked like the rest of the houses on the street. The houses were crowded together closer than the people had been to me in the newspaper office—an eccentricity of Baltimoreans, I believe. As I walked up to the door and hammered with the knocker, the young men were taking their box out of the carriage.

The lady who opened the door started to slam it again, but I caught it with my foot. I do not like to be unkind regarding people's looks, as the ugliest person can turn out to be quite worthwhile, but I have seen handsomer faces in a barrel of pickles. I inquired for Mrs. Pritchett.

"Mrs. Pritchett has been dead for twenty-five years," the lady said.

"I trust she has left someone to look after her school," I said.

"I am the house mother," said she.

"Then I wish to see Ellen C. Baggett," I replied and walked in.

The parlor was an ornate arrangement of sofas, carpets, paintings, and lamps. The lady followed me, protesting that Ellen was having a literature class at the moment. I walked down the hall toward where I could hear voices. The lady said she would call the police. I pushed open a door. A dozen young ladies turned in surprise to look up at me. Sitting near a window that opened onto a green lawn with trees was Ellen Baggett.

All those young ladies looking at me almost made me timid. But I knew this was no time to falter.

"Ellen," I said, "let's go home."

"Peter!" she said.

There was a great ruckus. I remembered to take off my hat. The teacher screeched at me. The house mother ran off to call the police. Ellen just sat there. "Pardon," I said to the teacher. Excusing myself at each step, I walked over to Ellen's chair and took her hand. She looked a bit older, not quite so plump, but still rosy.

"Come back later," she said.

"There's no later," I said.

"Come back later and we'll talk," she said.

"I can't do that," I said and hauled her out of her chair and began marching her out of the room. The teacher stood in the doorway with her arms outflung, barring us. "Pardon, ma'am," I said, thrusting her aside as gently as I could. She fell down and cried. Ellen was kind of balky. "You want to go with me or not?" I said.

"Peter, it's been three years."

"Then let's don't waste any more time."

She allowed me to guide her down the hall by her elbow.

"You want to pack?" I said.

"Pack?"

"We're going to get married and go to Texas."

She broke loose and ran away. There was so much screaming and laughing and scurrying around that I could barely hear what I was thinking about, which was that this was no place for me to be any longer than necessary. As I was standing there thinking, the front door flew open and the house mother rushed in with a hefty fellow in a blue uniform. He was dressed much like the doorman at my hotel but was wearing a badge. The house mother jabbered at me. I looked the fellow over. He was a policeman, all right, but he didn't even have a pistol, unless it was hidden in his hat. I could hardly see how he could hope to enforce any laws. The two young men had come in and they were talking to the policeman. I had about decided to forget the entire affair and go on home alone, when I heard footsteps and Ellen ran down the hall carrying a bag that had bits of garments sticking out of it. The policeman stepped aside and the young men ran outside again. I grabbed Ellen's arm and we hurried toward the door of the madhouse.

When I opened the door, somebody yelled, "Freeze!" A flash of light exploded in my eyes. I threw Ellen to the cobblestones to my right and dived to my left, drawing my derringer and shooting at the light. I rolled over and came up with the Bowie knife and moved toward the light in a swift crouch. Although half-blinded, I aimed to finish our would-be assassin. Ellen's voice halted me. I saw the two young men sitting on the ground, looking shocked, the wreckage of a box on legs lying between them. When the ruckus had quieted, Ellen explained to me that it was a camera. I apologized to the young men. We got into the carriage and they drove us to City Hall. There, to my amazement, was the editor. He had arranged for us to be married. I had forgotten the ring, but he sent a runner off to get one.

I glanced over at Ellen and began to doubt. Was she as attractive as I had thought? Would she be troublesome? Boring? I had been a bachelor for a long time. I thought about my high mountain camps, my hunting and fishing, my drinking and gambling. Was it possible that the addition of another person to my life would interfere greatly with my freedom? I started getting scared. But there was another side to it. She could be a help if she chose. Having my own family might be nice. Belonging somewhere could be an advantage of sorts, if viewed with the proper perspective. Anyhow, it was too late to get out of it. The runner had come back with the ring. We stood up for the ceremony, with the editor as best man and some woman I had never seen before as maid of honor. In a few minutes it was all over. I kissed Ellen. She was my wife. I had never formally asked her.

We spent the first night of our honeymoon at the hotel in Baltimore. The next day, when we checked out, there was a commotion in the lobby. At least fifty people were staring at us. Children asked me to write my name on pieces of paper. People shrank back as we walked through the lobby. Outside, a carriage awaited. The carriage was decked with flowers and had a banner that said *GOOD LUCK MR AND MRS MCGILL* on the side of it. A brass band was playing. I was bewildered but saw the editor in the crowd and he waved. Two bottles of champagne were in a bucket in the back seat. The bucket was marked *Compliments of The Sun*. By the time we got to the station, with the brass band marching behind us, the drums and trumpets had summoned a crowd of a thousand or more.

The editor asked us to go up on a platform that had a banner with my name on it. He introduced Ellen and me to the Mayor of Baltimore. "I don't understand this," I said. The editor smiled. The mayor made a speech. He recited a number of exploits usually attributed to Carson or Heycox and then said I had done them. I started to protest. "Our modest hero," the mayor called me. Ellen seemed to be very proud, so I sat back and drank champagne and let the mayor rave. Then they made me stand up. The people yelled, "Speech! Speech!" I couldn't think of a speech, and I sat down. They kept yelling. I got up again and when they were quiet I said, "Who's got some more champagne?" They laughed and clapped. The train whistle blew. Ellen and I shook hands with strangers all the way onto the train, where we found we had a compartment. Not until the last hiss of steam and the first jolting motion of the train were we alone, and still we could see people through the windows waving at us.

"They are very friendly folks here in Baltimore," I said. Then Ellen showed me the newspaper. On the front page was a headline that went down for rows, telling how the big frontiersman and Indian fighter, Wild Pete McGill, had come to town to marry the girl he had saved from the Comanches. The story went on and on with the most disgusting tripe. In some of it there was a grain of truth, but the writer had elaborated to such an extent that I could not identify myself. A large drawing of Ellen and me was beside the story.

That was my brush with the newspapers in the fall of 1876. Our journey back to Texas entailed the usual bouncing and railroad mishaps, but we did not mind. When we got to Dallas I booked a suite of rooms at La Grand Hotel. It was the swellest in town. They had a chandelier in the lobby that it would have taken me ten paces to walk around. Our sitting room and bedroom had buzzers which we could press to cause the appearance of a waiter or a maid. There was a telegraph office in the rotunda and an excellent billiard parlor in the lobby next to the Exchange Bank.

For our first dinner at La Grand Hotel, we had sea turtle soup and a goose liver paste Ellen had learned about at Mrs. Pritchett's, and she had lobster while I ordered roasted black bear from a menu that listed more than seventy items. We drank wine and were very pleased.

19

When we got back to Austin, I bought a farm in the hills across the river. The farm had a fieldstone house and a wooden barn already on it. They were the labors of a Dutchman who had died. As I had no trade that would adapt to the life of a family man, I cast about for a profession and finally went into the business of raising goats. I have made it clear what my opinion of goats is, but I found that being forced to do something you do not like can be profitable both financially and spiritually, as long as you do not have to do it often enough to get too humble. Goats were the perfect animal to raise in those hills. The grass was too scant to support large numbers of cattle, and bringing in feed would have been too dear. Goats, though, are tough and do not flinch from dining on anything they can digest, which covers a remarkable range. I had some good sheep dogs to help me, and there was a family of Mexicans not far off with children I could hire when cheap labor was necessary. Also I had some money left from my Santa Fe pile. I pretty much avoided Dutch John's and such places, and we had a fine year.

I wrote to my mother, who was still at San Juan Mission,

and told her I had got married and said I would like to bring Ellen to visit her, or else that my mother should come to visit us. After two weeks I received a brief reply that said my mother was involved with her holy duties but would let me know when it would be proper for us to see her. In March of 1877 I became convinced Ellen was pregnant. She had worked hard fixing up our house and caring for our garden, while I handled our two milk cows and took care of the goats. Taking care of goats mostly entails chasing them. The perverse little brutes have a way of getting up into the rocks on some inaccessible bluff and looking down at you with a mouthful of mesquite beans. More than once I was tempted to haul out my rifle and shoot the smirks off their faces. But my dogs could usually outwit the goats, and I doubt that I lost many.

The morning I decided Ellen was pregnant, she was pestering me for a hunk of sharp cheese. She had been ill before breakfast for several days. Then she began to make illogical demands for sharp cheese, which I had never before known her to eat. Thinking to humor her, I rode over to the farm of a Dutchman in the next valley and purchased a box of sharp cheese and a crock of buttermilk. On the way back, it occurred to me that Ellen was pregnant. I had heard tales of women demanding absurd items in such a condition, but always I had considered that a myth. However, I rushed into our house, gave her the cheese and sat at the table to watch.

"What are you looking at?" she said crossly.

"I am watching you eat this cheese you had a mad desire for."

"I don't want it. The sight of it makes me sick," she said.

So I put her into the wagon and we drove to town to consult a doctor. He confirmed my suspicion. We worked on through the spring and summer. One night in September, Ellen awakened me and said, "It is time." I put my ear against her belly. Beneath the warm flesh I felt a hard jerk. The baby was moving in there. I rode to get the midwife. She was the Mexican whose children I hired. After bringing her back, I rode to get the doctor in town. Galloping through the darkness on my Tennessee horse, I was thinking how glad I was that Ellen didn't have to have her baby in Apache fashion, squatting, with a midwife to bury the placenta to keep the animals from eating it. But I suppose there is not really much difference. I had watched Ellen rubbing her legs on the sheets until her skin was bruised and raw. She had bit her lips bloody, and her face was covered with sweat, and her eyes were big with pain. She had ceased to recognize me, but she called my name when the pains hit her. She screamed and cursed and writhed as though under torture, and there was nothing I could do, no contribution to make, no way to ease her or to share her experience.

Daylight was coming when I got back with the doctor. From the house, we heard a cry. I ran inside, prepared for trouble. There stood the midwife with a tiny bundle in her arms. Smiling, she pulled aside a cloth and showed me a small red ugly face that seemed to be peppered with mosquito bites.

"What is it?" I said.

"Your son," said the midwife.

"What's wrong with it?"

"Nothing is wrong with him. He's a very strong, healthy boy!"

I looked at the baby and wondered if he could actually be a part of me. I felt nothing for him except a sort of relief that he was here at last. I went to Ellen's bedside. She was pale and thin, but she knew me. "The boy is our foundation," she said. "We can build on him!" Then she slept. I went outside and watched the dawn strike the hills. I could hear the baby crying. He sounded very healthy.

A child causes a great change in your life. Where once I would have given no thought to jumping up and riding to Mexico, now I had a responsibility. To be honest, at first I did not take to it well. The boy, who we named Peter Paul McGill, was to me little more than a crying, slobbery, irritating creature, but to Ellen he was a source of wonder and joy. However, as the boy began to get older, as he learned to walk and to say words and to understand what I was telling him, I got more interested in him and more fond of him. By the time he was two years old and could respond to me with some degree of intelligence, I loved him. It is very difficult, I think, for a man to love a mewling little red baby. But a child that can reflect yourself, that is another matter.

I made a couple more efforts to see my mother, but she was too busy with her holy work. I wrote to ask if she wished to be present at the christening. She replied that she did not. As a result, we did not get around to an official Catholic christening. Ellen attended the Baptist Church whenever she attended any church at all, which was not often. As for me, I gave the Church little heed. It did not appear to me to matter whether the boy had water sprinkled on his head. For Paul's third birthday, we planned a trip to San Antonio and I wrote my mother once again.

Dear Peter, she answered. *I am glad to hear that all are well and the child is lively. But I do not think I could bear to see him or to meet your wife. The emotions would be too distracting. I must concentrate with all my mind and soul on loving God. Teach your son to love Him, and a miracle will befall you.*

She signed the letter "*María,*" which was one of her names although I had never heard her so addressed, and she had certainly never encouraged me to call her that.

For months the feeling had been deepening in me to return to the high country. Our goats were thriving and we were making a tidy living in the hills of Austin. But the mountains were drawing me. They were in my mind. I felt the need to climb. I wanted to be in the mountain air again and to see the big snows. Strangely enough, I wanted to be among The People again. I missed them; they had been a large part of my life's design. By the fall of 1880, there was hardly an Indian left in all of Texas. They had been driven onto reservations in Indian Territory north of the Red River. The chain of forts that once ran down the middle of Texas for protection against Indian raids had been abandoned or turned into towns rather than garrisons. The frontier had opened to all and was moving west. Austin was getting too tame for me. I was restless. The high country was beckoning.

Ellen's only relatives, her aunt and uncle, now lived in Memphis, Tennessee. We had made no close friends in Austin. When I suggested we move up to the land I owned on the plateau rim north of Fernandez, she agreed. The idea of it thrilled her. At twenty-three, she was a handsome young woman with a sparkling eye and an eagerness for life. We put our farm up for sale, took the train to Kansas City and then west to Santa Fe. The journey was exciting for all three of us. Little Paul was in a state of constant delight and amazement. Rather than tiring on the long trip, he seemed to get stronger and more inquisitive. It was plain he had my love for travel. Ellen was disappointed with her first sight of Santa Fe, but soon the charm of the place reached her.

The Atchison, Topeka & Santa Fe Railroad had come into the Lamy station, seventeen miles from town, a year earlier. The town had also changed in other ways. There were gas lamps on the plaza. Steam engines were operating. Prices had gone up. I had to pay four dollars a day to rent a horse and buggy. We spent a week at the Grand Central Hotel, and I gambled at Mr. Gold's without much luck. Señora Arias took Ellen and me to a grand *baile* at the governor's palace. The *New Mexican* was full of the exploits of William Bonny and the governor, Lew Wallace. Sheep and beef carcasses still hung in the open in front of the butcher shops. The mountains reared up to the north, urging me toward Fernandez. I bought a horse, a Morgan, the best horse I ever owned. I rode the Morgan up to Fernandez, then out to the rim and hired some Spaniards from Valdez to build my house and barn. When that was nearing completion, I returned to Santa Fe de San Francisco, bought a wagon and drove Ellen and little Paul up through the mountains, along the Great River, up to our new home.

Unfortunately, a reporter from the *New Mexican* wrote up the fact that I was moving to Fernandez and included some embarrassing stories of my adventures. We had scarcely got settled in our new home before two priests, alerted by the newspaper, knocked on our door. They were the two Franciscans, Fathers Higgins and Mulligan. Their Order had been expelled from New Mexico some fifty years previous, after the revolution, but had recently been allowed to return. Higgins and Mulligan worked in the mission and the church at the Taos pueblo, about ten miles from my home. There were two pueblos, each five stories high, on either side of a stream three miles from Fernandez. The place got its name from the Tewas, who called it Towih. The Indians at the pueblo had, of course, heard of me. They asked the priests to invite me to one of their ceremonies.

"I don't know how much you know about these Indians, McGill," Father Higgins said as Ellen was serving coffee in our parlor. I dare say I knew more about them than Higgins did, but Ellen knew almost nothing of them and I let Higgins talk. "They're an odd lot. Very superstitious. They believe gods live in everything. They think the idea of this life is to get through it without offending any of the gods, which is why they don't allow eccentricity or any change in customs or any show of emotion. Their gods demand visible prayers to mollify them. You see those in the sand paintings and the dances. It's very exasperating. When we get them into the church, they pay attention, all right, but sometimes I wonder if they're listening to me or if they just think they're helping me to mollify my own God."

"Oh, he goes into a rage when he thinks that," said Mulligan.

"The only thing that matters in this life is how you are prepared to face eternity," Higgins said. "I hate to see these poor children deprived of heaven."

"Well, they don't feel that way," I said.

"There is one heaven, McGill," said Higgins in a loud voice, with a glare in his eye. "These people believe there are four underworlds linked up somehow by a waterway. They believe Blue Lake, right up there on that mountain you can see from this window, is an entrance to the underworld. What kind of priest would I be if I had your attitude and allowed these people to be damned because of their ignorance?

Eternity is quite a time to spend in flames, my son."

"I never could see any point to death if it isn't final," I said.

Higgins leaned forward in his chair and opened his mouth, but Mulligan said, "What a fine-looking boy you've got there, Mrs. McGill," and we watched the sturdy, blue-eyed, red-haired Paul run through the grass with his dog and jump the irrigation ditch. Higgins sat back and stirred his coffee. He was a big, ruddy-faced fellow who had a popeyed, angry look, as though his collar was choking him. Mulligan was small, slender, and gentle. Both were Irish and not long in this country, but they had inquired into the history of the Taos area. To illustrate some argument, Higgins told about the Taos revolt of 1680, when the Indians who had been Christianized were washed with yucca suds to remove the stain. "You see, you see," he said. "And less than forty years ago they rose up again and killed Governor Bent in his sleep at Fernandez. The Army had to come and use cannons to blow down the walls of the San Geronimo Church at Taos and kill one hundred and fifty Indians. All that's left of that beautiful old church is a chimney. They need us here, McGill. They need to know we're right and they're wrong."

"That is a big job you're taking on," I said.

"There is no job more important," said Higgins.

He looked as if he would punch me to prove it.

The two priests began to call upon us every couple of weeks, and we found them good company. They worked well together. Where Higgins was constantly furious and on the verge of violence, Mulligan was quiet and soothing. Two days before Christmas, they arrived, riding their mules. Higgins was on the excellent Excelsior. The priests had made a number of visits to other houses along the rim and were quite drunk. Higgins was singing and shouting. Mulligan seemed to have slipped down inside his robes with only his eyes peering out, and occasionally he would chuckle.

"McGill!" Higgins yelled at me from the doorway. "Have you ever felt guilt?"

"Yes," I said.

"Then tell me," he said, "was it because of something specific, or your rotten conduct in general?"

He whooped with laughter and we sat beside the fire while snow fell on the mountains. I had some cognac that we drank with coffee. Both priests looked tired. They had told me their schedule: up at 4 A.M., pray an hour, study an hour, conduct Mass, do physical labor such as working in the cornfields for three hours, teach school, visit the sick, hold another Mass, more reading and study, go to bed at 10 P.M. in a cold little room. With my mother in mind, I asked Higgins how he could lead such a life.

"Because it gives me tranquillity," he said. "Discipline is the thing. Tranquillity is the result of discipline. I'll tell you a secret, McGill. I'm in love. Just as you might be in love with something of this earth, your wife, say, or your child, I'm in love with God and the Church. Shut up, Mulligan. Yes, McGill, I need the discipline of the Church and the ecstasy of being in love with God. When you can feel His presence, then you know how puny everything else is by comparison."

"So I've heard," I said and told them a little about my mother.

"You belong in the Church," Higgins said. "When will you come to us, McGill?"

"I don't guess I will," said I.

"Oh yes," Higgins said. "Oh yes. I've seen your type before. You'll come. Don't kick against the bricks, McGill."

Before that night ended, Higgins got hands and knees drunk. He ripped off his collar, flung it to the floor and danced on top of it, shouting, "I didn't want to be a priest! I didn't want to be a priest! My father made me do it!" We put him to bed at our house. I heard them leave while it was still dark, at least an hour before dawn. Mulligan later told me that Higgins drank a quart of wine, unmixed with water, at the Mass that morning and promised untold thousands of Hail Marys in apology for his dancing performance, which he claimed not to remember very well.

We went to many ceremonies at Taos. At Christmas we

watched the Koshares, painted like clowns, dance in and out of the rooms of the pueblos, their hair tied up with corn leaves, rattles on their wrists and ankles. In the spring we watched a corn dance around a Corn Mother, which is a perfect ear with four kernels in the tip. We saw a Turtle Dance, where the dancers were painted half brown and half white and crawled about as if they couldn't decide whether to live on land or in water. The Taos Indians called themselves Children of the Sun, and they called little Paul the Sun Boy. They allowed him to roam the pueblos almost as he wished, barring him only from two of the most holy kivas where they kept their sacred rattlesnakes. Winter came on again. Groves of aspens turned gold on the mountainsides. Water froze in the irrigation ditches. We went to our second Christmas cere-mony at Taos and Paul, now a husky lad of four, helped the Indian boys crack the ice in their stream to get drinking water. I attended several peyote rituals which were not revealed to the priests or, for that matter, to Ellen, as she had the usual prejudice against this Indian balm. Higgins and Mulligan continued to visit us. Higgins never ceased to try to talk me into the Church. It became a game for us.

So we moved into the spring and summer of 1882. I do not say much about our Taos years because they were happy ones. A series of happy events has a sameness. There were no great peaks of joy for us, though there were many bright moments, caused mostly by little Paul or by the satisfaction Ellen and I felt with each other. But neither were there vast depressions. The farming went well. I came to know our neighbors along the rim. There was never an intrusion, but I was comfortable with them. Ellen helped to nurse Higgins through a case of influenza. Paul and I fished for trout in the Rio Grande and the Hondo. We shot a bear in the mountains and made Ellen a rug of it. We went down the valley wall into Valdez and listened to the lisping Castilian speech of the Spaniards there. With Ellen we would sit on the bank of the Hondo and eat fried chicken and drink wine that had cooled in the fast water. I took Paul to visit other pueblos, but Taos remained his favorite. The Indians considered him one of them. Higgins regarded him almost as his own and would romp and wrestle with him and tell him Bible stories. The gentle Mulligan began teaching him to read, and Paul would examine my mother's old leather-bound Spanish books as though the words made sense to him. Paul would help me clean the irrigation ditches and hoe the corn and squash and pumpkins and milk the cows. They were very good years, very quiet.

For the Feast of St. Francis in October, Higgins needed a stock of candles. He intended to set up a display of candle-light, gleaming silver, paintings, and music that would make a profound impression on the Indians. As I needed to go to the bank in Santa Fe, I offered to fetch the candles for him. Promising to return within a week, I kissed Paul and Ellen goodbye and rode off on my Morgan. I remember them standing beside the house, waving.

I accomplished my business in Santa Fe and picked up the candles. On the way home, I stopped off at the pueblo in Tesuque—called the cottonwood place by the Indians—to watch a horse race. Some Comanches had come into Tesuque, about nine miles north of Santa Fe on the road to Taos, to trade horses for bread. A dozen or so officers and men from Fort Marcy were going to race the Comanches, who love to gamble. I had not been among Comanches in years. To my delight, I found these were Antelopes who knew of me and spoke of me in flattering terms. I inquired after Charlie Otter and was told he had been arrested by the Army and hanged for the murder of the buffalo hunters. We drank corn beer and whiskey and made speeches. At last the Indians were ready to race. They had bet blankets, whiskey, furs, and other items against rifles, knives, mirrors, etc., put up by the soldiers. The soldiers thought the racing would be easy to win.

The Indian ponies were not much to look at for the eyes of officers accustomed to Eastern thoroughbreds. The ponies wore leather boots up to their fetlocks to protect them from cactus. In the spring an Indian pony eats green grass, sheds his winter hair and shines with fat. In the winter the pony eats cottonwood bark and gets shaggy. The ponies have hard stomachs because of the lack of grain, can lope all day, can be ridden hard and cool off and survive in a way thoroughbreds never can. The Army officers looked at these little ponies and laughed. One captain brought out his Kentucky horse which seemed twice the size of the pony to be raced against. The pony was hammer headed, had thin legs and a rounded barrel, and looked mulish from the rear. The betting goods were piled up, the course laid off at four hundred yards, and a pistol fired to start the race. The pony barely won.

Incensed, the captain called for another race and beat the pony by three lengths. The Comanches requested a third race. All bets were doubled. One of the Antelopes winked at me. At the pistol shot, the Indian pony sped off as though the thoroughbred were tied to a tree. Halfway down the course, the Indian rider turned and finished the race riding backward, making obscene gestures at the captain who was using a quirt on his thoroughbred. The soldiers asked me if I would race my Morgan against the pony so they might win their equipment back, but I declined. "Save your money, boys," I told them.

I left Tesuque that afternoon, made a late camp, continued early in the morning, passed through Ranchos de Taos in the following afternoon, turned north out of Fernandez and arrived at my home at dusk. When I got there, my roof was still smoldering. Justo, Moreles, and some other men from the rim were putting out the fire with buckets of water. The neighbors had arrived quickly and almost no damage had been done to the house. But Ellen and little Paul were lying near the front door impaled on Lipan lances.

20

There are torchlights in the mountains tonight. They are moving very slowly uphill in a straight line. I suspect they are the Penitentes, who were once, according to Higgins, the Third Order of St. Francis before the Franciscans were cast out of the mountains. I have seen many of their meeting houses, or *moradas*, and the piles of sacred stones they call *descansos*. One night I was camped in the Sangre de Cristo when I heard reed flutes playing. Looking down from a ledge, I saw the Brothers of Light coming up the mountain, five penitents in a file, taking one step at a time, each penitent lashing his own bare back with a whip made of Spanish Bayonet fibers with cholla cactus spines in the end. Other men in robes carried torches and one had a blacksnake whip. I would guess his function was to keep the Penitentes from weakening and running off before they had been properly scourged of sin.

If those torchlights are not the Penitentes, I cannot imagine what they are. I doubt that Octavio would announce himself that way. The odds are that he does not trust me to do as I have said I will. It is a difficult promise to keep. I feel now somewhat like those Penitentes must feel, ready for this ordeal to be finished. Or perhaps they get a pleasure from it that I do not understand. I feel nervous, hurried. I don't know why. It could be that remembering the deaths of Ellen and Paul at this house six months ago has affected me more than I realize.

When I first saw their bodies, I could feel nothing. I could not believe they were dead. As was the case with my father's death, and with Barney's, the lumps of clothing lying there with the feathered lances sticking up from them had no relationship to the people I had loved. The neighbors were reluctant to talk to me. I went over and sat on the woodpile and lit a cigar. Finally Justo came to me and said he had seen a party of twenty-odd men riding along the rim road past his house. The leader, he said, was a big man with a black cloth tied over one eye. Justo said some were dressed like Indians and some weren't. He had run to get his shotgun, but they had gone on by. Then he saw the smoke.

When I could speak, I turned over the care of my livestock to Justo and asked him to tell Higgins and Mulligan what had happened. I came into the house here and packed saddlebags and blankets. I got warm clothes and ammunition. My Morgan was tired, so I selected a tough bronco, only recently saddle trained, and began to track Octavio. He had headed east into the Sacred Mountains of Taos. Tracking him was not difficult but I had to stop because of darkness and had to be wary of ambush. In the morning I found a mound of message rocks. Under the top rock was a note from Octavio. It said: *McGill now we are even*. But he would know I would never believe that until he was dead. Beyond the message rocks, the tracks split, half the riders turning north and the other half south. I followed the south turning and again the tracks divided, five riders going southeast and five southwest.

On a hunch, I went with the southeast track down along the Pecos River into the Pecos Mountains. The third day I caught up with them. I found them just at daylight. Three were asleep and two were making coffee. With my old Henry rifle, I shot them all. Octavio was not among them. I came down from the rocks with my Bowie knife to scalp them. One was not dead. I recognized him from the trip into Mexico and from Octavio's *ranchería*. He was badly wounded but conscious, still holding his coffee cup. He stared at me while spilt coffee smoked on the back of his hand.

"Where did Octavio go?" I asked.

Rather than answering me, he began to sing:

> *"I live, but I will not live forever.*
> *Mysterious moon, you only remain,*
> *Powerful sun, you alone remain,*
> *Wonderful earth, you remain forever."*

It was a Kiowa death song. I cut his throat.

There is no use in detailing my search, as it was a very long one. I went down to El Paso, where the Army, which of course had intensified its own quest for Octavio but with no success, informed me the Rurales had raided his *ranchería* and driven him out of Mexico. I went to Tucson and up to the Gila River and searched the San Carlos Reservation. I thought I had him once, but he avoided my snare. From San Carlos I traveled the Salt River, then north to Fort Defiance, up to Canyon de Chelly and back into New Mexico Territory to Chaco Canyon, where the Navajos told me Octavio had gone to the Spanish Peaks north of Raton.

However, at Raton Pass I heard hc had doubled back down toward Taos and I turned once again into the Sacred Mountains, where I found him.

A blizzard had holed me up for two days in the mountains not five miles from Arroyo Seco. I shared a cave with a bear that snored. I emerged into a white, silent landscape and, thinking to go to Taos to see the priests, I was riding down a canyon when I crossed the tracks of a dozen horses. The

dung still sizzled in the snow. I was carrying my Henry out of
its scabbard and without the protection of the fleece its
action froze and I had to pause to urinate on it. I had no more
than finished when I heard voices and looked up to see them
coming toward me.

Evidently they had struck deep drifts and had been forced
back. They were bent over their horses' necks, heads bowed
and wrapped in blankets and robes, and before they could
get their weapons out I shot Octavio. The Henry boomed in
the canyon and snow fell from the pines. Octavio shouted,
his arms flew up, and he toppled out of his saddle, causing
me to miss my second shot.

Two of them stopped with Octavio, but the others came
after me. I heard their shots rattling and popping and the
bullets snapping as they went past. My horse was plunging
recklessly down the already beaten track. Shooting a rifle from
the back of a running horse at a target that is moving away is
a highly difficult stunt. It was only the worst sort of luck, for
me, that one of the shots struck me. A wallop hit my left
shoulder blade and I heard myself say, "Uunh," and my left side
was numb. I gave the horse a needless kick in the ribs. We
came down from the canyon onto a flat white field that
stretched to a line of trees along a stream. My horse was
heaving. I considered getting off to let him rest, but the
outlaws were too close and I was afraid that the loss of blood
might make me too weak to remount. With the yips, screams,
and shouts of Octavio's men to urge us on, we raced toward
the trees. I reached the trees two hundred yards ahead of
them. I looked back, fired one shot at Eagle Dancer and then
heeled my horse onto the ice, across the stream, through the
trees on the other side and onto another flat. Behind me I
heard the outlaws yelling as they rode onto the ice and then I
heard a great splintering sound and a splashing and threshing.
Several had hit the ice at once, and it wouldn't hold. I was
getting very dizzy and my back and shoulder were starting to
hurt. It seemed to me I could feel my collarbone poking out of
my coat. I tied myself to the horse's neck with a piece of
rawhide, aimed the gasping animal south, and passed out.

I awoke smelling whiskey and peppers and looked up into the ruddy face of Higgins, who was breathing on me.

"Thank God, he's alive," said Mulligan.

I was in their little mission at Taos. As the whitewashed walls came into focus beyond Higgins' face, I saw several Indians sitting around. "These chaps found you and brought you in," Higgins said. "They won't leave until they see whether you're going to die or not."

I knew I was not going to die because I had not heard the sounds nor seen the spirit trying to leave, but I was extremely weak.

"What is this blasphemous thing we took from around your neck?" said Higgins.

He held up my silver chain. With a forefinger he flicked the lion's tooth so that it spun around.

"Put it back," I said.

"McGill, you are a blasted heathen," he said.

"Please, Michael, the man is sick," said Mulligan.

"That's my point!" Higgins shouted. "The man is shot and at the gates of heaven and he's behaving like a blasted heathen! I warn you, Mulligan, if we allow this man to die an unrepentant heathen, it will go heavy on us. I don't know if my conscience could tolerate such a heavy blow as that."

"But he does, after all, have Our Lady and St. Jude also on his chain with that lucky charm. There is goodness in him," said Mulligan.

"You see," Higgins said, turning back to me, disgust on his face, "Father Mulligan believes men are good. Nonsense! Men are swine and they must be driven into heaven like swine into a pen!"

The Taos Indians who were crouched around the wall with blankets draped over their round flat faces began to stir. Some could understand a bit of English but the Irish accents of the priests confused them.

"It is all right, friends," I said in Spanish. "The Fathers mean no harm. I owe my life to the people of Taos. You are good people."

"No, you do not owe us your life. We know that you will never die. But give us your blessing," said one old Indian.

"I do not have that power," I said.

"Yes, we know you do," the old man said.

I glanced at the priests, neither of whom could speak Spanish.

"Very well," I said. "My blessing on the people of Taos."

The Indians got up and each in turn came past my bed and said, "Live forever and protect us," or "May your corn be always ripe," or "May your feet be swift and your arms strong," or other such pleasant sentiments. The priests watched curiously. If Higgins had understood, he likely would have strangled me.

"What was that about?" Higgins said when they had gone, but I pretended to sleep.

I was laid up more than two months. The bullet had gone through my shoulder blade, turned up and cracked my collarbone and had fallen into my shirt pocket. There were torn muscles. I bled a lot inside and was sore. Indian women stayed with me day and night as nurses. They would pray for me to their mysterious gods and would place kachinas beside my head. An old man, Diego, came and danced and touched my wound with a magic stick tipped with snake rattlers. Higgins and Mulligan visited me twice a day, at least, usually coming at regular hours during what had been their study periods. The Indians knew when to expect them and would hide their kachinas and bags of magic. One afternoon, as an Indian woman was giving me a cup of herb tea, Higgins came in and found a red and blue kachina on the window ledge. "What devil is this?" he said.

Frightened, the woman grabbed the kachina and ran out. It would have been a very bad thing for the pueblo if Higgins had insulted the kachina, which he of course knew but was of the temper to do anyhow.

"Since you don't believe in the kachinas, then they don't hurt anything," I said. "Don't get upset."

"Don't hurt anything? What do you mean they don't hurt

anything? They stand between these people and the true God."

"It's hard for them to see the difference in praying to a kachina or praying to a statue of the Virgin," I said.

Higgins looked at me in horror. "McGill," he said, "if I were you I would start praying myself."

"In my life, whenever I wanted to pray I didn't have time to," I said, "and when I had time to I didn't need to."

"You need to now and you have the time," said Higgins.

So I quoted to him a Navajo prayer that I had learned with Paul:

> *"Oh our mother the earth*
> *Oh our father the sky*
> *Your children are we and with tired backs*
> *We bring you the gifts that you love.*
> *Then weave for us a garment of brightness*
> *May the warp be of the white light of morning*
> *May the weft be of the red light of evening*
> *May the fringes be the falling rain*
> *May the border be the standing rainbow.*
> *Thus weave for us a garment of brightness*
> *That we may walk fittingly where birds sing*
> *That we may walk fittingly where grass is green.*
> *Oh our mother the earth*
> *Oh our father the sky."*

"That," I told him, "is the nicest prayer I ever heard."

"More of your heathen rubbish," he said.

As I got stronger, I began to get up and, with my left arm in a sling, go out and sit in the sun. I remained at the mission because I had no place else to go and it was good there. The tiny children would come around me and play while I watched their older brothers and sisters work in the cornfields with the adult women and the priests. Higgins and Mulligan were breaking the hard ground with wooden plows to prepare for the planting. There were still chunks of ice in the stream, and the mountains beyond were white with snow, but the pines on the lower slopes were green. When they finished their three hours, Higgins and Mulligan would come and talk to me before going to teach in a small room at the rear of the little church.

"McGill," Higgins said one morning, "I have been thinking. Maybe I know what is preventing you from coming into the Church. You are wondering why God if He is all-wise, all-merciful, and all-powerful should have taken your wife and child."

I could see he was warming up for a lecture on His mysterious purposes.

"Father," I said, "as far as I can tell, God didn't have anything to do with it. My wife and boy were murdered by that stinking savage, Octavio."

"You're not much of a thinker, McGill," said Higgins.

During this time my heart was still occupied with hatred for Octavio. Bitterly, I understood that I should have gone after Octavio as soon as I returned from Mexico and killed him for what happened to Barney. My father had tried to teach me never to let down a friend, but I had done so and had brought forth the result upon myself and my family. My hatred for Octavio could not be disguised, even if I had wished to. I would sit after dinner and sip wine and clean my rifle and my pistol and sharpen my knife for hours, wishing I had not already shot Octavio so I could do it again.

"You must not allow yourself to hate," Mulligan told me.

"Yes, you must," said Higgins. "You must hate evil. You must fight it. You could do a great service for the Lord in fighting evil all over this territory, McGill. You have a tremendous influence on these Indians. They regard you almost as a prophet. If you went out to spread the word of the Lord among them, they would listen. In that way, you could do more to fight evil than you have done by merely killing that outlaw. You could make the deaths of Ellen and Paul mean something. They weren't killed at random, McGill, unless your actions make it so."

"These people don't need the word of the Lord," I said.

"They need for you to let them alone. They were doing better before you priests came than they are now."

"But you are overlooking something," said Higgins, wagging a finger, surprisingly not angry. "The priests came with the Conquistadores. Once the Conquistadores landed on this continent, the Indians were finished. The Indians now have to choose whether to perish or to be absorbed. Being absorbed is better. To be absorbed, they must adopt our faith. Attitudes like yours are a hindrance. If you are as fond of these people as you claim to be, you should be helping them prepare for the inevitable rather than fighting it."

"I don't believe being absorbed is better." I said, but I saw what he meant and I ruminated on it most of the night. As a result, I slept late. When I awoke, I heard Higgins in an argument with a visitor as they entered my room. Higgins kept raising his hand as if to swat the visitor, who was less than shoulder high to him and would have looked even shorter had it not been for the plume of ribbons that descended from the peak of his cork helmet.

"This filthy barbarian insists on seeing you." Higgins said.

"Badthing!" I cried, leaping out of bed and stuffing my nightshirt into my pants.

We embraced. The little Karankawa smelled like a wet possum, but he was wearing his fanciest garb—nose ring, butterflies painted on his face, an elegant silk dressing gown that trailed on the floor, a white loincloth, a yellow tunic with lightning bolts on it, moccasins ornate with beads.

"Do I hear correctly that this person is calling me a barbarian?" Badthing said in Tex-Mex.

"More or less," I said.

I hung the coffeepot on a hook over the fire. Badthing looked up at Higgins. "Ask him why he so addresses a wise man, a man who knows the secrets of all life, a man who chats with the gods, a man of magic?" said Badthing.

I asked and Higgins said, 'Well, look at his clothes for one thing."

"Look at his," said Badthing. "Why else?"

"Does he believe Jesus Christ is the Son of God?" Higgins said.

"No problem there," said Badthing.

"Does he believe in the Virgin Birth?" Higgins said.

"Why not? Do you believe Jonah was swallowed by a whale and got spit up?" said Badthing.

"I surely do," Higgins said.

"Do you believe Joshua blew down the fort with his trumpet?" said Badthing.

"Yes, I believe that," Higgins said. "Do you believe Jesus Christ was crucified and arose from the dead?"

"I have no trouble with that," said Badthing. "Do you believe in the Holy Ghost?"

"I do," Higgins said.

"Then I see little difference in us," said Badthing, who went on to list the Geranjé, the Worm Theory, the Peyote Road, talking owls, wise coyotes, personal visions, and various apparitions that I did not translate, for Higgins was sitting down to coffee and looking at Badthing as if God had sent an eccentric missionary to this humble church.

With no reluctance, Badthing agreed to stay for lunch. Mulligan joined the three of us. We had coffee, bread, and cheese, and Badthing and I talked in Tex-Mex of the things that had happened to us. He had escaped Mexico and gone to southern California, where he worked at the mission in San Diego until he was able to steal a horse. Then he had gone back to the Texas Coast and lived for a couple of years as shaman to a hidden tribe that lurked in the marshes. I could hardly tell him a thing about me that he did not know. He would nod and say, "Yes," when I reached each successive stage of my life since I had seen him. As I spoke of Ellen and Paul he looked sadder and then sadder still, and at last he lifted a hand to stop me.

"I have come here for a reason," he said, blinking his eyes so that the butterflies flapped. "It is a bad reason. Recently, I went into the Jemez Mountains to look for gold, one of my old failings. There I was captured by Octavio."

"But I shot him," I said.

"Indeed you shot him, but he did not die. He was wounded as you are. Now he is well, as you are. With thirty men, he is on his way to Taos. He says you must surrender to him or he will destroy this mission and this pueblo in punishment for them having saved you. He will blow them up with dynamite and will kill every person here. That is what he says. You know he can do it."

"What's wrong, McGill?" said Higgins.

With another voice, I told them. I suddenly was tired, more tired than I had ever been. I wanted to sleep.

"We'll get the Army," Higgins said.

"The Army has been trying to catch Octavio for ten years. They'll never get him," I said. "He will wait in the mountains until they are gone, and he will do what he says."

"He can't," said Higgins. "The Lord won't let him!"

"When does he want me?" I said.

"He wants you to go to your house tonight," said Badthing.

"He does not say when he will arrive, but he wants you to wait. He will send a messenger for you when he is ready. The messenger will take you down into the valley of Valdez, he says, though that may be a trick. I am sorry to tell you this. I told him my woman was responsible for the spots, but he said you were. He sent me to tell you this because he knew I could reach you. I am very sorry."

I went over and sat on my bed. The two priests stared at me. Badthing chewed a mouthful of bread and poured brown sugar into his coffee. With a brand from the fireplace, I lit a cigar. "I won't let you do this," Mulligan said, but I barely heard. I had never been so tired. There was nothing left. My wound began to throb, and there was a pain in my stomach. I thought of Ellen and Paul and Barney and my father and my mother, wherever she was, and I looked around at Higgins and Mulligan and Badthing, and the prospect of death did not seem so bad.

"Could I borrow a horse?" I said.

The moment I said it, I felt better. I could feel my strength returning. There is nothing to compare with resolving a problem for making a man's blood flow.

"Take Excelsior," said Higgins.

"We can't let this man go," Mulligan said.

"The Lord will protect him," said Higgins. "Pray, my man. Have faith. With faith comes strength, and with strength paradise."

Higgins went down on his knees on the dirt floor of the little room and began to pray. After a moment, so did Mulligan. Their voices droned, and I could hear Badthing chewing. Outside the Indian children were yelling as they played a game with a ball. I sat and smoked, quite calm now. It was not difficult. There was really no other choice. Every accident of my life had worked in combination to bring me here, and there was no way out. When I went to mount Excelsior and ride across the fields, between the mountains, along the rim to my home, the Indians were assembled beside the stream that divided their pueblos. Higgins and Mulligan had given me the Last Rites in the little church, which I considered useless but did because it pleased them and could not hurt me. A dozen Indians sang in the choir loft and then followed me outside carrying candles and singing, but those assembled on the bare ground beside the stream were silent. They knew what I was doing and regarded it a solemn occasion, but also they believed the old Comanche tale that I could never die. Higgins kissed me on the cheek. Mulligan made the sign of the cross. As I swung up onto Excelsior, my medallions hung out of my shirt. The lion's tooth clicked against Our Lady of Guadalupe and St. Jude, and I rubbed them all for luck.

Now it must be past midnight. I have been outside and the night is cold and clear and the torchlights are gone from the mountainside. Excelsior seems restless. I scratched his ears and fed him sugar, but he is too intelligent a beast to be bribed out of agitation. I wonder why Higgins and Mulligan have never visited me in these weeks. I wonder if anyone will ever see this chronicle. I must stress and stress again what a comfort this chronicle has been for me. I have never been a lonely sort of man, have never understood those who are lonely because they are alone, but in this particular scrape I have

(Here the journal ends)

Editor's Note

Peter Hermano McGill (1850-83) was the first North
American to be declared Beatified, or Blessed, by the Sacred
Congregation of Rites of the Roman Catholic Church. He was
venerated by Pope Pius XII in a Mass at St. Peter's, in Rome,
where it was declared that he died heroically as a martyr to
his faith. Since Beatification, at least two of the three miracles
necessary for sainthood have been attributed to the Blessed
McGill, whose being is of particular significance to the Indian
tribes of the American Southwest.

Until recently it was thought the Blessed McGill left no
writings. Other than a few newspaper clippings and tales
passed on by people among whom he wandered, all that was
known of him was in the petition submitted to Rome by a
Franciscan priest, Father Higgins, who attended the Blessed
McGill in the winter of 1882-83 in a mission in New Mexico
Territory. Subsequent investigations of the Blessed McGill
were based on testimony of Father Higgins and other priests
and citizens of the area.

Last year, however, as an abandoned adobe house north
of Taos, New Mexico, was being demolished, the bulldozer

blade turned up a tin box that had been buried in the fire-place. In the box was this journal that the Blessed McGill apparently wrote in his final days. Prior to publication, the manuscript was edited for spelling and to a lesser extent for punctuation and grammar, of which the Blessed McGill had an amazing grasp for a man of his education and period. In no case was the structure altered, nor was any comment or idea expressed by the Blessed McGill changed or deleted in any way. The editor has divided the narrative into chapters, using as a guide when possible the author's own pauses.

The afterword is based on newspaper stories and the notes of Father Higgins.

Afterword

It is assumed that the Blessed McGill was interrupted by the messenger of the Lipan Apache, Octavio. Evidently, the Blessed McGill heard the messenger approach, for he had time to remove a mud brick from the fireplace and hide the metal box. By consulting the notes of Father Higgins and a newspaper story in the Santa Fe *New Mexican*, it is possible to reconstruct McGill's death. Both accounts agree that the mule, Excelsior, was found killed by several shotgun blasts near the barn. Probably, then, McGill walked down the path into the valley of Valdez where Octavio was, indeed, waiting.

"Heroically," wrote Father Higgins, "this brave Christian refused the savage's offer of life. McGill was told if he would renounce the Christian God as being of no benefit to mankind and deny the divinity of Christ and the possibility of salvation, he would be spared from a horrible death. Witnesses who later repented and came into the Church told me McGill replied, 'I refuse to deny my faith. The love of God is too sweet to me. I believe in the one true Church and in the power of faith in our Savior Jesus Christ to transcend the grave.' McGill's martyr death has had a profound influence upon the red Indians of Southwestern North America. Everywhere I have gone, I have told the story of how this man defied the bestial forces and thus gained his place in heaven."

The *New Mexican*, in April 1883, reported McGill had been crucified upside down and burned alive. The outlaw Octavio was never captured. It was rumored that he died in the Mexican Revolution of 1910, but that was never confirmed. The latest miracle attributed to the Blessed McGill was the curing in 1956 of a Zuñi called Randolph Fat Toes who claimed to have leukemia. The Indian visited the holy man's death site daily and ate handfuls of dirt. At last, he testified, the Blessed McGill appeared in the clouds and said he would recover. Thus far, the disease seems to have abated. Several other cures are under investigation.

About the Author

Edwin A. (Bud) Shrake, Jr., novelist, journalist, sports-writer, biographer and screenwriter, was born in Fort Worth, Texas on September 6, 1931. He attended Paschal High School where, along with Dan Jenkins (*Semi Tough, Baja Oklahoma*), he wrote for the *Paschal Pantherette*. In 1951, Shrake joined Jenkins at the *Fort Worth Press* Sports Department, run by legendary sportswriter Blackie Sherrod. While working for the *Press* full time, Shrake earned a degree in English and Philosophy at Texas Christian University.

In 1958, Shrake moved to the *Dallas Times Herald* as a sportswriter. The rival *Dallas Morning News* hired him away in 1961 to write a daily sports column. In 1964, Shrake moved to New York, again joining Dan Jenkins, this time as a writer for *Sports Illustrated*. While in New York, Shrake and Jenkins kept company with Billy Lee Brammer, Larry L. King, Willie Morris, George Plimpton, Norman Mailer, James Dickey, William Styron and many other literary lights of the day. Shrake was later to reminisce that this period consisted of "exciting, mostly idealistic times and…everybody seemed to know everybody else among the crowd of writers."

Shrake returned to Texas in 1968, making Austin his home. He continued his association with *Sports Illustrated* until 1979 while also writing novels and screenplays. In addition, he wrote an occasional article for other magazines, notably "The Land of the Permanent Wave," published in the February 1970 *Harper's*. Then-editor Willie Morris considered it one of two pieces published during his *Harper's* tenure that gave him "special pride. ...[It] struck a chord in me that I have never quite forgotten, having to do with how clean, funny, and lambent prose caught the mood of that moment in the country and mirrored with great felicity what we were trying to do at *Harper's*. To me few finer magazine essays have ever been written."

Shrake has published several novels. Almost all are set squarely in his home state and, as A. C. Greene once commented, "seemed to be reaching for some truth about life (Texas life) that needed to be explained." Representative of Shrake's fiction are the heavily-researched, wry western, *Blessed McGill*; the searing portrait of Dallas during the days of the Kennedy assassination, *Strange Peaches*; and *The Borderland*, an historical novel covering the violent years immediately following the Texas revolution.

In the late 1980s, Shrake turned to the writing of celebrity as-told-to autobiographies, beginning with his friend, musician Willie Nelson. *Willie: An Autobiography* was followed by *Bootlegger's Boy*, the story of the controversial former University of Oklahoma coach, Barry Switzer, and *Harvey Penick's Little Red Book*, tips and tales from the accomplished golfer. All three of these works made the bestseller's list, the Penick book becoming the bestselling sports book in American publishing history.

Shrake's versatility as a writer extends to screenwriting. Productions on which Shrake is credited include: *J. W. Coop* (1972), with Cliff Robertson playing a rodeo star adjusting to a changing west; *Kid Blue* (1973), a comic western starring Dennis Hopper; *Tom Horn* (1980), with Steve McQueen as the legendary shootist; and *Songwriter* (1984), a film about the country music business directed by Alan Rudolph and starring Willie Nelson and Kris Kristofferson.

A. C. Greene listed *Blessed McGill* in 1981 as one of Texas' fifty best books and in so doing, fairly described much of Shrake's writing in general—it shows "an appreciation for the absurdities of existence, a recognition of irony's major role in the world, [and] highly suggestive humor."

Shrake holds a lifetime achievement award from the Texas Institute of Letters and the Bookends Award from the Texas Book Festival. He is a member of the Texas Film Hall of Fame and a recipient of the Distinguished Alumnus award from Texas Christian University.

Shrake presently resides in Austin, Texas and continues to write.

Publisher's Note:

The above is largely derived from material in the Southwestern Writers Collection at Texas State University in San Marcos, Texas. Founded by Bill and Sally Wittliff in 1986, the Southwestern Writers Collection has become a distinguished and steadily-growing archive, charged with preserving, exhibiting, and providing access to the papers and artifacts of principal writers, filmmakers, and musicians of the Southwest. Mr. Shrake has donated his papers to the archive.